ELSEWHERE

in

SUCCESS

Iris Lavell is a psychologist and writer. She lives in a suburb of Perth, Western Australia. This is her first novel.

IRIS LAVELL

ELSEWHERE
in
SUCCESS

FREMANTLE PRESS

For Sarah, Peter, Alison, Shawn,
Kuyan, Lachlan and Joshua

He knew where to dig. He'd been given the tip-off by one of their neighbours just a couple of weeks after he and Louisa moved in to the house in Success.

He'd been surveying the garden, thinking of excavating the building rubble that had been left on site, and making plans for incorporating it into a retaining wall. The man, whose name faded from memory almost as soon as Harry had heard it – something beginning with a B – had seen him from across the road, and wandered over for a yarn. As he was leaving, he'd mentioned the buried lawnmower.

'It's just to the left of the bougainvillea.'

'You're kidding,' Harry had said.

Louisa seemed to find the news unsettling. 'You should let sleeping dogs lie,' she said, but Harry wasn't one for appreciating the value of sleeping dogs. In the cool of the late afternoon, he took out his shovel.

Louisa came outside to watch. She told him she was half expecting to see someone attached to the other end.

'No, nobody,' he said.

'Why would he do that?' she asked.

'He couldn't get it started. According to Bevan.'

'Who's Bevan?'

'The guy across the road.'

'Brian.'

'According to Brian.'

The excavation wasn't easy. It took it out of both of them – Harry, physically, and Louisa, in the emotional sense. When the job was done, they poured themselves a glass of wine and stood before the unearthed relic until the light was almost gone. It stayed there for a week, as a bizarre reminder of something, Louisa had said.

Of what, she couldn't be sure.

CHAPTER ONE

Harry usually does the gardening, but he's out today; Louisa is cleaning up outside, sweeping the driveway. Across the road, kids are playing cricket. The boy with red hair makes contact, and yet another tennis ball skims across the road, catching the local flock of cockatoos by surprise. They fly off. Louisa fetches the ball and throws it back.

'Thanks.'

Play resumes. Next door to the cricketers, Brian starts up a chainsaw, preparing to eliminate his final tree before the onset of winter. It's autumn already, but still feels like the middle of summer. Louisa is tempted to give up on the sweeping and go inside, but she sticks it out.

The noise from the chainsaw stops and starts, but the noise goes on longer than the periods of quiet. When the chainsaw stops a mower will start up. That's how it always is. One power tool triggers another.

As she sweeps, Louisa vaguely wonders about the secret lives going on in the surrounding houses – what the women do while the men are outside with their power tools. Nothing comes to mind. Her thoughts inexplicably jump to the man who buried the lawnmower in their front garden those years ago. She thinks she understands how he must have felt. She considers her own meagre efforts – her lack of any real interest, patience, perseverance, when it comes to the gardening. He might have been something of a kindred spirit. Or maybe in a suburb called Success, he thought that failure was the only possible alternative.

Harry has taken off for an afternoon alone with Buster. They drive to the dog beach where Harry swims, with Buster watching anxiously from the shore and rushing at the waves to bark and bite at them. Harry keeps an old roasting tray in the car for Buster's drink after he has dried them both off with a ragged beach towel – a gift from Yasamine twenty or so years ago. He drives towards the Round House in Fremantle. The old convict lockup, cast as tourist attraction, is too sanitised for Harry's taste, but it's a destination with a view over the sea. They park, walk, and climb the hill to look down on Bathers Beach. He lets Buster off the lead as soon as they are out of sight and the dog races ahead.

Today, when they reach the top, there is a man playing didge, with a hat in front of him. It's not the best place for buskers, pretty slim pickings today actually, but this doesn't seem to worry the guy. He makes the didge talk and poke fun at them as they pass. Buster responds by barking and baulking at the end of the instrument, and the musician obliges by matching his sound, confusing him, and giving Harry such a buzz that he reaches into his pocket and drops a small note into the hat. He tells the guy that he used to play the sax. No more about himself, but they talk generally of music, mixes, production and fusion. It's a story he'll share with Louisa when he gets home. These small things make life worth the effort – not that he's depressed as such. There are fewer moments like this to hold his interest as he gets older, moments worth keeping for future reference. Harry and his dog hover until self-consciousness intrudes. Then they wander on down the steps and across the road, before looping back towards the carpark. It's almost five o'clock and time to be getting on, but it's still hot, and even here, right by the ocean, there is no relief.

The chainsaw has stopped, and a mower has started. People are going about their business. Louisa continues to sweep.

Past midnight the soundscape is bound to change. Security guards will be patrolling the streets. Hoons will be doing burnouts at two or three in the morning, leaving their oversized rubber tags between speed humps on the straighter sections of road. Occasionally, rubbish bins will be set alight.

These are the nights that Louisa holds her breath, waiting for the crash, tempted to pray, willing them all to calm down and go home to bed. She'll lie staring at the outline of the lump that is Harry asleep on the side of the bed nearest the window. He'll have taken something on top of something else to make him sleep. As she lies awake she'll be sending out this thought: What about your mother? Think what you're doing to her. Just think.

Technically Harry knows he shouldn't have let Buster off the lead, but he likes to see him run free. Those white-collar psychopaths on the local councils prefer to keep everything under tight control, or else it's a cynical ploy to extract funds from an unsuspecting public. They have their bloody signs erected everywhere – do this, don't do that – enough to make a perfect saint break the law.

By the time he sees the ranger it's too late. Women in uniform have never done a thing for him. It's possible she senses this and it feeds her resentment. In hindsight he realises he made some stupid mistakes from a distance that just ended up making her more determined to hunt him down. Women are particularly good at picking up on body language. He'd tried hiding himself and Buster behind some scrub, not in a furtive sort of way, more casual than that, as if they'd decided to take the long way round, but the woman had spotted them, was onto it, and was making a beeline. If Louisa had been with him, she would have told him to smile and act nice, but she wasn't, and he didn't.

Louisa moves around to the side pergola and starts sweeping there, cleaning up the leaves of the constantly shedding evergreens, marri and jarrah, mixed with flowers from the bougainvillea. There must be a slight breeze higher up, because more leaves drop as she works. A flock of galahs passes overhead, swings round, and lands on her side of the street, where the cockatoos were earlier. She likes these birds because they're so ordinary, and because they have a funny walk with their big heads and squat bodies. She stops sweeping and watches them waddling around, picking at the grass. She wonders how she looks to them.

The woman is not amused. Harry tries charm, compliments her on the uniform. She wouldn't trust him as far as she could throw him. (By the look of her she could throw him some way.) To make things worse, Buster is now crouching to relieve himself in the middle of the footpath, and Harry hasn't brought a plastic bag.

'The council should supply them,' he says, making a grand, sweeping gesture with his hand, to indicate where the fault really lies.

'Didn't you read the signs?' she counters with what Harry considers to be an unnecessary level of aggression in her voice.

'I didn't see any signs.'

Her upper lip slips into a cynical smile. She has a notebook with her for writing out fines, which she does with practised efficiency before ripping out the page and handing it to him. She's caught quite a few today, she tells him. Don't quote me. She was just about to knock off – five more minutes and she would have missed him altogether. Rubbing salt into the wound. He's made her day. She's ruined his.

He takes a detour, swings past Clancy's and settles Buster on the back seat of the car with a biscuit bone before going in.

Louisa is creating small mounds of dirt and leaves which she will later shovel into the bin. It's been some time since they have done anything to the backyard apart from the watering. There are leaves everywhere. It's not the best weather for physical activity, but something needs to be done. Today the air is so dry and hot that the eucalypts could be easily set alight with a careless match. She stops thinking that, afraid a person can give thoughts the power to make things happen, just by thinking them. The image of a bushfire, a wildfire, jumps into her mind. Forget that, she tells herself. Think of something else – the colour of leaves changing. The leaves catch alight. She puts them out with a bucket of water.

The sun is lower in the sky. She wonders where Harry is.

Harry's thinking to have a quick drink to calm his nerves before driving home under the limit. He's just turned away from the bar with his pint when he spots Carole and Gordon in the corner of the room. Carole has seen him at the same time and is waving him over to their table, where they are waiting for a meal to be served.

'Why don't you join us?'

'Why not?'

He places his beer on the table and goes up to order. Normally he'd have made some excuse, but he's feeling burnt and welcomes the opportunity to debrief. When he returns to the table he brings the conversation round at the earliest opportunity.

'What a bitch!' says Gordon.

'The power goes to their heads,' says Carole. 'They love their rules, don't they?'

Harry immediately warms towards them both. He's met them a few times before, but they're Louisa's friends rather than his. She catches up with Carole on a regular basis, and every now and then they bring the blokes in.

Without Louisa there, the dynamics are different. He's enjoying himself more as the evening deepens, and Carole seems more attentive than usual. Time passes quickly. Gordon turns out to be a great bloke, and Carole is becoming increasingly attractive as the night goes on. It's the beer goggles, Harry supposes. He watches himself, but Gordon seems pretty cool with the whole thing, as if he's used to it. Harry's eyes linger on the hint of cleavage in the V of her dress. Not that anything happens. Not that it will.

Still, he can't help feeling a bit guilty. They will part reluctantly after several hours. By the time he gets home Louisa will be fast asleep, or pretending to be. She'll have left the front light on for him. She's not such a bad old stick. Not bad at all.

Louisa is sweeping, sweeping, sweeping. One spot is extremely clean, a little oasis of calm in a desert of shifting dunes. She is no longer in the moment. Victor is standing bent over Tom, who is at the kitchen table doing his homework. With effort she pushes the image down and covers it up.

'Stop it,' she says. 'Just stop.'

This happens every time she does housework or works in the garden. She can't afford to think too much. She should get someone in once or twice a week.

Disciplined thinking is different at work where she communicates using PowerPoint. In the public service, she keeps it simple with dot points – none of that thing with words sweeping in from every direction in an attempt to keep people awake. It doesn't work, and anyway, she can't be responsible for everything and everyone. All she needs to do is follow the script she's been given and stick to the rules.

It has been some time now since she decided that she doesn't mind rules after all. There is safety there, keeping everything in its place. It's not easy, and that's good. It takes focus.

As Harry takes his leave, Carole leans in and plants a good one right on his lips. He feels somewhat embarrassed, but Gordon seems not to have noticed.

'We should all catch up soon,' Gordon says, and his Scottish accent exaggerates the goodwill that the invitation suggests.

'Yes,' says Carole, and then, making Harry doubt the significance of what has just happened, 'Tell Louisa I'll give her a call.'

'Okay,' he says. 'Okay, I'll let her know.'

'Take it easy,' says Gordon. 'Keep an eye out for any flashing lights.'

'No. No, I'm right,' he says. 'I'm good.'

Harry pulls into the driveway. The television is on and the door is open. Louisa is still up. He turns off the engine and sits listening to the radio before he goes in.

Louisa has the television on, but it's just background noise. She is hunched over her cup of hot chocolate, warming her hands. Surprisingly, the temperature has dropped suddenly with the onset of evening.

There is a problem she has been trying to solve for a long time now, but she can't articulate it. It's something she feels, something wordless. It's been there since she was a child, but this getting older seems to intensify things – emotional things. It occurs to her that she might be pinning everything on to Tom when it's not to do with him at all. She doesn't like the thought. It feels disloyal, as if she's been using him somehow. Things distort the more she thinks them through, the more time passes.

Sometimes she wonders about that. What if she has been trapped here forever, in endless cycles of wax and wane? What if her boy never existed, if she imagined the whole thing? What if he is a trick of the mind? Can she trust her senses, her memories of events?

She seems to remember herself as a small child travelling in the back of a car towards a mirage on a distant piece of road.

'Water,' she says to her father.

'Let's see if we can catch it,' he says.

But when they get there it has moved to the next rise, and then to the next.

They never do catch it. It makes her want to cry.

CHAPTER TWO

Harry considers himself to be a good listener, but not when he's under attack. Over breakfast, Louisa hasn't stopped talking for at least ten minutes. She's on a roll.

'I don't suppose it ever occurred to you that I might like a nice night out at Clancy's, catching up with friends?'

'It wasn't exactly planned, Louisa.'

'And why do you have to deliberately rub people up the wrong way? You'd think you'd have learned a little diplomacy by now. By this time in your life. I suppose you expect me to pay the fine.'

'I don't expect anything of the sort. I pay my own fines.'

'You don't pay your own fines.'

'Well, I don't expect you to pay them.'

'And what then, Harry? You leave it and the next thing you know, everything descends into chaos. Next thing we're getting threatening letters. The phone gets cut off.'

'It's got nothing to do with the phone.'

'Same thing.'

'It's not the same thing.'

'Leave it to me, you said. Leave it to me.'

'Well? What does it matter who pays the phone?'

That throws her, the art of the non sequitur, his strategic amnesia, his sheer dogged refusal to engage in her version of reality. Besides, Harry has a theory: a point is never won unless it is conceded. She seems to recognise the ploy. She takes another tack.

'While you were out kicking up your heels, I had a horrible day trying to clean up the mess.' She's looking upset. 'It's not easy you know.'

'I do most of the gardening,' he points out.

'That's not what I'm saying, Harry.' She's exasperated with him. He knows her well enough to see there's no point talking when she's like this. Better to cut his losses.

'I know,' he says, patting her arm, looking around for a way out. 'I know.' It's not what she wants, but it's the best he can do. His eye catches the appointment card on the fridge.

'What date is it today?'

'Why?'

'I thought you were supposed to be seeing that Lucy woman today. Have you cancelled your appointment?'

Her face tells him what he'd suspected. She's forgotten again.

'That's just great, Harry! Why didn't you say something?'

'I just did.' He smiles. It doesn't come out quite right. There is something too smug in his tone of voice. So smug that he notices it himself. So does she, apparently. She stops.

'We'll need to talk about this some more, Harry, when I get home.'

'And what time will that be? Just so I know when to make myself scarce.'

He squeezes out the last word as she turns away, but she doesn't look back.

Lucy has flowers on her desk: purple, yellow. This startles Louisa. She's told her about the flowers. Is it coincidence?

Is the counsellor playing games with her? She gives her the benefit of the doubt. She decides to recount the thoughts she's been having again, about the roadside memorial. Lucy tells her to close her eyes and counts her into a state of deep relaxation.

'Tell me about the memorial, Louisa,' she says.

Louisa speaks with some effort. 'I'm driving straight up to it, but it isn't any closer. I'm getting out of the car. There's a big hill in front of me. I'm climbing this hill – it goes on forever. There are ants crawling up my legs.' Louisa stamps her feet in a frenzy.

'What's happening now?'

'Biting me.'

'They've stopped,' says Lucy. 'They've gone away. They've all gone away. Go on, keep climbing. You're at the top now. What can you see?'

Louisa calms down, becomes still. 'A cross, white cross. There's a name.'

'What name?'

'Tom, I think. I can't see for sure. I'm finding it hard to see it.'

'Try. Tell me what you see.'

'It's very old, very old. The wood is split and the paint is cracked. Yellowing and peeling off. There are dead flowers about. Nobody has been here for a very long time.'

'How can you tell?'

Louisa speaks slowly. 'Feels abandoned. The ground is hard, gravelly, as if the keeper of the memorial has gone away. No, more than that, there's ... a feeling of abuse. It's as if a bouquet were carefully placed here, and then kicked to pieces. There's a curled-up photograph lying on the gravel at the base of the cross, but I can't see what it's of.' She's agitated again. 'I don't want this. I don't want this, Tom.'

'What's happening?'

'He's walking away from me. Come back here, young man! Tom, you come right back here this minute! How can you be so stupid?' Louisa shifts around in her chair impatiently. 'It's not necessary.'

'What's not necessary, Louisa?'

'This ... this cross here. This pain here.' She pushes her fists into her stomach. Her face is tight with grief.

'You're okay,' says Lucy. 'You're all right, Louisa. You're relaxed and in control.' Lucy is silent for a moment, leaving Louisa waiting with her eyes closed before she speaks again. She pitches her voice low, to reassure. 'As I count to ten I want you to gradually come back to this room, this place, feeling calm, relaxed, energised. One ... two – feeling more relaxed – three ... four ... five – calm and in control – six ... seven ... eight – energised and alert – open your eyes when you feel you want to – nine ... ten – fully awake, alert, relaxed.'

Louisa sits absolutely still and heavy in the chair. After a moment she says, 'I can smell formic acid.'

Lucy stares at her. 'Tell me what's happening for you right now.'

'I'm devastated, as ever,' Louisa says, but guards her face with the hint of a smile, attempts to stop her darting thoughts, to slow down, to think of nothing but her own breath going in and out. She breathes, but it's not easy.

Silence follows. With some effort she meets Lucy's eyes.

'No. Sorry, I'm not ready,' she tells her. 'I thought I was, but I'm not. My mind's a complete blank.' She laughs apologetically. 'It's a blessing really.'

No response. Lucy uses silence like a knife, cutting into Louisa's attempt at humour, exposing it for what it is. Once she has registered that Louisa has seen her point, she speaks.

'And how are things with Harry?'

'He's infuriating, as ever.'

'Why, what happened?'

'Oh, you know, it's nothing really. It's me, I suppose, expecting something and then getting annoyed when he doesn't deliver. I just wish he'd back me up a bit more, that's all.'

'Anything specific? Can you give me an example?'

'I don't know. There was this thing about him going out for the afternoon and not coming back until, you know, late. Midnight, when I expected him around five. He didn't have his mobile with him.' She punctuates the statement with a laugh. 'I mean that's the whole stupid thing about it. Here I am really trying to make some sort of connection with him and he doesn't even think to take his mobile with him when he goes out, so what chance do I have?'

'Weren't you worried when he didn't turn up?'

'No, not really. I might have. I don't know. No, he can take care of himself.'

'Sure.'

Louisa says nothing, shifts in her seat. She wonders how much more time she has.

'Where was he?'

'It's a whole long story. He got a fine in Fremantle for having his dog off the lead and then thought he'd pull into the pub to drown his sorrows, and a couple of my friends were there. So instead of letting me know, he sat drinking with them all night, while I was stuck at home on my own.'

'Have you talked to him about it?'

'I tried. Not really. Don't look at me like that, Lucy. It's not that easy trying to pin him down. Any hint of an in-depth discussion and he wriggles out of it. He thinks I'm arguing with him. I'm not. I'm just trying to make some sort of connection. Talk to him heart-to-heart, you know, but he gets annoyed with me. I said I was going to discuss it further when I got home, but I don't think I'll bother. I don't want to push it too far.'

'Push what?'

'My luck, I suppose.'

Louisa closes off her face and her voice, ending the line of questioning. She glances at her wristwatch, crosses her legs and jiggles her dangling foot up and down in a kicking motion.

Lucy stares at her foot. Louisa holds it still then replaces it on the floor.

'I've got something else on this afternoon,' she says. 'Sorry.'

Lucy opens her mouth then changes her mind about what she was going to say. She looks concerned.

'Do you want to stop there for today?'

'I think so. I'm so tired. I didn't get much sleep.'

'Are you still listening to your CDs?'

'Not really.'

'You don't have to. Only if it helps.'

'I know.'

Lucy closes Louisa's file and pushes it to the corner of her desk, stands and smooths out the wrinkles from her skirt. 'You have to work at it, of course.' Still smoothing.

'I love your skirt,' says Louisa.

Lucy looks pleased.

'Thanks,' she says.

'I wish I could wear skirts like that.'

Lucy smiles.

'I'll be away for the next few weeks, as I said. You have the locum's number if you need to make an appointment in the meantime, don't you?'

'I'll be okay.'

'Have you started doing your art yet?' asks Lucy as Louisa is leaving.

'I've been thinking about it.'

'Fantastic!' says Lucy. 'Next step is to do something about it.'

Louisa drives from Lucy's West Perth office to a vantage point in Kings Park where she can see the changes in the city as the sun descends, the peak-hour traffic builds, and the lights switch on. Despite the heat, the days are getting shorter.

A man walks past the front of the car, glances sideways, catches her watching him, bows his head and hurries on. Louisa carries an unused visual diary and a box of coloured pencils in the glove box. She opens the diary but can't bring herself to make the first mark, so she leans back in the seat and falls asleep. By the time she wakes, feeling chilled, the traffic has already built up and died down. Harry doesn't bat an eye when she walks in hours late. He glances up from the TV.

'Good session?' he says.

CHAPTER THREE

Overnight it pours. The small front passes, leaving everything sparkling and refreshed. Outside the sky is clear and the day is warming up. Harry has turned the radio on to his usual community station and a local Elvis impersonator is doing 'Love Me Tender'. Harry sends it up, singing along in his best generic American accent, drops to one knee and holds out his arms for the big finale. He bellows the last note and holds position, waiting for her applause. She's not in the mood.

On the table is a vase of flowers from the weekend before. Louisa touches one of the yellow flowers lightly with her left index finger and watches its petals drift onto the lace surface.

Harry struggles to his feet. He looks a little disappointed by her lacklustre response. He whips a tea towel over his shoulder, draws on his extra-large rubber gloves, starts the dishes and switches to the song that is now playing on the radio.

'You can have my sheila but don't touch my akubra,' he sings.

'Oh for goodness sake!' she says in mock exasperation. She smiles, and he is encouraged to sing more loudly. 'Stop it,' she wails, deciding to throw herself in completely. 'Next thing you'll have the dogs joining in.'

Today there are two dogs, one borrowed. Louisa rises

awkwardly from the table, stepping over them. They have defied the rules of the house and entered the restricted area of the dining room. They have a doggy smell that she tries to cover with citrus room freshener, but the dogs won't have it. They smell even more, out of spite.

She claims she's not a dog person, but her hand goes out to give each of them a pat as she passes. They wag their tails and look for food.

She stands by the sink to watch Harry do the dishes.

'What are you doing?' she asks him.

'What do you mean?'

'Are you making all that noise because you think I should be doing the dishes?'

He is rattling away with the cutlery, creating a sort of washing machine effect in the water that he insists is an efficient way to clean the knives and forks. She is distracted by thoughts of having to do them again once he leaves the sink. He doesn't care. Her presence gives him the opportunity to perform.

He sings loudly. 'The guy with the perfect grin is standing imprudently still.'

She laughs. 'Talking about yourself?'

'An oldie, but a goodie.'

'An oldie,' she says, but her mind is elsewhere. What was she thinking a moment ago? She was imagining a more innocent time, a happier time, thinking about something that happened when she was at school, but she can't remember what it was. The past slips away. The future on the other hand seems relentlessly fixed, as if she is walking into an ever-narrowing funnel of – of what? Possibilities? Impossibilities?

That's it. She was thinking that she should have been more pig headed, because at school she'd wanted to be a pilot, or an archaeologist, but her parents had dissuaded her. Only very clever boys became pilots, and only rich people became archaeologists, they'd told her. That was just the way it was.

'Why?' she'd said, but can't recall the answer. The real question is why wasn't she more argumentative as a teenager? Perhaps she was. When did she learn to be so acquiescent?

'The way we were,' murmurs Louisa, prompting Harry to throw in a verse of 'Memories' before falling into silence again.

The radio has also dropped out.

Perhaps it is too quiet.

Harry has loosened his grip on a wet glass. It slips through his glove to the ceramic tiled floor and explodes.

'Shit!'

He has a very loud voice and seems to enjoy overdramatising everyday events.

'SHIT!'

He has put too many suds in the water. He does this all the time, and glasses often slide from his grasp. Louisa sighs heavily, gets the brush and pan and brings everything back to equilibrium.

'Do you want me to finish off?' she says.

He doesn't respond. She doesn't know whether he is going a bit deaf or ignoring her.

'Do you want me to finish off?' she says, raising her voice, and speaking clearly.

He gives nothing away, goes back to his singing, mumbling the words this time. She watches him. He seems okay.

He sinks back into his task, apparently refreshed by the little burst of adrenalin, an occasional extrovert living with a frequent introvert. She wonders, not for the first time, how he would react if something really big were to happen. He wouldn't have anywhere left to go.

Harry decides it is best to be careful with what he says. He is thinking about Yasamine, so it's best he says nothing. He doesn't want to slip up and call Louisa the wrong name, so there are times when he avoids calling her anything at all. Sometimes he calls her 'dear' for fun, or when he's annoyed with her, or wants to present himself as if he is in an old-fashioned movie.

He agitates the sudsy water even more than before. The water slops over the edge of the sink and runs back along the grooves of the draining board. Some splashes on the floor. He imagines Yasamine doing the washing up. She is wearing an apron, and has her hair done up in some sort of thirties or forties style.

Sometimes he thinks he was born a couple of generations too late. He could have been a Cary Grant or Humphrey Bogart. He glances across at Louisa, at the stain on her top where she has rubbed against something grubby, and at her untidy hair. He can't think what sort of movie he should put her in. He decides that it's best to try to stick to the facts after all, here and now, things right in front of his face, in his face.

'In yer face,' he mumbles. 'In yer face.'

'I don't know about you sometimes, Harry,' she says, but he won't be sidetracked.

He feels himself sinking. He needs to surface. He needs to shout out and thrash about. He thinks about the value of primal scream therapy and wonders if she might not be better off doing that. At least it would give her a bit of something. Life. She needs to stop holding things in.

'GAHHH ...' he bellows out of the blue, but this time she ignores him, ignores his larger expressions of anguish. She has grown used to him. She can't even be bothered humouring him anymore.

He often sings and makes jokes for her and deliberately drops things to wake them both up. He tries to kickstart his mind but it winds up slowly, resisting at every point. He wants to stir things up. She tries to calm everything down. It's a battle of wills.

He'll pointedly ignore her. She probably thinks he's going a bit deaf. He smiles to himself. He wonders about boiling point under pressure. He should take bets. He chuckles. He feels a little guilty.

Louisa stares out of the window. The roses will need pruning in the next month or two, but they never stop flowering long enough to allow her to choose the best moment. As her gaze falls on Buddha, she decides she is meditating.

Buddha in the garden is a recent addition, but he might have been there forever. He sits unmoved among the falling rose petals, or when the rain falls. Yesterday he sat unmoved as a snail travelled across his generous earlobe.

When Buddha first arrived, Buster approached him cautiously, tail pointing straight out, as if his instinct were to back off in that direction. He finally gathered his courage, tentatively leaned in, sniffed Buddha, relaxed and refrained from lifting his leg, thus pronouncing him benign yet deserving of respect. Later when Jessie, the borrowed dog, came to visit, Buster introduced her to Buddha, but she was more interested in the tennis ball that Buster had provisionally discarded. He let her play with it – tennis balls appeared in the yard on a regular basis. He wasn't particularly attached to that one.

Louisa is not a Buddhist, but she is attracted to the idea of non-attachment. She tries teaching a version of it in her work. As far as rules go, she says that they are a choice and that it is a good discipline to follow them to the letter, but not to be too attached to them. It's good to step away from them occasionally to see if they are still working.

'It is important not to be too rigid about that,' she says to her workshop with middle management.

'I'm no hippy,' she says, 'but even so it's good to be a bit flexible sometimes. It's useful to practise adjusting your thinking, to allow for some leakage, a level of uncertainty. It works for me,' she tells them. 'As messy and complicated as it gets, I always allow for more than two possibilities. Even when there are obviously only two possibilities!'

This is where she pauses and waits for a response. It's her one little joke, but nobody smiles.

'So,' she says, 'in management, flexibility is more important than anything else. That means being able to respond quickly, which isn't so easy if you're always thinking in absolute terms of right and wrong.'

There's the inevitable dissenter, the guy who butts in all the way through and makes the workshop run behind time.

'I don't agree with you,' he says. 'If I did that I'd never make a decision. I wouldn't get anything done.'

She nods as though she's considering what he's said, then presses on. 'When I was younger,' she says, 'like most young people, I was caught up in the seeming incontrovertibility of binary logic – black and white thinking for those unfamiliar with the jargon – and I didn't understand the implications of containing the world in oppositional thinking. Depending on your premise, you can win an argument from either side. You can justify anything at all, even if it is highly destructive.'

Tom pushes against her line of thought, interrupting.

'Each judgemental idea embraces its enemy,' she says, 'as much as you might try to deny, or challenge, or expel it.'

She loses her train of thought. There must be a discernible gap in her presentation because people begin to shift in their seats. She's losing them. She smiles. It is important to keep things together at work.

She calls a tea break.

'Morning tea. Apparently we have Danish pastries, coffee, tea and chocolate biscuits out there. Yum,' she says. 'Fifteen, twenty minutes?'

Louisa stares at the Buddha, seeking answers. He smiles back. A magpie lark is pecking at something on the ground next to him. Harry is rattling away at the front flywire door, trying to fix the latch.

Tom used to say, if you win, you lose. Then he'd laugh. When you lose, you win. What did he want to win? What did he think he had to lose? With Tom, everything was always the wrong way round. He opposed everything she tried to teach him. He'd say, 'Don't plan for the future. Put yourself first. Act first, think later.'

He'd always been impulsive. It was in his nature. If something occurred to him, he'd do it regardless of pain. When he was quite small, he'd repeatedly hit his forehead against the wall. She'd distract him and, a couple of hours later, find him doing it again. When he was older, he'd hold his hand over a candle flame, to see how close he could get.

'All right. You've proved your point,' she'd say.

'There is no point.'

No point. Words hold clues. Her sister Zoe used to follow her opinions by a question: 'Does that make sense?' When did she start that? Had someone once challenged her ability to make sense so that she had to keep checking back? She'd use it like punctuation at the end of a sentence. It's the sort of thing that doesn't let a person off the hook. It makes them pay attention, like a kid that might be singled out and tested on what the teacher just said. It gets stuck in a person's head like an ear worm. Does that make sense? It makes a person feel quite irritated, because even when things are obvious it makes them have to confirm that. Of course it makes sense. Except that these days Louisa also increasingly feels that it is important to check the same thing. The virus of self-doubt is easily caught.

Seeing is believing – there's another one. Louisa thinks of Tom, switches it around, says, I'll see it when I believe it.

Believing is the hard bit. Seeing follows.

What can she see?

She sees some sort of fuzzy stuff in the space between herself and the wall. After she cleans her glasses it is still there.

She reaches her hand out, into the space. Her hand tingles. Her heart and her jaw ache.

'Is that you, Tom?' she says. 'Is that you?'

The space doesn't answer.

Neither does Harry. He is out of earshot. He has stopped rattling at the door and has gone into the bedroom.

Sometimes when she is semi-relaxed, Louisa allows herself the luxury of trusting that things are as they appear. On those rare days she holds Harry too long in their goodnight embrace. He has his own issues. After tolerating her uncharacteristic intimacy for a few seconds he shrugs her off.

Louisa hears the water start. He is taking a shower. She considers walking in on him, standing beside him beneath the falling water, bringing them both back to life, but she thinks better of it. He has the door to the bedroom ajar but that to the en suite closed behind him. He has started singing something unrecognisable and apparently wordless – a kind of tortured yodel. Buster sleeps in the passage. The other dog follows Louisa about, looking hopeful. She holds out her empty palms to show that she has nothing to offer, but the dog misses the point completely, and persists.

A moment later, both dogs have started barking because a van has pulled up outside the house. A man, a stranger, sits there in the driver's seat, not getting out, speaking on his mobile phone. It is late afternoon.

Louisa pushes the vertical blind aside and watches him. He looks young, around his late twenties, about the same age that Tom would have been now. In a parallel universe Tom might be sitting in a white van outside some woman's house, talking on his mobile phone. He might be living his life somewhere. He might have a wife and a child at home. It looks as though this young man has dark hair and is wearing a white business shirt. Louisa thinks that if he weren't sitting in a van, he could easily be a real-estate salesman or a Mormon. He doesn't turn his head, but perhaps he senses her looking at him, because he finishes his conversation, and drives off. The dogs settle down.

Harry calls out from the shower to say that he has forgotten his towel and could Louisa get it off the line for him. Buster barks to reinforce his request, just in case she missed it. The other dog struggles to her feet to be on stand-by in case she is needed.

Nothing else of note happens today.

CHAPTER FOUR

Wednesday morning. The mid-autumn rain has hardly begun before it's gone again. Now a hot spell is back after too short a reprieve.

Some time after Louisa has gone to work Harry notices a van parked in front of the house under his tree, which is annoying because he's been thinking about moving the car to the shade, to cool it off before he went out. The fact that it's warm, and isn't raining, adds to his frustration. He walks to a spot where he is visible to the driver and stands his ground, with his hands on his hips. Buster takes advantage of the open door, pushes past him, and hoons off down the street. The driver notices Harry and the passing dog, and winds down the window.

'G'day, mate,' he calls out.

'G'day.' Harry acknowledges his good intentions.

'You don't mind me parking here while I have an early lunch, do you.' It isn't a question.

'No,' says Harry. 'No worries. But I need to water around there soon.'

It is an obvious lie given the water restrictions, the day,

and his house number, but it saves face, and avoids a sticky confrontation for both of them.

'I won't be long,' says the man. 'Good tree.'

'No worries,' says Harry, checks the mailbox, whistles the dog back, and goes inside.

The guy is good to his word. After about five minutes, Harry hears the engine start up and when he looks out the spot is clear.

When Harry tries to start his car to move it into the shade it won't turn over. This always happens in the heat, so it probably has something to do with the solenoid heating up. This is what he tells Louisa. He's no mechanic, but neither is she. Once the car has cooled down again it usually starts. Now Harry is stuck there for the rest of the day – unless leaving the bonnet up will help.

He curses the van for causing the problem, opens the bonnet, waits five minutes and tries to start the car again, but it's completely dead. Harry is sick of this heap of junk, and thinks about his missed opportunities for a regular, middle-class life.

He decides to call the mechanic when he gets around to it, but later in the day lets it go when the car has cooled down, and starts first go.

It's Monday morning. Louisa has the day off and Harry has gone out somewhere with Buster. At about ten she glances through the front window to discover the man is back, in the same van, parked on the verge under a tree that she and Harry planted for Tom just after they moved in. It looks as if he has the seat tilted back and, from what Louisa can make out, he appears to be sleeping.

She could ignore him. It isn't as if he's officially on their property, but it's odd that he's parked at the front of their house again. And Harry said he was there just the other day. She ought to confront him. She's feeling restless, and a bit reckless, so she decides to take a closer look. She'll check the box for letters, and work out what steps to take from there.

At the mailbox she sneaks a quick look and finds that he is, as she initially thought, asleep at the wheel. He's wearing a baseball cap pulled down over his eyes so that only the bottom third of his face is visible. His mouth looks as if it is smiling, but it could be a trick of the light.

She thinks what she might do if she were a braver kind of person. She might walk across to the van and knock sharply on the window. She imagines the man startling and sitting up, pushing his cap back to reveal a boyish face. She imagines him around twenty-five or thirty, no more. She'd indicate to him to wind down the window. She should do that.

'Hello,' she'll say, and wait.

'Hello. What do you want?'

'What do I want?' she'll say. 'What do you want?'

'Nothing.'

Then what?

The man shifts in his seat and turns awkwardly onto his side, as if he is trying to get a comfortable position in his sleep. He has his back to the driver's window now.

Louisa looks at the advertising material she has taken out of the letterbox. Someone has opened a beauty salon in the local hairdressers. She should try it out sometime. She returns to the house and positions herself by the front window so that she can keep an eye on the van.

What next?

'I've noticed you seem to have taken up residence lately,' she'll say to him.

'What?'

'You've been hanging around on our verge.'

'I didn't know verges were private property,' he'll say, looking uncontrollable. No, not uncontrollable. Looking uncomfortable. That's right.

She'll start feeling awful because she's gone too far. She'll wish she'd pulled the curtain across the window and ignored him, but something has started now, travelling with its own impetus.

'No, it isn't private property,' she'll say. 'No,' she'll say. 'I'll put the kettle on. Shall I?'

Is he safe?

'You might as well come in then,' she'll say.

'Sure.'

He'll get out of the car and follow her in.

'Que sera, sera.' She'll start singing the song to herself as she walks ahead of him. He'll recognise the song and hum along, his voice familiar, almost childlike. She used to sing that song to Tom when he was a toddler. He'd join in with his baby voice, getting the words wrong. They'd sing when Victor was away. That was her, trying to create a world of safety and predictability for him. For Meredith and him. What if Tom had grown up to be this young man parked in his car on the verge? Come on in, son, she'd say.

I should stop, she tells herself, but she can't. She gives in, and continues with the story she has made for herself. He's not her son, but he could be someone her son would have become.

He'll say something nice to her. He'll have been brought up by a good woman who is proud of her boy. He won't be a drug user, not even recreational. He won't be filled with anger and hate. He won't be the sort to blame his mother for not being perfect. He won't have pain that needs anaesthetising. He'll be an ordinary, decent young man. He'll be a bit cheeky.

'I like your house,' he'll say, 'and your tree. It's a nice place to sit just there. There aren't many quiet shady places to sit and meditate.'

'You looked like you were asleep,' Louisa will say sharply, 'not meditating.'

Why would she needle him like that? To see how he'll react? To put herself at risk? He might attack her and steal all her things. She doesn't care. He could kill her for all she cares. The reality of pain, of death probably, is less than its anticipation. It's the people left behind who suffer most. In her case there would be no one. Not really anyone to care. Not for long.

'You decided to wake me,' he'll say. 'I wonder why?'

She'll say, 'We've noticed you sitting out there before, not meditating. We wondered what you were doing.'

This will be an excuse to say 'we', so he knows she has a man in the house and doesn't get any ideas about attacking and robbing her. She'll sneak a look at his face as he takes a seat, but it will be blank.

She wonders again if he has a mother somewhere, if his mother knows where he is and if they keep in touch. She wonders again if he's ever got involved in anything bad and if he's okay now, if he's straightened himself out and got himself a good steady job.

'What sort of work do you do?' she'll ask him.

'I'm a salesman.' No, something less everyday. 'I'm a merchandiser. I hate my job.'

'Hate's a pretty strong word,' she'll say.

She tries to conjure up his face as she says this. Her mind jams, turns digital – half picture, half coded pattern. She tries to make out the picture, gets an inkling of something she doesn't want, tries to move it on, but it is frozen, forcing her to look. Her heart begins to pound. She thinks: One day you'll give up hating. It takes up all your energy. What is the point really? What point does it serve? There really isn't any point. She is struggling to speak her thoughts aloud, but her voice has dried up. Now she can see the man standing before her, grinning. He looks older than she first imagined him, more hardened.

She is in the kitchen, staring at the bench. She can't remember moving from the window. She feels as though she is being watched, as if someone can read her actions, can see right inside her head. She'll confound them. She gives her change of position meaning, puts the kettle on, shakes her head, and chastises herself for being so silly. No one is watching – no one but herself. She is indulging in a harmless fantasy. She's just fine.

She attempts to conjure him up again, to control his coming and going, the way she wants it to be. A vague picture appears. She's given him a friendly smile this time, made him more relaxed. She's made him younger again.

'What next? What next?' she murmurs.

There'll be something else, not specified, and then it will be time to go.

'Thanks for the tea,' he'll say, 'and for the charming company. I'm John.' No, 'I'm Brad.' You are not, Louisa says to herself. It's the name Victor insisted on when Tom was born; Tom's middle name. Of course her mind is playing tricks on her. And people don't use words like charming any more – it was old-fashioned even when she was young. Brad will straighten his cap and leave. That's it. He'll straighten his cap and he'll leave.

Louisa watches the man from the window. He seems to have woken up. He sits up and it looks to her as though he is wiping his hands over his face. There is some reflection on the car window. He starts the van, revs it a couple of times and drives off. She stands there, looking out, feeling disturbed.

CHAPTER FIVE

When Harry's number came up he felt as if he'd won the lottery. Others told him he'd lost, but they were wrong. Life had been all right but he'd been starting to drift, and the call-up gave him a sense of purpose.

He thinks fondly of his days as a conscript in Nashos during the Vietnam War. He never got to see active service because the Whitlam Government was voted in before he could go. At the time he was relieved – he'd seen some of the footage by then and had been starting to have his doubts – but he's since looked back on his National Service with a certain amount of nostalgia, especially when he watches the Anzac Day parade on television.

'I don't know why you're so proud of it,' says Louisa.

'Us blokes are just designed that way,' he says. 'We're hardwired to protect our territory, our women and our children.'

'Us women are hardwired to protect our children, our homes, and our men.'

'I'm trying to make a point, Louisa.'

He goes on to explain to her how good it felt to be tested

in that way. He tells her how fit he was from playing football at school so he didn't find the basic training as hard as some, and how being in the army taught him what they meant by mateship.

'All the boys together,' she says. 'Doing boy things.'

'And your point is?' he says.

He watches the parade and the rising of the sun at Gallipoli. The cameras pick out faces in the crowd, young and fresh, kids learning about respect and duty and filling his heart with hope and pride. These young blokes must understand what he's on about better than Louisa – the value of sacrifice and mateship. There are girls there too, a sign of the changing times.

'What is mateship anyway?' she calls out from the kitchen. 'I mean, does it include women?'

'It could do,' he says. 'The way I see it is this – mateship is how society should be organised. Men work together and women do their own thing. See, men and women could mostly work and live separately and then come together for sex, family celebrations, and so on. But the strongest bonds would be outside the family, between men. And a similar sort of thing between women I guess, like they used to have with the Country Women's. Or whatever. We'd be more or less equal but different.'

'What about the kids?'

'What about them?'

'Who'd look after them?'

A red herring. He treats it with the contempt it deserves. But a separation between men and women – the more he thinks about it, the more he likes the idea.

'They ought to bring back a separation of male and female roles,' he tells her.

'It's not going to happen,' she says, handing him his tea.

The conversation is leading nowhere. He shrugs it off, goes back to remembering his youth. It's the prerogative of an old soldier. She leaves him to watch the parade on his own.

In Nashos it was good to be a man among men all working together towards a common goal. It was hard work and straightforward. You'd be just fine as long as you followed orders. It took away all of the uncertainty, and all the anxiety. There was no time to think. You fell asleep as soon as your head hit the pillow, and then you slept like a log, physically exhausted from the day's work. That was the best sort of tiredness you could have. He'd wake refreshed, feeling strong and energetic, ready for the next challenge.

Plus his early success as a musician gave him a certain amount of kudos with the blokes. There were times when he'd take out his sax and jam with a few of the others who'd brought their guitars with them. There was one bloke with a tin whistle and a couple of guys with harmonicas. Not that there was much time for that with long days, short nights, and sadistic NCOs bursting in on them. Not a lot of privacy, but that was intended to cultivate a sense of joint purpose. You had to know you could rely on your mates. What you saw was what you got. There was no room and no real desire for reflection or sedition, unless you counted the guy who took off and ended up in gaol as a conscientious objector. No, they didn't want to give you too much time to think. Everything they did was done for a reason.

Watching the dawn service at Gallipoli he feels a wave of emotion come over him when they get to the 'Age shall not weary them' speech. The night sky gradually lightens throughout the ceremony, former foes come together in a spirit of mutual respect and friendship, and the dead are appropriately honoured for the ultimate sacrifice they made. Louisa has returned to watch with him. She is standing in the doorway.

'I'm glad you didn't go to Vietnam,' she says. 'It was awful for the soldiers when they returned, and for their families. Just awful.' Her voice is measured and her face is turned away from him. 'They were just young boys sent to the slaughter.

Vietnam was another pointless war,' she says, 'a product of poor decision-making and simplistic thinking. Greed, power, mistakes, politics. Just like Gallipoli. What kind of damage does that do to a person?'

She is talking about herself, of course, and about Victor. So he keeps quiet. He could say that one bad apple doesn't necessarily ruin the entire barrel, but he won't – not today, of all days. He doesn't want to hurt her feelings. He reaches out his hand, but she's gone again. His eyes drift back to the screen.

Now he's thinking about his years on the planet. He's wondering how his own life might measure up to the best of the unlived ones of those fallen soldiers. This leads him to reflect on his life as a series of non-conclusions – careers, army service, marriage, parenthood – all terminated before he could see where they'd lead. And really now he thinks it wouldn't have taken all that much. If he could have taken what he learned in Nashos and pushed a bit harder, then he'd be in a very different place now.

Finally, as the sun rises in the Gallipoli sky, Harry thinks about women, how they sap your strength, how they make simple things more complicated than they need to be, how they are cold when you would expect them to be emotional, and they cry over trivial matters. Then he wonders whether it's just him, and if he was meant to be alone, an old salt or an old prospector. Men like that have always been around. There have always been hermits living in their hermit caves. That's who he was meant to be all along: just him and Buster against the elements.

CHAPTER SIX

Louisa has gone to visit her mother. By the time she gets home, Harry plans to be in the garden pruning trees and bushes to prove he hasn't been wasting his time. The garden will grow back. He'll prune it again. It'll grow back, and so on, the story of his life. He'll have the radio on. He'll be focused on the here and now. The local footy-tipping competition. The list of jobs still to do, stuck on the fridge with the magnet advertising the veterinary hospital. The list has barely diminished since Louisa put it there three or four years ago. He'll see if he can cross something off, and when Louisa gets home she'll give it a big tick. Day will lapse into evening, he'll walk the dog, watch the news, then something funny, this and that, go to bed.

The rain has stopped and a weak sun had found its way through restless cloud. Harry turns up the radio and goes out to the shed to find his gardening gloves and secateurs. Buster is lying in a sheltered hollow that he has dug under the zamia palm. He appears to be sleeping with his eyes half open. His chest rises and falls in a slow, steady rhythm. Harry starts work on the hibiscus.

The radio is much of the same. Nothing holds his attention. As he snips, his past circles. He could distract himself with a drive to the beach and a walk. He could call Louisa to tell her he'll take her out to dinner later, then go on the computer to search for BYO restaurants. Given his last look at the joint account, he probably won't.

Money – the not so well-kept secret to freedom and a better kind of life. And superannuation. They make such a big thing of it these days. He hadn't thought about it when he was young. He thought about money in general, of course – had fantasies of making it big, with everything that brings. Nice cars. Recognition. Justification for the risks taken. The alternative seemed to be a steady, boring kind of life, gradually accumulating assets, and an early, comfortable retirement, if you played your cards right. As it turned out, he'd done neither.

If he'd stayed working at the Chemistry Centre he'd have a reasonable payout by now. He wouldn't be with Louisa, of course. He'd have a different life, a different car, his wife, daughter, and a son by now. They'd have been great mates. The son would have fixed his car for him and they'd have all gone fishing together – him, Yasamine, Bella, and the son. The girls would scream and protest when someone caught a fish. He'd pretend to chase them, teasing. The son would join in. It could have happened. He could have made it happen.

In a way he'd had a son of course – Louisa's boy – but he hadn't taken enough time to really get to know him before it was too late. At the funeral he'd stepped up and been consort and comfort – an outsider playing the part of an insider. He'd held himself strong, never wavering, not allowing the pain of that day to penetrate. In truth, he felt like a bystander who'd forfeited the right to grieve. He'd stood by as a world collapsed, realised in retrospect that it's possible he'd seen some signs, and done nothing. So he did what he could to salvage what was left over. He'd stayed. He'd been there for her, even when she retreated from him, which was better than nothing from a man who'd never committed to anything. She stayed too – he's not sure why. Because it was the line of least resistance. If he'd taken another path he might have raised his own son with Yasamine, and they might all have fared better. Tom might still be alive. Everything a person does shifts the future, just a bit.

After they had Bella, Harry told Yasamine he'd need to find something that he liked, something that he'd be able to do for a long time, before they had another one. He knew even as he said it to her that it wouldn't happen.

A normal father would have bonded with his daughter. If he's honest with himself, he'd probably have to admit that he's always felt more bonded to his dogs. He makes an effort and focuses on Bella, a memory of a memory. The little girl that she was back then doesn't exist any more.

He wonders whether the person she turned into is all right, if she's married now, what she looks like, if she's an interesting person, what she'd do if he turned up on her doorstep, if he's got any grandkids. He thinks all this in a detached way. He guesses his detachment is some sort of psychological protection. Louisa would probably be only too happy to tell him if that's right – she'd talk it over with Lucy, and then tell him. He wouldn't ask her anyway, because she'd take it as an invitation and move in to the buffer zone that he's constructed around himself. What he feels, or doesn't feel, about Bella, or anything else, for that matter, doesn't need endless explanation. It's just the way it is.

It's different when he thinks about Yasamine. She still exists for him, even more clearly than Louisa does. She has grown older with him. In his imagination they have come to understand each other perfectly. She has forgiven him. There is still raw feeling there, something that he avoids naming, and desire. He feels loyalty towards her, towards her memory, and knows that his avoidance of closeness with Louisa is partly to do with his loyalty to Yasamine.

And partly to do with his need for space, lots of space.

Harry has had enough of the pruning. He peels off his gardening gloves and puts the long-handled secateurs away.

Buster is still asleep in his hollow, eyes closed now, snoring lightly. Harry has the house to himself. He turns off the radio, washes his hands, splashes water on his face, stares at his reflection in the mirror, sees that he's still not bad-looking in that particular light, heads out to the kitchen and puts the kettle on. He waits until it boils then decides that he doesn't want a coffee. He could probably do the dishes. He might have a lie-down first, and make the most of his time alone, guilt free. He stretches out on the lounge-room floor and conjures up a picture of himself and Yasamine in the kitchen, his arms around her. She's pregnant. Next thing she's pushed him away and they're arguing.

It might be a different argument he's recalling. It might have been the time he accused her of trying to palm someone else's kid off on him. He never seriously believed it: it was just something he said. As soon as he saw the pain in her eyes he was sorry, but it was too late to take it back.

That was just before they split up. He was thinking of the money. He was hurt. He was young. He was a bloody idiot. He ought to be ashamed of himself.

Still, it was understandable. Back then he was exhausted and constantly on edge. Bella cried for the first three months with colic. His wife cried too. He pictures her face. He pictures her crying, tears running down her face. He feels nothing. He has pictured it too many times before. It has lost its meaning. A beautiful face, nevertheless; the gift of her particular heritage – her father had been Greek-Irish and her mother was from the Torres Strait. Her parents had moved to live in Cyprus by the time he met Yasamine. She'd stayed on in Australia to be with her friends, and to make her own way. He met her folks when they came back for the wedding, and again when they came to see Bella when she was two. They kept in touch occasionally, on birthdays and Christmas, but pretty much left them to their own devices. He didn't hear from them again, after the separation.

Harry pours himself a drink. He picks out the particulars so that he can call up the sensation of being with her. Yasamine, with her smooth, olive skin, curly hair, dark eyes, long legs, small breasts. She was moody – up and down all the time; she had a temper. There was a quirky dimple at the corner of her mouth on the left side of her upper lip. As he thinks of it now he gets an odd feeling, a mixture of pain and joy ... and something else. Love, he supposes. The French probably have a word for it. Like melancholy.

'Melancholie.' He says the word out loud with a pseudo-French accent. 'Melancholie.' The word seems to echo in the empty house. Harry's voice sounds strange when he hears it back like that. He switches the radio back on to catch the Dexter Gordon Quartet playing 'Autumn in New York'. He smiles and shakes his head. His band used to play that back then, when Dexter Gordon was his gold standard.

Yasamine was indifferent to jazz, but he only found that out afterwards. In the end, she didn't like him playing his sax. One day he came home and found it in the outside rubbish bin.

'I hate it,' she said. 'I hate the bloody thing! I can't stand it.'

'Do you know how much it's worth?' He didn't care how much it was worth, but he'd been wounded. Music was who he was. 'Do you have any fucking idea of how much it's worth?'

'How much am I worth?' she said. 'How much are we worth, Harry? Hey? What? What?' Slapping him around the shoulders, getting hysterical. 'You bastard!'

He cleaned the sax and played all night to prove a point. Then he put it away. He had hardly picked it up since.

At first it was to demonstrate how hurt he was. It wasn't long before they separated. Then she left him, and it became a sort of thing to punish himself. As his anger subsided it stopped mattering. He'd changed. He seemed to have lost his drive. He could take it or leave it. Occasionally he'd pick it up, have a blow, put it down. Nowadays he doesn't even try, probably out of habit or something. Apathy. But he's never stopped listening.

The band had a big line-up with a couple of horns, a double bass and drums and Sassy out front on vocals and keyboard. They'd got themselves a regular gig in Fremantle on Friday, Saturday and Sunday nights. That first night, Yasamine was there with a group of girls, all giggling and elbowing each other in the ribs, except for her. She looked straight at him the whole time. She was drinking some sort of pink or blue cocktail with a silly umbrella and staring at him while she sucked on her straw.

He tries to remember the colour and decides it was blue. No, it was definitely pinkish. It could have been a tequila sunrise. Not that it matters now. He can't remember her liking a particular cocktail over the years that followed. They would drink the odd glass of beer together. Still, back then she was a complete mystery to him. She outstared him with her mouth around that straw. He wondered if she recognised him from an earlier encounter, but he was sure they hadn't met. He would have remembered her for sure, with those eyes and that mouth.

She was shameless, not worried about how her staring looked to anyone else. It was unnerving, but kind of sexy too. Every time he looked back she was still looking at him. He was dating Sassy at the time. Sassy was amused at first but after a while she started to get annoyed, and it showed in the act. It wasn't necessarily a bad thing because it gave them an edge that changed the feeling in the room. People stopped talking and started to take notice, trying to work out what was going on.

Yasamine came back the next night by herself, and the night after, so he went up and talked to her. At first it was just to keep Sassy jealous, but then there was something about Yasamine that started to grow on him and he knew it was going to be serious. She became a bit of a groupie. After Sassy found them making out at the back of the toilets she pulled the plug on the band so they lost the gig. They got another singer and another gig at another pub, and Yasamine followed them.

Back then she said she thought the saxophone was the sexiest instrument around, but after the baby was born she changed her tune. He thought later that it was the idea of it that she liked, not the music itself. She started buying Madonna records just to annoy him.

Still, she was cute all right. When she laughed he found that dimple of hers distracting, and he used to tune in and out as she talked, jazz abstracting through his mind the whole time. Now it occurs to him that he used to joke about it, that silly dimple at the corner of her mouth, just to make her smile so that he could see it come and go. It made her mouth look lopsided. Her mouth *was* slightly lopsided. It was his favourite thing.

If he'd stayed at the Chemistry Centre and they'd had another baby, things would have been better and Yasamine would still be there with him. She'd have kept her figure. She'd still look a bit like Cassandra Wilson. She'd have aged well. Her hair would be long and curly, with some grey. They'd have a life now with their kids and maybe a grandkid. They'd have a caravan and a four-wheel drive; they could afford the petrol. Or they'd have some sort of classy hybrid, good for the environment. They'd have great friends – someone to mind the dog when they went away. Or the cat. She always preferred cats.

Harry goes to the filing cabinet and pulls out a box wrapped in a grey plastic shopping bag. He takes out the photographs. He doesn't know how long he has been sitting there when he hears Louisa pull into the drive. Her return comes as something of a reprieve. He's wallowed enough today. He stashes the package and when she comes inside he is waiting by the kettle with two cups and coffee.

Louisa gives him a kiss, kicks her shoes off and puts her bag away. He hands her a mug of coffee.

'Good day?' he asks.

'We went into the city, had tea at the Barrack Street Jetty. And a muffin. We watched the rain on the water. You couldn't see to the other side, just the ferry suddenly appearing when it was only a few metres away. It was like looking at a painting.'

'That's good,' he says. 'How's your mum?'

'Oh you know. Okay.'

'I did some pruning.'

'I noticed. Well done. You've made quite a big pile.'

Harry seems pleased that she's noticed. He meets her eyes, glances down at her dress. She finds it hard to read the gesture.

'What?' she says.

'Nothing.'

'What?' she says.

'You look nice. I've always liked that dress. You should wear it more often.'

'Thanks. I like it too. Are you going to have your coffee?' It sits untouched on the bench.

He takes a sip or two and tips the rest down the sink.

'It's awful,' he says. He has an idea then, and he puts it out there before he can think it away. 'I don't suppose you feel like going out again today? It's a while since we went out. It looks like it might be clearing up.'

'Does it? Where?'

'I don't know. We could have a meal and catch a movie. Or catch a movie and have a meal. It would be a shame to waste that dress.'

'We could do something,' she says.

'What do you want to do?'

'I'd like to go somewhere with music.'

'What sort?'

'I don't mind. It doesn't matter.'

'Okay, leave it to me,' he says. 'Music sounds good.'

Harry searches the 'What's On' section of the local paper and finds an obscure production, touted as 'an improvisational musical': *Antigone Crashes on the Beach*.

'Looks like a student production. What do you think?' he asks her.

'I'm game if you are. It's not actually *on* the beach is it?' she asks. 'It's a bit cold.'

'I don't think so.' He looks. 'No, it's at Kidogo in Fremantle, you know that little building on the other side of the railway line. Hey, we're in luck. It's the last day! Oh, it's a matinee – starts at four. Hopefully they'll still have tickets. There's a mobile number here.'

Harry disappears into the next room, rings, and comes back to tell her it's all arranged.

'He sounded surprised to get a call, like he was just waking up. It doesn't augur well. We might need to grab a stiff drink beforehand,' he says. 'Just to take the edge off.'

She laughs. 'It'll be good for you,' she tells him. 'It's about time you got a bit of culture.'

CHAPTER SEVEN

The production is highly stylised with papier-mâché masks, figure-hugging lycra, projected images and an obscure storyline. They arrive just as the lights are going down, and are ushered in by a flustered young woman wearing black. There is a scattering of empty seats – not enough of an audience to beat a quick retreat if the production becomes unbearable, Harry whispers to her. The acoustics are good and the venue is small. A woman, who Louisa imagines to be the director, or producer, overhears him, glances across, and coughs. The music is experimental too, but over dinner Harry tells Louisa that he thinks this has been the show's saving grace. He says it reminds him of when he used to mess about with the guys trying to create a new musical genre. 'We tried something we called "punk-rock jazz!"' He laughs. 'The things you do!'

He tells her they'd rehearse in an old garage on a large semi-rural property. They'd lived there for about a year, when he and Yasamine had ideas of starting some sort of alternative lifestyle. The guys would come down and stay in an old cottage, and they had a great time working on their music every day.

'You don't talk much about Yasamine, or Bella,' Louisa says. He frowns.

'Or your music. I'd like to hear more about it, Harry.

Sometimes I wish you'd get back into it again. Why don't you?'

'It's gone, Louisa,' he says, to finish the conversation.

'Yes, but why? You were good. You must have been good, and you must have loved what you did. It's only gone because you decided that it was, sometime back there. You must have loved it.'

'Can we talk about something else?'

'I don't get it,' she says. She never knows when to stop.

'We should be getting back,' he says. 'You've got work tomorrow.'

He stands, pays, and they drive home wordlessly, with country music playing in the background.

It's still early when they arrive home, not yet nine. Harry says he's pooped, and goes to bed. Louisa washes the cups and then decides to tidy up the study. She has barely started when she comes across the box of photos. She sits back, holding it on her lap.

'This is not such a great idea, Louisa,' she tells herself. 'You won't sleep tonight.'

She removes the lid, and settles back on the floor with her legs outstretched and her back against the wall. She is looking for a picture of Tom, but finds her daughter instead.

Meredith was eight when Louisa left Victor. There is a photograph of her about the age she was then, or just a bit younger, holding her cat, her face half buried in its fur. Louisa can't remember taking it, but it must have been her because Victor wouldn't have allowed her to put the animal up to her face like that.

Did she tell Meri to smile and is that why she is hiding behind Ginger? Later Victor backed over the cat with the BMW, not realising it was sleeping under the rear wheel. Louisa and Harry don't have a cat, but Louisa always checks under the wheels before she backs out, just in case.

Meredith was Daddy's girl. How horrible for her, Louisa

thinks now. How awful, the way she had to be all right for her father's sake. He said he was sorry, but that she should have kept the cat out of the way, and that if she were a good girl he'd buy her another one from the pet shop.

It seems to Louisa that there is deep sadness in her daughter's eyes. Was it a fleeting unhappiness, or was it the way she had always been? Louisa hadn't seen it at the time. The photograph has picked up something that her daughter hid well. It is no wonder that Meri seemed older than she was, and yet as Louisa looks at her now she knows that she was just a little girl, with a small child's interpretation of the world. That would have been the time to be there for her, when she was looking for some sort of direction, when she needed some sort of stability.

Louisa rings Meredith on a regular basis, but the conversations go nowhere. These days Louisa hears more about the details of her daughter's life from her sister, than from Meri herself. Zoe tells Louisa that on the surface everything is fine, but she worries about the girl and says it might be a good idea to give her a ring.

'I do ring her,' says Louisa, 'but she never tells me anything.'

It's true. Whenever Louisa rings, Meredith is polite and guarded. No, there's no special news. Todd is well. They are both working long hours to get more of the house paid off. Yes, they're coping just fine. Louisa and Harry should come to Sydney some time, but it's difficult arranging a time, with work and everything. There's someone at the door, she has to go. Thanks for ringing. Yes she'll keep in touch. She'll ring home next time. Home? The line clicks shut.

It's a frustrating and pointless exercise that only seems to make things worse. After Louisa hangs up she feels empty.

Harry seems fast asleep, but he half wakes when she crawls in beside him, and rubs his warm feet against her cold legs, reaches his arm around her body, and nuzzles into her neck.

'Night,' she whispers, but he is in deep sleep again.

The following week Louisa tells Lucy about Harry's unwillingness to talk about his music, and about the photographs, and Meredith, and Victor. Lucy advises her to keep trying to reach Harry, not to let herself get shut out.

'Because, what is the point otherwise?' Lucy says.

'I try,' Louisa says, 'I know I need to try harder. I do want to find more opportunities for us to talk, so that he feels comfortable to tell me things, so I can tell him things, so that we get closer, but I bend over backwards, and agree with him quite often about stupid things that don't even matter, even when I don't, but then he turns around and takes the opposite point of view which turns out to be what I thought in the first place, only then I can't say it, can I? So he's deliberately contrary. It doesn't matter how nice I am.'

'Well, no,' says Lucy. 'You need to try something else. You need to get a bit more angsty.'

Angsty? What's that? Grumpy? Angry? What has that ever achieved, Louisa wonders, but it's too hard to explain. 'Yes, I suppose,' she says. 'I guess so.'

Just the same, Lucy's comment precipitates something.

Louisa finds the first occasion she can after her session to tell Harry more about Victor and how what he did to her made him feel powerful, which she thinks he must have needed, because underneath it all he was weak. Why else would he pick on a person half his size, not to mention his own children who he should have been protecting from harm? She tells Harry, with a little too much feeling, that it makes her sick, what he did to them all.

Harry apparently takes her brief attempt to communicate as an oblique criticism of all of his sex, and gets moody for a while.

'Oh, for Pete's sake,' he says.

He goes for a walk around the backyard, does some light pruning. He comes back inside, puts the secateurs down, and takes up where they left off.

'I'm not Victor!' he says.

'I know.'

'For one thing, I actually care about you Louisa,' he says. 'Believe it or not.'

This surprises her, the fact that he would say it in so many words.

'Do you?' she says.

'Of course I do. I'm here, aren't I?' And he gives her an awkward squeeze. 'It doesn't have to be said.' His voice breaks over the last word, suddenly uncertain. Her eyes fill.

'Sometimes it does need to be said,' she says.

A short silence, then:

'We could have sex more often I suppose,' he suggests, hopefully.

'Could we?'

'Yes.'

'No time like the present,' she retorts.

Harry misses two beats, fixes her in the eye, strips off his gardening gloves, begins to hum the national anthem, and dances her towards the bedroom.

'What about the pruning?' she says.

'Bugger the pruning!'

As they make love, Louisa slows him down, luxuriating in the generous heat of his body and the ever-surprising tenderness of his touch. There is something subtle and new for her here, as if her body, even at this late stage, is still learning.

Afterwards, when they are lying lazily on the bed, with his arms loosely holding her, and the late sun filtering in, she tells him, 'You know, Harry, I do love you.'

His arms tighten fractionally, before he lets her go. He rolls over, sits up on the side of the bed, and stares out of the window. A cloud must have slipped across the sun. The light in the room softens.

'I know,' he says, 'me too.'

He stands with his back to her, naked, vulnerable, desirable. Her body aches for him, but he is gone, already moving on to the next thing. The end of the day is upon them, and tomorrow things will be as usual.

He begins to dress. 'It's getting late,' he says. 'I'd better take the dog for a walk. Want to come?'

CHAPTER EIGHT

Buddha cost seven dollars and ninety-five cents from a retail outlet that Louisa and Harry have difficulty categorising. The store sits near a south-of-the-river market and sells a range of goods including a substantial quantity of fruit and vegetables, lollies, cheap ornaments, antiques, bric-a-brac, multi-denominational religious items of devotion, fairies, artificial flowers and pot plants.

Buddha had originally been priced at fifteen dollars, but because he had a small chip on the big toe of his left foot, he was marked down. It was the bargain that drew Harry's eye, and a love of imperfection that drew Louisa's. Louisa held him and said no to the plastic bag, as Harry counted out eight dollars and told the shop assistant to keep the change because he was so pleased with the price. They drove straight home while Harry hummed along to Peggy Lee and 'Fever' playing from the CD stacker.

There was no debate regarding Buddha's place in the grand scheme of things. For once they were agreed. It was as if the spot beneath the pink rose tree had been waiting for him all along. A welcoming of petals had been prepared by the breeze.

Buddha's chip glinted white against the dark green paint that covered the rest of his expansive body. At first when they looked out onto the garden from the dining room window they could see it clearly, but after only a week it had begun to disappear. Dirt was covering it, and a petal from the rose had bandaged it. The petal shrivelled and stuck, and eventually dried out and was blown off and absorbed into the general background. By this time, the white had virtually disappeared, leaving an interesting black scar that could be discerned only at close quarters. Although the wound healed with the passage of time, Buddha retained a triangular mark on the tip of his toe, a point of focus for the observant to meditate upon.

They each noted the event as a minor miracle, and independently wondered about its significance.

Louisa stands in the mist watching the drops of water form and trickle over Buddha's bald head. He smiles. The winter grass has almost obscured him from view, but it doesn't seem to matter.

'Let nature take its course,' she murmurs, on his behalf. 'You don't seem to mind, do you Buddha? Of course, you're not actually alive. That might have something to do with it.'

At that the rain gets heavier, encouraging her to go inside.

There was a man, Floyd, who worked on the station for her father when she was very young. He used to play tricks on her and Zoe. Part of his job was to kill sheep for the homestead meat. It's not a pleasant job, her father said when she came crying to him that first time, but it has to be done. Floyd actually seemed to like it though. He liked other things too – making her feel safe and then ridiculing her for trusting him. Zoe seemed tougher, more able to handle things like that. She stood up to him a bit more.

It takes a long time before a person looks back at the child and the adult and realises that, logically, the child can't be held responsible. It takes even longer to feel it is true. Responsible for what, she's not sure.

'Come on,' says Floyd. 'Come with me.'

Zoe is there too. She must be about six years old. Louisa is four.

'Where to?' says Zoe, tripping after him.

He's walking away. He has the dog with him – a bitzer, part kelpie, part several other things. A bit of dingo. He expects them to follow. They do, of course. They might have an inkling about Floyd's tendency for mischief by now, but they are curious. The yard, which is attached to a smaller pen, is a short distance from the homestead. Mostly it stands empty, but today it holds about a dozen animals including some ewes with their lambs, already weaned, but with some still trying for milk.

'Pick one,' he says.

'What for?' says Zoe.

'Which one do you like best?'

'That one is cute,' says Louisa, pointing to one of the bigger lambs.

'That one it is,' says Floyd.

Louisa hasn't thought of Floyd for years. She wants to approach the subject obliquely, talk about it generally, and not get into the particulars. She doesn't like to think about Floyd, but he has emerged in her consciousness for a reason. He might hold a clue. Louisa thinks of Buddha then. He could be the bridge she needs. She tells Lucy that she's interested in Buddhism because it doesn't shy away from the subject of death, and how she thinks she might be looking for some sort of spiritual or philosophical answer. 'What do you think?'

'About what?'

'The meaning of death.'

Lucy says, 'The meaning of death? I think that we can dwell on it, or just acknowledge it as a fact that helps us to appreciate our experience of living. I suppose it's not just about an individual's life or death is it? I mean we're all a part of something bigger than ourselves, don't you think, even if you think of it as just being part of the community? If you have the opportunity to contribute something positive to that, that's good. I see you doing that, Louisa – making your contribution rather than just curling up in a ball. Not that I could blame you if you did. But remember, the aim is to keep moving forward. Isn't it?'

'I guess.'

'I'd like you to try focusing on the future for a change. Some goals for the future. Do you want to continue with the hypnotherapy to consolidate your commitment to moving forward?'

'Not this week if that's okay.'

'It's your time, of course. It's up to you.'

'Not sure that it's the best approach for me.'

'At all?'

'I'm not sure.'

'All right. That's fine with me now.'

'I need the big picture.'

'What do you mean by the big picture?'

'The meaning of life.'

'It's what you make it.'

'No.'

'There is no need for a big picture in psychology.'

Louisa's heart sinks. 'I thought there was.'

'It's a distraction, Louisa. I mean, what's the real issue here? You need to be prepared not to run away from the small picture. Why do you continue to hurt yourself? That's worth thinking about.'

On the way home and over the next few days Louisa grows increasingly irritated with Lucy. Angsty, in fact. Lucy seems to think everything is so much more simple than it is. It's not what she meant, this logical linear type of thinking that Lucy seems to specialise in, as if life is a problem to be solved with a right and wrong answer. Besides, it's a bit facile to imply she should just let go and move forward, as if history isn't a part of her life, as if it isn't her present and her future. As if Tom didn't even exist. She owes him that at the very least, an element of prolonged suffering. He'd expect it of her.

If she were to be perfectly honest, all that last session did was to make her feel worse. She'd wanted to talk about meaning, not her personal failings. What she needs most is a grand scheme of things, some sort of higher order so that there is a point to everything, despite all the suffering.

The mere thought of it makes her feel agitated. It's hard to watch the television news. She has to walk out of the room to find something else. She has to get her mind onto another track. Harry tells her not to be so sensitive. That's life, he says. The mortality rate is one hundred percent. Which, he says, begs the question: what does it matter anyway?

There are times when Harry says things that make her wary of him, even suspicious. She says nothing, forces her mind onto something else.

She thinks of the grasshopper with the broken leg. She would have been about seven or eight. She'd picked it up and brought it to Zoe to see what could be done. Zoe said give it to me, dropped it on the ground and stepped on it. Then she ran off to get on with her play. Louisa stood there looking at what remained of the grasshopper, not sure what she should feel about what had just happened. It was still twitching slightly. She stepped on it again, finishing it.

She should have known. Zoe was like that. Not unkind exactly, but tough and realistic. Once they had to pluck a chicken after it had been decapitated. Floyd chopped its head off and the poor thing ran around headless with Zoe laughing until she wet herself. They'd plucked the chicken with its body still warm. Louisa has a fleeting experience now of the smell – wet feathers, and steam from the water coming to the boil in the old copper. It slips by and gives way to Floyd.

'Sit on the fence here. This is going to be funny,' he says.

'It'll make you laugh. You'll see.'

He whistles to the dog and it goes into work mode, crouching down, sorting and dividing the small flock. The dog seems to intuit his intention. It doesn't take Floyd long to catch Louisa's sheep, her lamb.

He drags it from yard to pen, and her emerging realisation hardens into certainty. He takes the knife from his belt. She wants to run, but can't move. She is drawn to watch, impassive, as the frightened animal struggles and cries out for its mother. It struggles, stumbling around in Floyd's grip, until it gives in, throat exposed, eyes rolled back. The blood gushes. All the while, the lamb's mother is frantic, running up and down the fence line, trying to break into the killing pen. The rest of the flock bunches together. Floyd turns to look at the girls. Louisa sees that Zoe's face is blank. Her own is hot.

'You're horrible!' she shouts. 'You're mean and horrible!' Her tears won't stop running. Floyd begins to laugh.

'See,' he says. 'I told you it would be funny didn't I?'

Louisa left school at fifteen, started her training to become a nurse's aide, and not long afterwards was shown her first dead person. The clinical instructor pulled the curtain back after preparing her charges for gravitas that Louisa failed to feel. The body in death was a transitory token at best – a temporary link to the life that had gone. She would see many more corpses before she left the hospital to marry Victor. She would lay them out, think about them, forget for a while. They came back to haunt her after Tom died. Death in all its various forms.

Sometimes she sat with people as they died, when there was no one else. She felt their souls depart. Presence. Absence. She found one man too late, after rigor mortis had set in. He was set in the foetal position with his arms folded up and crossed over his chest. She thought of ancient ritualistic burials. He looked as if he were preparing himself for birth into the next world. That one returned to her sometimes, just before sleep. He'd been brought in off the street and nobody knew who he was. John Doe. It was difficult to tell how old he was – old to her mind then. He moved in and out of delirium.

That night he'd grabbed at her hand and read her palm as she prepared to straighten his bed. He told of her forthcoming marriage, the children she'd have, her unhappiness, and about Harry. Not by name; something about a musician. The details have become vague. Subsequent events have merged with memory. Perhaps there was something else about a mysterious man in a white van.

She is making it up. She wonders again about the man parked in front of her house. She wants to believe that there is more to life than she can see, and a stranger who can predict her future would suggest that. The man in the van might be significant.

The old man held her hand, talking in full flight, but suddenly looked startled, stopped and let her go.

'That's enough,' he said. 'Could you get me a bottle, nurse? I need a bottle now!'

Afterwards Louisa wondered if he had seen Tom's fate in her hand. Had he wanted to spare her, or had he suddenly wondered whether he was really seeing the future at all?

It's possible he just needed to urinate and couldn't hold on any longer.

CHAPTER NINE

Harry ventures out to the backyard to discover that one of the bigger trees has pruned itself during the night, leaving a jagged edge that will rot if not tended. He calls several tree loppers listed in the local paper and finally secures the promise of a quote later in the day, timing vague. It means he has to hang around. Louisa has put on her corporate clothes and gone to work so he does the dishes and cleans up a bit. He is domesticity personified. If his friends could see him now, if he still had his friends, they wouldn't know him. He has only himself to please these days, Louisa of course, and Buster.

He can't think what's changed him specifically, can't put his finger on when it happened, but it's true: he is a different man these days. His body has slowed down, and he's become more domesticated than he was. It's not as bad as he would have thought twenty years ago, or ten. Now he could happily have that life with Yasamine and Bella. Back then he couldn't sit still. He thought he needed something, but it seems it was Yasamine that he needed all along. Eventually she got fed up with him and left. He blamed her but if he was honest with himself now he'd say he engineered it.

Bella was three. Perhaps she still has vague memories of him. He had a beard then, and long hair. Her fourth birthday was coming up because he'd already assembled the red and yellow swing set they'd picked out while his mother babysat. That was how quickly it changed from Yasamine staying and her deciding to go, or telling him, at any rate. It happened somewhere in that few days between when they bought the present and the day of the birthday. Yasamine fronted him one day and said it was over. They hadn't even been arguing. The dull echo of that old hurt still threatens to entrap him, and he sidesteps it to walk straight into thoughts of Bella.

What sort of birthday did she have in the end? He can't remember. She didn't get the swing set. Yasamine didn't take it with her, or he hung onto it just in case. Then he carted it to the rental property, just in case, and there it stayed until he moved on again. That time he left it behind. He wonders if it's still there. After Yasamine and the bloke moved north with Bella, he never saw any of them again. He had the address for a while because of the papers he was served.

That day he'd just got home from whatever work it was that he was doing at the time. Making fibreglass covers for utes? Or that could have been later. His brief stint as a landscape gardener. Whatever it was, he was in his paint-splattered overalls and steel caps. That much he knows because he felt the difference between himself and the guy walking down the driveway in his clean shirt and tie, and later the mammoth self-control it took not to kick him in the head.

It was too late by the time he realised what was going on, that the guy parked opposite his house had been waiting to serve him. He didn't sense the wrongness of the weasel scurrying down the driveway and catching him off guard at the door with his keys out. He probably thought the bloke was some sort of salesman, still thought it for the few seconds after he confirmed Harry's name and pulled out the envelope. It took a moment or two to dawn on him, even though everything was in slow motion like just before a car crash.

He refused to sign her documents for months – a compulsive

stretch of time where his furious calls alternated with her insistent cajoling. If the truth be told, he kept it going as long as he could because it let him feel that it hadn't finished yet. But it was a sickening game: literally making him sick – in the body and mind. He started seriously fantasising about what he might do to them, all of them. Then what? Then what? Finish himself? But guys who do that, he'd always thought, should do themselves first. They're weak and they're mean. They've got no dignity. You can't own someone else after all, not even your wife or kids. Ellington was playing on the radio, reminding him of another sort of life. The feeling subsided. They were dim days with few points of reference, but he must have been moving slowly through. And not far below the surface he knew that he was who he was, not defined by his connection to his wife, or his daughter, or anyone else for that matter.

One morning he woke up early and decided it was all just so much bullshit and that he didn't care anyway – they weren't worth it. Or they were worth it. He'd been getting there for a while, scared of what he was turning into. He finally gave in and signed. The other bloke adopted Bella officially and gave her his name.

Yasamine told him it would be the last thing she'd ever ask of him, that he could keep everything else, she didn't care. He wouldn't have to pay child maintenance. It was insulting, as if his intentions were so mercenary. That was more her style than his. He signed anyway, ending the conversation for good.

It's one of those days when he can't stop thinking about it, so he decides not to try. He indulges, makes another coffee and stares out the window. The rain has stopped.

Harry tries to conjure up Yasamine's face, but this time he can't. Instead he remembers a photograph of her sitting in a boat tied to a jetty. After he took the photograph he stepped into the boat and one of the oars fell into the water with the movement that he created. He tried to catch it but only succeeded in pushing it further away. She got mad at him; she called him an idiot, and got out of the boat. Then she came back. They must have got the oar back and gone for a row. He can't remember the rest of it. But there were other things on that holiday. Good things. He remembers walking through the forest at Pemberton and the cool, musty smell of the bark.

There was a time when it could have been different, when he could have kept everything together, but for some reason he hesitated. He found it hard to make a commitment, even when she threatened to leave. He couldn't give in.

It all sounds stupid now. Other people, normal people, plod on, mend their differences, accept that life isn't perfect. He's spent his adulthood looking around for the perfect job and the perfect lifestyle, but has succeeded in scraping together just enough to pay the bills. He's always been dissatisfied.

By three o'clock the rain has cleared and the sun is shining. The tree guy still hasn't arrived. He's probably not coming. It's been a miserable day – can't blame him. Harry decides to take Buster down to the dog beach. He leaves a note for Louisa: *Lou, Gone to the beach. You might want to get a couple of frozen dinners. H xx*

When he gets to the beach there is one small parking space available so he eases in there, between two urban assault vehicles. These days, spaces seem to be getting smaller in inverse proportion to the growth of vehicle sizes, and he feels a twinge of jealousy at the ostentatious affluence of everyone, it seems, except him. He feels like he's the only one who can't afford to live in a big house and drive a fancy car, although he notes with satisfaction that while the cars next to him would do nicely for the grey nomad life that he aspires to, they look as if they have never left the bitumen.

As he opens his door, Buster shoves past him and the driver's door is pushed onto the vehicle in the next bay. Harry checks and can see nothing, no damage at all, but when he returns to his car after their walk, he finds a note on the windscreen. Scrawled in capital letters on both sides of a piece of paper torn from a small notebook is the following:

THANKS FOR THE SCRATCH ON MY CAR YOU FUCKING FUCKWIT. LEARN HOW TO FUCKING PARK YOU FUCKING IDIOT. I WOULD FUCKING KEY

Harry turns the note over.

YOU'RE FUCKING CAR BUT IT'S OBVIOUSLY SUCH A FUCKING PIECE OF JUNK THAT YOU WOULD'NT EVEN NO IF I DID. YOU FUCKING FUCKWIT.

The spaces on either side of him are now clear. Harry looks around to see if anybody is sitting in a vehicle watching him, but there is no one. He wonders about the occupant of the vehicle that was next to him. Did he walk past him on the beach with his dogs or his surfboard?

The note has obviously been left by someone with a great command of the lexicon, some fucked-up adolescent dealer, no doubt, who can afford a sixty-thousand-dollar vehicle through his ill-gotten gains.

The carpark is emptying out. Harry checks to see if his car has been keyed, but he can't tell, so he screws the paper up into a ball and tosses it over his shoulder. Obviously he would have known if he'd scratched someone's car, so either the bloke (he assumes male) has got his car scratched elsewhere and just noticed it, or he enjoys leaving notes around for the perverse pleasure of upsetting decent law-abiding people. Either way Harry wouldn't want to give him the satisfaction.

He thinks about how he will talk it over with Louisa when he gets home, and how they will both have a good laugh about it. They'll speculate about the note-leaver and reduce him to the ridiculous dickhead that he is. She needs a good laugh. She hasn't been laughing much lately. Harry should take the note to show her. He looks around but it has rolled away somewhere, or been caught by the wind.

'Never mind,' he says to himself. 'Never mind. Leave it.'

He whistles Buster to the car, turns on the radio, and switches to the jazz program.

'It's strange,' he thinks, 'that note seems familiar.'

He's sure he's seen something like it before. Déjà vu. He wonders if Louisa has brought one home. He seems to remember her, or someone, claiming that she hadn't even touched the car next to her, had actually gone out and come back in to leave more room, and had returned to some such note. Maybe it was Yasamine. Could it have been that long ago?

Then it occurs to Harry that this note could be like a sort of virus being passed on in the community by an organised group, a sort of suburban terrorist cell that has designed it as a way to stuff up a person's day. This thought makes him angry again. Sure *he* can take it, but what if it happened to some sweet little old lady or some old guy with a dicky heart? Or some good person who has already been through the mill and is on the brink of giving it all up? This sort of thing could push them over the edge. Or what if he was a good person like a doctor – or no: a carer, or someone like a welfare worker who earns next to nothing for the privilege of trying to make life better for no-hopers like that guy when he falls on hard times? This thought gives him some satisfaction, imagining the guy dirty and unkempt, down and out, asking for a few dollars for a bus fare, getting knocked back, going on to the next person. This train of thought leads nowhere. Harry is feeling more annoyed than he was before. He drives home and catches every red light, thoughts of the guy circling through his head as he waits. He misses a green and someone beeps him, causing him to jump.

'Bastard!' he thinks. 'I should have keyed the shit out of his fucking car. I bloody should have.'

Louisa gets home at a quarter past three, reads Harry's note, and is exasperated by his dinner directive – more than the situation warrants. It's been one of those days. She's felt strange since she woke in the morning. She forced herself into the routine of getting dressed, going to work, struggled through the day, and now she's arrived home to this. The more she thinks about it, the more it stresses her. Her heart is beating uncomfortably and she has broken out in a sweat. She needs some sort of release.

'What's wrong with you? What's wrong with you!' she shouts at the empty room, at Harry, at herself. It doesn't help. She desperately searches for a skerrick of advice from Lucy that might help. Deep breaths, deep breaths, she tells herself. She breathes slowly and deeply. That brings it down a notch.

She pulls herself together, changes into comfortable shoes and goes out again. She looks around the shops for an hour or so and chooses fish dinners from the frozen section of the supermarket. When she gets back, Harry hasn't returned. She decides she'll make an effort so she sets the table with a cloth and candles, before going out to the tree to see if she can find a usable lemon. One has fallen on the ground and a small snail is stuck to it. She could detach the snail but its shell is thin and would be crushed. She leaves the fallen lemon and picks a greenish one from the tree, but her heart is thumping. There are signs everywhere that Tom is still around.

'I know, Tom,' she says to the air. 'I remember everything.' Her hands are trembling and a chill has spread over her body.

One spring morning Tom discovered a snail under the lemon tree as they walked around her parents' garden. He would have been about two or three. The snail was hiding by a fallen lemon beneath the tree. Tommy let out a squeal of delight and was about to stamp on it, but Louisa held him back.

'Don't hurt the snail,' she said. 'Poor snail.'

She rescued the snail and put it in some greenery, where it would have to deal with new challenges, she supposed. Even a snail deserves a fighting chance.

Later when Tom told her mother that he had found a snail, her mother said she hoped he squashed it.

'No, Mummy saved it,' he said.

'Yes, that sounds like Mummy,' said her mother.

These are the things she remembers. 'Do you remember, Tom?' she says. 'You were too small.' Her heart sinks a little.

That day, Louisa realised that no big hand would come down from the sky and rescue her and the children. She would have to save herself. She would have to stop being passive. It took her another three or four years to work up the courage to leave. She was waiting for something bad to happen to her husband. She was waiting for him to get his just desserts.

But that was wrong, and anyway the world doesn't work like that. He had a right to live his life. Everyone has a right to live a life – to follow it through to its natural conclusion. Everything. She stares at the lemon picked green from the tree, remembers dinner, returns to the feel of her feet inside her shoes, hard against the brick paving, the shifting leaves on the rosebushes, the distant sound of traffic.

She has just walked inside when she hears a familiar engine sound. The vehicle pulls up outside the front of the house and stops, with its engine still running. She goes to the window. The van is back. She jumps away from the window and sneaks a look from the side, trying to see what he is doing. The man, who she now recognises is a cross between Tom and Victor, is looking in her direction. His window fogs up. He wipes a patch clear, and continues looking in the direction of the house.

She is unnerved. Her heart begins to beat irregularly, threatening to stop, and alternately racing to the point of bursting. Her forehead is damp, and the back of her neck is prickling. She shivers. He is looking, at the house, at the window. The engine is running. She wonders if he can see her. She edges further into the corner and, holding the lemon like a hand grenade, drops to the floor, crawls along the wall beneath the sill, and takes cover under the coffee table. Her eyes are fixed on the passage that leads to the front door. She can hear the engine, louder now, revving. What if he is aiming to drive straight through the front wall? She crawls out from the coffee table, across the floor to the far corner of the room. The front wall will slow him down. He won't get at her there in the corner, not if she makes herself small enough. Then what?

Now her thoughts are spinning, winding tighter and tighter to the only possible conclusion – Victor. He has paid this man to do his dirty work. He knows where she lives. He's got this man watching her, and he's employed him because of the man's resemblance to their son. It's a new kind of torture, something to keep her hanging, to get her back in his control.

She will not be intimidated! She is finding it hard to breathe. She curls herself into a ball, closing off every point of access. She seals herself in.

CHAPTER TEN

The rain has forced a new hole through the gutter just outside the bedroom window. Each time it rains, the water funnels down, causing a minor flood. Harry leaves a plastic bucket under the waterfall – a temporary fix until he can get someone in. He would try to do it himself, but he's getting stiffer, and he feels as if he's got enough on his plate with Louisa being the way she is.

Since the day he returned from the beach to find her huddled in the corner of the lounge room clutching a lemon, she seems to be functioning, just. She's been going through the motions, keeping her work going, but how, he doesn't know. Even to his untrained eye, she needs some serious time off to sort herself out. She's been to see Lucy since, and come back wearing a fixed smile, saying she's fine, when it's obvious that she's not.

'We did more hypnotherapy,' she said. 'I think she's trying to manipulate me. It's a kind of brainwashing. I know who's put her up to it. She thinks I don't, but I do. I won't let her do that again.'

'She's just trying to help,' he said, but was rewarded with a darting look of suspicion, and after that Louisa clammed up.

She didn't speak to him again for days.

Harry has tried to get her to make an appointment with the doctor, but she won't go. She acts as if things are back to normal.

It's taking its toll on both of them. When she's not working, she's taking something strong, something that she's hiding from him. He can't sleep, and she sleeps every chance she gets. That is, until today.

Today she was up before him. When he ventured from the bedroom into the hallway, she was already on the way out.

He worries. She needs to settle down. He is at a loss. He wonders whether he should try the tough love approach – to treat her as normal, as though nothing happened, as though he didn't find her shaking and crouched on the floor with her arms covering her head. As though when he finally coaxed her into a standing position, she didn't slide furtively along the wall, peer for a full minute through the window into the empty street, and mumble that she knew what he was up to.

'Who? Me?' he'd asked, but she hadn't answered, just pushed past him to check that the door was locked. She sat in a chair that she dragged into the corner at the side of the window, and rocked herself all night. That's how she was each time he got up to check on her. The hot chocolate he brought her sat cold and untouched on the table beside her in the morning. She went to bed then, and slept all day. He stayed home and watched over her, tried to get her to see someone, but she wouldn't budge – not, he suspects, until she could convince the world that she was all right. She had her pride. A part of her must have known that the way she was behaving wasn't quite right. Finally she relented. She'd gone to see Lucy then.

And after a week of him calling in to say she had the flu, she'd managed to pull herself together for work, for appearances, wearing a bright smile, calling out a little too loudly as she left the house - see you later, see you – and anyone who knew her well could see that she was ragged around the edges, but she seemed to be managing for that short period of time. She'd come home, exhausted from the day's performance, and do nothing. She'd sit and stare, take whatever it was, go to bed, and sleep for hours longer than was healthy, twisting and turning, voicing enough of the horror of her fractured dreams to really concern him. Eventually she'd seen Lucy again, at his insistence.

'Give her another chance,' he'd said.

This time she'd come back a little better. The days went by, and slowly, bit by bit, she'd begun to re-emerge. He wondered if she'd seen the doctor, if she'd started taking antidepressants. He did a quick search of the cluttered bathroom cabinet, but found nothing.

Finally, today, Harry notices another subtle change, as though she might be back to normal. She's almost cheery, not overly, her normal active self, and she's on her way out. He's still not sure. He'd like her home where he can keep an eye on her, but he doesn't want her to feel like he's mollycoddling her.

'Why are you rushing off?' he says, briskly. 'It's a nice day. We could get some washing on the line while it's fine. Look, there's a good stiff breeze out there. It'll dry in no time.' She switches from almost cheery to appropriately bristling.

'In case you haven't noticed, I was up early. I already have a line full. I think you should start rushing around a bit more yourself.'

So he gives her the finger. Half in fun, half relieved. It looks like she's finally back.

'Yes, very mature,' she says. 'Fine. I will stay in for a bit. But only because I've just thought of something else I need to do.' She puts her keys and her bag down and disappears through the back room to the laundry, and beyond.

The back door slams and she comes back into the room carrying an armful of dry washing from the line. She is still feisty. She dumps it on the couch and starts to fold but then she stops and looks at him until he is forced to look back.

'I'm sorry,' she says. 'You really do a lot. I shouldn't have said that.'

'Said what?' says Harry.

'Anyway,' she says, 'I think you need to remember I do plenty too, you know. I do my fair share.'

'I never said you didn't.' He grins. 'You must be feeling better.'

'I am better!'

'Good. I can see that you are.'

She slumps onto the couch amidst the clean washing. 'Why should you care?'

He sits beside her and puts his arm around her shoulders.

'I care.'

She stiffens, shrugs him off, stands and starts on the washing.

'Well don't just sit there,' she says. 'Help me fold.'

He stands and they fold in silence. After a while he says, 'What happened, Lou?'

'I don't know.'

'Talk to me.'

'I'm so tired, Harry. I started losing control of things again. No matter how hard I think about it, I can't seem to work it out. I don't know what else to do. I'd rather not talk about it.' She stares at the tea towel in her hand. 'How did this get in here?'

He shakes his head. She continues to stare at the rogue tea towel.

'I let my imagination run away with me a bit, I guess,' she says. She seems unsure of what to do. When Harry moves to take the tea towel from her, she pulls it close to her chest. 'I'm okay now. I just needed some space to sort it out, and I have.'

CHAPTER ELEVEN

Harry finds the weeding ritual strangely satisfying. It gives him time and space to think, but sometimes it takes him to places he'd rather not be.

He knows that his memory is selective, but sees that it is like that for a reason. There's no use beating yourself up about what you didn't know, about what you did or didn't do, now that you're older and wiser. You learn what you can and move on.

He is kneeling on a patch of grass next to a blue letterbox. Another place. Another time. There's the sound of the young couple across the road arguing again. Her name is Suzanne, and his is Gary, or Greg, or something. Harry's smiled at her once or twice, but she's kept to herself. She's a sweet little thing. Gary or Greg has a problem with men smiling at her. He doesn't believe in smiling.

Suzanne is screaming and crying, and Gary or Greg is shouting. At one point he drags her out the front door by her hair to wash blood off her face at the outside tap. It's hard to know why he makes the private so public. He's overdone it on some sort of chemical concoction. He wants to humiliate her. He doesn't care. Or he wants someone to stop him.

Harry stands to make himself visible, puts his hands on his hips. 'Hey!' he calls out. Suzanne keeps her head down, afraid to look, afraid to make things worse. The guy looks across, draws his index finger sharply across his throat, and drags her back inside. The door slams shut. Harry hesitates momentarily, and has just made up his mind to go over when Yasamine grabs him by the arm and tells him not to get involved. He hadn't noticed that she'd come outside and was standing behind him.

'You're not thinking of going over there, are you?' she says.

'Why not?'

'You don't know what he'll do. You've got your daughter to think of. And me.' There is some panic in her voice.

'She needs help,' he says. 'We can't do nothing.'

'It's none of our business, Harry.'

'I'll call the police,' he says.

'He'll know,' she says. 'He'll know it was us that called.'

Harry calls the police. They take their time. He calls again. They're on their way. When they get there Suzanne apparently is able to answer the door, apparently says she's fine and asks them to go away. They do. Their hands are tied. Harry has done his duty and leaves it to the professionals, but he feels uneasy. Later he discovers that Gary or Greg has gone on beating Suzanne after the departure of the police, until she is dead. She's twenty-one. He's twenty-two. Now he has more things to think about than who called the police.

He gets a couple of years in the end. Another neighbour tells Harry they had kids who were staying with the grandparents.

That was years ago. Suzanne should be pushing middle age now, getting fat. Maybe Greg or Gary is still around, hasn't learned, is still a junkie, still beating women, his brain stalled at adolescence, living in denial. How else could you go on?

But that young girl, she didn't deserve it. And Harry realises with some misgiving he could have been more of a man. He could have taken that risk for the poor girl. He won't make that mistake again.

Harry's had enough of the weeding for one day. He washes, changes, and retreats into his office, a converted bedroom that lately has been giving way to the forces of entropy. Since Louisa's episode, she's stopped tidying his space and it has been transforming itself into a store room – hardly the image he should be promoting to the occasional client who insists on visiting. For some time now, he's been thinking he should market himself more aggressively. He needs to get back to where he started. He needs to do a good clean out and start the whole thing from the beginning again.

The business was conceived over drinks at Gordon and Carole's one night, not long after he and Louisa had moved in together. They were socialising quite a bit more then. She'd been introducing him to her assortment of friends. He couldn't return the favour since he'd lost touch with his own.

The whole thing was Gordon's idea really, drawing on what Harry had told him about his former career. Gordon seemed to know what he was talking about, and he had all the trappings of success around him, which added the feel of credibility. They were younger of course, still visualising a future. So Harry went for it.

He still uses the same spiel he worked out back then. When people ask him what he does, he tells them he operates a distance mentoring service for adventurous young musicians travelling to the sticks from the bigger centres, interstate, and, on occasions, overseas. Asia mostly. The idea is that they make their breakthrough here, become biggish fish in the West's nursery pools, so to speak, launch their careers. 'From deserts the prophets come,' he quotes, although he struggles to remember where the quote came from, and what it actually means. It seems to persuade though. He provides young hopefuls with local knowledge – advice tailored to their circumstances – on reasonably priced accommodation, information on rehearsal rooms, introductions to venues for gigs, contacts with session musicians, and the latest on recording studios. He charges them next to nothing, but he was always supposed to get a cut when they made the big time, take the pick of the bunch, take on their management. That was the plan.

In fact, the business started well. Louisa encouraged, and was right there with him. They agreed she'd keep the books. In the first six months they'd provided services to five groups and a couple of singer-songwriters. Some had grants, or a loan from a supportive relative. He even signed one group that had a bit of early success, and a couple of nice fat deposits went into his business account, before the promising musicians disappeared into obscurity.

Harry felt inspired, mixing with them and feeding off their youthful enthusiasm. He got back into the scene and began to think about picking up the sax again. He and Louisa started considering opportunities everywhere: for services where there were gaps, and for new markets – actors, artists, groups of all kinds. They made some grand plans, and even met with the bank to discuss taking out a loan. Luckily, they hadn't signed anything, because of what happened next with Tom.

Louisa dropped out and never really got back into it. And Harry might have looked okay, but he was damaged too. That's clear now, although instinctively, he played his hand close to the chest. He'd been too new, and guarded around the boy, to claim any sort of affiliation. He didn't know how long the relationship would last after all, and he hadn't been the boy's father. Afterwards he tried to keep up the impetus of the business, but it all felt too hard. It must have showed, because the calls dropped off.

Even so, there'd been enough of a start to create a thread that connected then and now. The business became whatever the demand required. They lived modestly on what he'd saved, and on Louisa's earnings, supplemented by the occasional bit of business. Periodically someone would ring and say they'd heard from a friend of a friend that he could help them out with the organisational aspects of a prospective country tour. So he'd do that. He'd continued to build on his networks, picked up the odd contact in regional areas, kept up knowledge of some of the more obscure musical trends. He could still sound as if he had his finger on the pulse, so the calls dribbled in. Each time he thought of calling it a day, he'd get another small flurry of interest. It had been just enough to justify renewing the business name every three years, just enough to do his bit towards household expenses, and just enough to stop him from throwing in the towel.

When Harry wants to indicate he's at work, he keeps the door closed and the window open. There is a small knock on the door, barely audible. It's something she does when she's dropped in confidence – as if she's afraid to disturb him. She's giving him the option to pretend he hasn't heard.

'Who's that a-tapping on my door,' he says. He rises from his chair and swings it open. She has tea for him, and a small saucer of biscuits.

'To keep you going,' she says. 'I'm bored.'

'Why don't you go out?' He takes the tea and biscuits and sets them down by the keyboard.

'Where?'

'I don't know. You could go shopping.'

This seems to surprise her. She holds her hands palms upwards and produces a heavy sigh.

'No, Harry.'

'What did I say?' he says, feigning ignorance.

'You're encouraging me to shop? Really?'

'I suppose it makes you happy.'

'What are you saying?'

'Nothing. No ulterior motive. You should knock louder,' he tells her.

'You're right. I might go out. I should go out.'

'Catch up with friends.'

'I'll think of something.'

She departs. Harry sucks on a biscuit and surfs the net.

Fifteen minutes later he hears her leave the house, hears the car drive off. He takes a long, deep breath, stands up, does a jog on the spot and shakes out his hands. It's hard work keeping up this supportive Mr Nice Guy thing. It's time she got better. He has a sudden, familiar feeling of restlessness, overcome by the urge to run away. He attempts to pin down the source, fails, slumps back into the chair, closes his eyes, and wonders about this particular self-destructive characteristic of his, and why it hasn't burnt out by now. He wonders about his ancestors, and whether Yasamine was right, that he has gypsy blood. She'd based the theory on nothing more than that, his tendency for impulsiveness, as far as he could ascertain. And the music.

Yasamine didn't seem to want to get involved in the world at all. 'Why can't we all stay home together and watch TV like normal families?' she'd ask. She resented outside influences pushing in on their family, whether it was trouble with the neighbours, or the guys in the band.

Of course he wanted to escape. What young bloke wouldn't? She was forever going on at him about money and helping out with the housework, but the baby was always crying and he was exhausted. She was too, but he couldn't help that. He would have helped her if he could, but he couldn't. He was too young. She might have been younger, but women seemed more mature, more able to cope. It seemed born into them. He was just trying to survive, and he was always feeling angry. He constantly had to stop himself from blowing his top, from hitting out.

In his weaker moments he could imagine getting just like his father. Somewhere at the back of his mind was that worm of doubt. He wasn't sure what he might be capable of doing if he lost it completely, his discipline, his self-control. He couldn't bear the thought of what might be lurking inside him.

It wasn't what he wanted. It wasn't who he wanted to be.

The old man died more than fifteen years ago. Harry recalls the day he finally got up the courage to visit him in hospital. He was going to get some things off his chest. He was going to be heard. He was going to make the old man acknowledge what he'd done; hear him apologise for the damage. Harry might forgive him then. He might not. He'd see how it all played out.

When he saw the old man in his bed he didn't recognise him at first. He could have walked right past and never known if it hadn't been for the name on the wall. He'd looked so small. He was all swallowed up in the cold, stiff, white sheets. His blue eyes stared out at Harry without recognition, helpless and needy.

His liver was shot by then, and his organs were shutting down. That's a strange expression, shutting down, as if someone is doing the final walk-through of a vacated house and turning off the lights. The old man's brain was just another empty room. He would call out, but it was a reflex action. It didn't mean anything. It was disturbing.

Harry realised with some shock that he'd been cheated out of a final showdown. He couldn't talk to the old guy. His father hadn't come to any great realisation and now it was too late to make him. He just lay there in that big hospital bed, uncomprehending. He would never see his own part in how things had played out.

The old man was left to die in a four-bed room in that old public hospital. He was dying, everyone knew it, he seemed to be signalling for a drink, but he wasn't allowed a drink even then. One human being to another, it was cruel to watch. He was sixty-one, too young in some people's minds, but Harry thought, if anything, he'd been alive too long. It wasn't as if he was getting any better. It wasn't as if he had some blinding flash of insight in those final years, or months, or weeks. The damage had been done long ago – to himself and to them.

Harry decides it made him what he is. He had his father in him and that was that. He'd pushed it away from him when he was a kid, but discovered it was still there, just under the surface, right after Bella was born.

CHAPTER TWELVE

It's part of their DNA, apparently, not confined to Louisa. He is flicking between radio stations and hears that it is every woman's fantasy to shop till they drop with their man at the ready to catch them, push them back out there, and urge them on. Like some kind of shopping coach. Harry takes a deep breath and suggests that they spend a day of shopping together. Louisa puts on her new dress, and does her hair up in a new style. The sun is shining.

At the centre they bump into Carole. Harry is embarrassed. He hasn't seen her since that night at Clancy's. She gives no sign – seems to have forgotten all about it. She is pushing a trolley containing nappies and other age-inappropriate items. She invites them both to lunch.

'We're babysitting Gordon's niece,' she tells Louisa, 'for a week! But she's a good kid. Give me about an hour or so to get things sorted – let's say around one? It should be fun. Gordon won't be there because he's not back until tomorrow, but Harry will still be needed to keep you company when I have to attend to her, you know.'

'We'd love to,' says Louisa, ignoring Harry's raised eyebrows and other facial signalling. Why does she do that?

Why does she have to make decisions for both of them without consulting him? She knows he's not comfortable around kids.

Two hours later, Harry finds himself awkwardly seated on a low sofa with the baby pulling herself up on his trouser legs to achieve a tottering stand. Her small hands are wet and plump and she leaves marks from a biscuit that Carole has given her. From the smell that is wafting upwards she needs changing.

To his annoyance she has the same dark curly hair that Bella had as a baby. Her eyes are almost black and there is a distracting level of openness in her gaze as she watches his face. The whole experience is uncomfortable and inconvenient.

'Isn't she cute, Harry?' says Carole. 'She's so cute.'

'She's all right I suppose,' he says. 'I'm not really into kids.'

'You have a daughter, don't you?' Carole persists. 'What happened?'

'Carole!' says Louisa.

'Not everyone is cut out to be a parent,' says Harry. 'You know that.'

Carole flushes. 'What is that supposed to mean?'

'I thought you'd had a falling out with your own.'

'Harry!' says Louisa.

'No,' says Carole, looking at Louisa, her eyes widening, 'we didn't have a falling out.' She laughs. 'I'm hardly the sort of person to say never darken my doorstep again, am I?'

'No, I suppose not,' he says.

'Anyway, part of being a good parent is letting kids make their own choices. There is a big difference between that, and falling out. Independent kids are precisely those who are secure enough to take off by themselves to explore the boundaries of the world. Personally, I think it's a good thing.' Carole barely loses her composure. In reality, his comment seems to have piqued her interest. She smiles into his eyes. 'I must admit, I do miss her. And the children of course.' Her gaze wanders to the photo gallery on the wall above his head. 'Anyway, we've been talking quite a lot lately, on the computer. We've been using the social media to share photos.'

'Oh, that,' says Harry.

'The kids are really happy and well adjusted. They're doing amazingly well in school. It's hard to believe. Such a relief! I think it's a credit to them.'

'Sure,' says Harry.

'Jenna has been chosen to play lead violin in the school concert. How about that! I don't know where she gets it from. Well, I do. I learned the cello, only I was lazy with my practice. You'd know all about that, Harry. Just kidding!'

Harry smiles, and shrugs.

'Viscount is a great little gardener, apparently. Tomatoes. They put the time in, of course. They don't buy them too much rubbish. Gordon and I are planning a trip over. We might combine it with Scotland. If Gordon can't get the extra time off, I'll go on without him.'

Carole gazes at Harry. 'Every decent relationship has to go through its ups and downs. That's what keeps it honest. Don't you think?' Her voice is calm, but she challenges him with her eyes. He finds it vaguely stirring. She's not bad looking even when he's stone cold sober.

'Oh well,' he says. 'Sorry.'

'What for?' she says, still smiling.

'I'm not much into computers,' says Harry, 'or this social networking. I'm a bit of a Luddite.'

'You should,' she says. 'You need to come into the twenty-first century.'

'It's not compulsory. I do what I like.'

'Getting stuck in your ways,' she says. 'That's the fast track to getting old. Not good.'

'I think the baby needs changing,' Louisa observes. 'Do you want me to do it?'

Carole beams. 'Oh, would you? I don't think I could face another one today.'

'You should stop feeding her biscuits,' he says.

'I'm allowed to spoil her. I'm her auntie.'

At that Carole disappears into the kitchen, using the excuse of making more coffee while Louisa changes the child. Harry takes a stretch and a closer look at the photographs along the wall. As photographs go, they are marginally more interesting than most. They all feature Carole's daughter, her children, and a younger Carole and Gordon in various combinations, each caught seemingly unawares in the act of living or relating to one another. Not all smiles. A few normal, posed ones, here and there. One in which they're all laughing, except for Gordon.

Harry turns back to the room and looks around. The last time they visited, Gordon and Carole lived in a different place. The new house is immaculate, ultra-modern, and apart from the small gallery of photographs, there are no other pictures, or wall hangings, no ornaments or knick-knacks, and no clutter other than the play pen, and few scattered toys.

When Carole comes back, they drink half the coffee and prepare to leave. Louisa looks as anxious to go as he is.

'She's exhausting,' she says once they pull out of the driveway.

'Who? Carole?'

'The baby.'

He suddenly feels dog-tired. On the drive home his mind is flooded with memories of Bella, memories that he didn't even know were still there, things she did, as fresh as if they happened yesterday.

'Bugger!' he says, and he feels Louisa stiffen in the seat next to him.

'What?'

It takes him a moment to respond.

'I forgot to take the DVDs back. I'll need to go out again.'

Neither of them says much on the way home. Louisa is wondering what that was all about, the odd dynamic between Carole and Harry. It's unsettling. She feels more unsettled when she jumps as Harry loses his cool.

Victor is in her thoughts again. She hopes that he is not thinking of her. She hopes that her thoughts are not giving him some power over her. She stiffens.

'What?' says Harry. 'Relax, why don't you?'

She shakes her head, opens her eyes, and stares straight ahead. She needs to stay vigilant so she doesn't fall back into that dark place. Self-respect, she tells herself. Wake up, Louisa! Keep your hands on the wheel and your eyes on the road. Except that Harry is driving now and drifting too close to the median strip. The road is wet and potentially slippery.

'You're a bit close,' she says.

It annoys him, she knows, but too bad! She has to keep pushing forward so that she doesn't slip back into silence.

Even so, the journey is long, Harry is off in his own world, and she slips. She is caught and held on the whirling plane that flattens and spins her thinking into a familiar sickening loop. They are the same thoughts she's had over and over again, the ones that she's had ever since Tom's short life disintegrated. The force of that shock cracked the seals on the small, tight casket pressed in her mind, where the worst memories of Victor had been held. Victor the lawmaker who created and recreated the rules so that she never knew what they were; who made sure that the ground was always moving with no shared meaning, no sense of predictability – unless it was the way her body invariably reacted against his; in pain; immobilised; and blocked off on every side as he enclosed her whole world. She feels the familiar sense of rising panic, the feeling of being sealed inside without a line to the outside, her body a container for her anxiety and fear, her half-formed thoughts bumping around blindly inside her skull, and how Victor just stood there watching her struggle. She'd assumed he was waiting for some improvement in her, but eventually it dawned on her that he was just watching, the way he'd watch an insect, fallen into a cold cup of tea.

Why was it that she kept trying to be the person he wanted her to be, until finally she understood that she already was the person that he wanted, cracked and broken? Imperfect in every way.

She'd figured he couldn't help himself. She took his word for it.

'I love you,' he'd say, while she cowered on the floor, humiliated, bleeding. The kids always seemed to be somewhere else, in their rooms asleep. She would try to be damaged quietly so she didn't wake them up. He'd be the one making noise, yelling first, crying afterwards. 'I love you so much. I don't know what I'd do if I lost you.' His voice would tremble and break and that would be enough to keep her hanging there. He knew exactly what he was doing to her. He understood the torture of uncertainty, of waiting. He'd been to war. He'd been through it himself.

Harry pulls into the driveway and sits a moment after turning off the engine.

'You don't say much these days, do you?' he says. He laughs. 'Not like Carole, that's for sure.'

'You want me to be more like Carole?'

'No,' he says. 'Don't be ridiculous.'

'I'm not.'

She flushes as she says this. He's made her a little bit jealous. There could be some romance later if he's lucky.

'I better take the dog for a walk before the weather closes in again,' he says, as he gets out of the car. 'I don't suppose you'd like to come with us?'

'Not today. I've got stuff to prepare for work.'

This doesn't auger well for later.

'Fine,' he says, and the car door closes after him with a little too much force. She opens hers and calls out after him, 'What was that for?'

'At least Carole looks like she hasn't given up on exercising,' he says.

'Is that supposed to be some sort of encouragement?'

'What sort of encouragement do I get? At least Carole gives –'

'Oh, blow it out your arse, Harry,' she says.

'What?'

'You heard.'

'Right!' he says.

'Right!' she says. She glares at him.

He suppresses the urge to smile. He picks up the dog's leash from its usual place just inside the hallway. 'Come on Buster,' he says. 'Walk.' He begins to chuckle as he walks off down the street, with Buster racing ahead of him.

CHAPTER THIRTEEN

When Harry rings he has it in his mind to apologise to Carole over how he pushed her buttons at lunch, but he finds himself flirting instead. Or he's kidding himself and that's what he had in mind all along. He'll take her cues and whatever opportunity presents. He doesn't mind being labelled an opportunist. He's a team player, and that's exactly what's needed – opportunism – which to his mind is great timing, the ability to pick up on someone else's cues and improvise around them.

'Do you want to talk to Gordon? He's not in,' says Carole.

Harry lowers his voice an octave. 'I don't mind. I'd rather talk to you. How are you anyway?'

'Oh well,' says Carole, picking up on the vibe and capitalising immediately, 'I'm okay except for this slightly, oh I don't know, restless feeling that I've been getting lately.'

It's encouragement. He moves in for the clinch.

'That's strange. Me too.'

'Really?'

'Yes.'

'That's interesting,' she says. 'What are you going to do about it?'

'I'm not sure. What are you going to do about it?'

'I don't know. Let's see, we could help each other out.'

'We could.'

'Well then ...' says Carole, and as easily as that, it is arranged.

It's a bit of fun. Nothing serious. She reminds him of Yasamine for some reason – nothing like her at all really, but she looks all right. She's lively and doesn't hold back, although he could only take her in small doses and on a temporary basis. It might have been different when he was younger but he's used to a bit of peace and quiet these days, and he's never liked having too many expectations placed on him. Carole is what they call high maintenance. She'd expect him to keep his feet off the coffee table, and she'd want endless nights out, trips away and so on, not to mention what that sort of thing would cost. Plus she'd need attention, which is okay for a while, even sexy, and brings out his protective side. But it takes energy he doesn't have.

Gordon has more of what it takes for her, but he's away a lot, and probably getting his own bit on the side. They'd have some kind of an arrangement, which is fair enough, and their business. He likes Gordon. Gordon likes to stir things up. He reminds Harry of himself before he began to learn the value of stability. Before he started getting old. He chuckles to himself. He's not dead yet. It's time for him to shake things up a bit.

Louisa has driven to her favourite vantage point in Kings Park. She gets out and leans against the side of the car, gazing along the line of trees, taking in the feel of the wind against her skin, the litter of leaves and sticks at her feet, the sound of the crows and magpies as they call out to one another across the trees, and the damp scent of eucalyptus mixed with melaleuca and acacia.

When they were kids living on the station, she and Zoe would put old bits of lino on the ground to make cubby houses under a cluster of twisted grey trees that grew just past the outer edge of the homestead garden. The trees had grown stunted and bent horizontal, as if they'd been permanently caught in a strong gust of wind. She wonders how they would have looked if they'd grown somewhere more conducive with plentiful water, and less wind. The same trees might be planted somewhere in Kings Park. She'd check it out, if she knew what they were.

She is parked by an avenue of lemon-scented gums with broad white trunks, and towering foliage that springs back each time the wind drops. At the base of each, for as far as she can see, is a small brass plaque stuck in the ground, bearing the name of a young man killed in an old war. She is standing under the tree for Private John Jones killed in 1917, aged twenty-three.

She feels okay really, right now, today. There is beauty in the shifting light of the late winter gloom, something very nice about the sound of the wind, the sight of swaying trees and the chill in the air. She feels calm. Right now she is happy to be alive. Something must have shifted.

When she first booked in with Lucy she'd been having ideas about suicide. It would have been so easy to slip away, not that she wanted to die, but she was exhausted. Tom was gone and it was getting harder, if anything, as time went on, to live with that. She was overwhelmed by the stress of trying to get to something she couldn't have. She imagined a world where it would be possible to see him again and make everything all right, but only if she were to die. The idea expanded until it used up all the available space in her head, routing alternative scenarios.

'What about your daughter?' Lucy had asked her.

'Of course that's what's stopping me from going through with it,' she'd lied. In truth she hadn't allowed herself to think too much about Meredith and she'd told herself that Meri wouldn't particularly care anyway. She'd moved away a long time ago. Meredith had built a life for herself on the other side of the country with her husband, career and up-market friends. No room for Louisa or the past there.

Still she must have been telling Lucy an element of truth about not wanting to hurt her daughter. It was in her mind when she fronted up to therapy, that this would be proof she'd tried. She wanted to leave something behind for Meredith, to distance her from any feeling of responsibility, by making it a failure of therapy. She hadn't expected to feel bad about leaving Lucy in the lurch.

Louisa had gone to talk about Tom, but after they'd been meeting for a few sessions Lucy must have felt obliged to point out the monster in the room, Victor, and the story around all that.

'I'd rather just talk about Tom,' Louisa had said.

'It's part of the same picture.'

No they are two quite separate pictures, Louisa thought, but it was too hard to explain. She allowed herself to be convinced.

'Sometimes you have to lance a boil,' said Lucy.

Over the week that followed, Louisa worried about what Lucy's line of questioning would open up. She thought she might ring and cancel. In the end, she fronted up.

'Where do I start?' she said.

'Anywhere.'

'It might not make sense.'

'It makes sense to you. That's the main thing.'

Louisa considered for a moment. She said, 'Do you ever watch those wildlife shows where a predator is stalking a herd? It watches, picks one out, and then separates it from the rest, because the herd provides some sort of protection. Some animals are sufficiently connected and bonded not to let that happen. They close ranks, don't they? Elephants. They turn and face the threat together. The predator attacks at its peril. Others don't do that. They scatter. They sacrifice one of their own.'

'Herds can be a powerful force all right. What happened with your herd Louisa?'

'It wasn't big enough or strong enough to protect me, I guess. Or I was too young and stupid to see the danger signs. I got drawn away.'

'I see. What did he do to draw you away?'

Louisa heard an accusation in the question. 'Yes I know it's my own fault, Lucy, but he was very manipulative you know.'

Lucy looked slightly surprised, but remained unfazed. 'I didn't say it was your fault Louisa. I'm just interested in breaking down his ... tactics, if you like.'

Louisa took a deep breath. 'Oh, well that's easy. It's all about what you're connected to, isn't it? Victor made me lose my connections with what was outside our marriage. I lost my connections with everything, my friends. Family. He shrank my world down to just him. And the kids. He even resented the kids a bit. I think I lost touch with other people's day-to-day reality – the ordinary stuff of being able to catch up with friends and have a bit of a laugh – that sort of thing. Sometimes it's just easier to give in. Something wouldn't let me though. I kept fighting to survive.'

'Tell me how you did that. How did you fight to survive?'

'Before I figured out what was what and got out of there, you mean? I guess I tried to survive in the world according to Victor.'

'Okay, that's interesting. Tell me about that.'

'I suppose I tried to get inside his head, so I'd know what to do. It's not that I wanted to feel what he was feeling, but I thought I ought to try, so I could understand where he was coming from. So I knew how to keep safe, me and the kids. Only I didn't really love him, and he was bound to find out, so that was scary, like I was keeping a secret from him. He had a way of seeing every little bit of doubt. You have to be a good ... actor, I suppose. I was scared for the kids too. I had to prove it to him, somehow, that I loved him, so I tried to convince myself that I did. You see? That way I wouldn't be keeping a secret, because I might be able to actually feel what I said I was feeling. It sounds crazy doesn't it?'

'No.'

'It was awful living like that, walking on eggshells all the time. I didn't have time to think things through back then. I'd lost the ability. I gave up everything – my power, myself. My children. And a part of me must have thought I would break through to him and find his heart in there somewhere, and then we'd all be all right. Only I never found it. It was as if he didn't have one.'

'You did survive. That's the important thing, Louisa. You survived long enough to change your lives.'

'I'm not sure how. In a strange sort of way I felt sorry for him, because he couldn't have been happy, being what he was, and doing what he did. So that's a kind of love, isn't it? It's hard talking about this. Putting words to this makes it real. It's hard to think of that person as me, someone who allowed that, with my children there, trying not to hear or see. I did that, didn't I?'

'Or he did.'

'Yes, I know he can't get off scot-free. It's mixed up in my mind, what happened, whose fault it was: my pain and his arousal, pain and sex, pain and passion. I think he liked feeling whatever it was that he was feeling while I suffered. Plus I thought he needed me, but eventually I realised it didn't really matter to him that it was me. If it hadn't been me, it would have been someone else. Carole for that matter. No, she would never have put up with that crap. She might have dated him though, in his younger days, if she'd seen him first. He was good-looking, but I hated his looks. He made me sick. And charming – a real charmer. They thought I was the lucky one. Outsiders.'

She stopped talking then, all of a sudden, felt herself drifting off, almost to sleep.

Louisa is making more of an effort to walk with Harry. Today they have taken to the beach. He and Buster go ahead, at Buster's pace, leaving her to walk alone with her thoughts. There is a strong sea breeze, but the sand where she is walking is wet, saving her from the stinging sand higher up the beach. She walks barefoot, just inside the water line, and keeps her head down, watching how Harry and Buster's footprints are alternately covered and exposed by the rhythmic movement of the sea water. The water washes away the edges, smoothing their prints into impressions, or erasing them completely.

She looks up to see a single gull hanging above the water, buffeted by the wind. Harry and Buster are far ahead, and increasing the gap. Her eyes fall again to the sand, to her bare feet, to the uneven track she is creating with each step, to thoughts of the session with Lucy when she talked of Victor, and to the early days.

She sees him dressed up in a tie and suit that he wore with the indifference of someone for whom a suit has always been standard dress. He was from a wealthy family. She must have had something he wanted though: something from her very ordinary background. He stood awkwardly on the threshold of her parents' modest house, with a bunch of flowers for her mother, a redundant sweetener. He might have been older but her mother was already bowled over by the fact that a handsome law graduate was interested in her younger daughter. Her father was pleased too, she suspects, but didn't give as much away.

She was only sixteen, and living at home, commuting to the hospital by train, or being driven by her father. She was amazed that this man, twenty-five and on the way up in life, was apparently interested in her. Later he would tell her he had a fantasy thing for nurses. He seemed nervous too, so she felt more at ease and warmer towards him. He seemed that way. He seemed many things. It was difficult to pick apart what was and what something seemed to be.

Was she in love? It is hard to remember, but she tries to be honest. She was excited and flattered, but recalls a feeling of reserve. That night she was careful choosing what to wear. Lurking at the back of her mind was fear of encouraging him. She was in too deep already.

On paper, he looked good – handsome, successful, passionate. He didn't yet drink excessively, or he hid it well. He'd been to Vietnam, his number came up, but he reckoned he did it easier than some. Later he told her something closer to the truth. He was pissed off by the reception they got when they came home. It didn't seem fair after what they'd been through.

He said that in the army, he got into a few habits. They all drank and smoked some weed. When he got back, the government paid for his degree. His folks were happy they didn't have to fork out yet again, even though they had plenty, and he was glad he didn't have to go crawling to them. He didn't talk about the people he killed. He didn't really talk about the war at all, just his mates. He was twenty-five but he seemed so old to her, and he joked that she looked like a kid to him. She didn't even look sixteen until she got all dressed up in her lipstick and high heels. Everyone stopped talking and studied them when they walked in together.

There he was on the doorstep with flowers for her mother. It was the night they went out to dinner with his friends. Not friends exactly. Louisa never saw any of them again after that night, until the day of the wedding.

CHAPTER FOURTEEN

Harry imagines Carole soaking in a bubble bath, her breasts bouncing like playthings just above the water line, cushioned in the bubbles. Jazz is playing in the background, her eyes are closed and her lips are slightly parted. Her hair is falling down, wet on the ends, pointing like a sign to her nether regions. He walks in fully clothed. He is wearing his khakis from when he was in Nashos, slouch hat, flowers stuck in the end of his rifle. He is feeling fit and strong. He has his sixpack back. He towers above her. She opens her eyes and smiles at him.

'Get in, soldier boy,' she says. Her voice is husky. He says nothing, being the strong, silent type.

He leans his rifle against the wall and starts to unlace his boots, but she becomes impatient.

'Don't make me wait,' she begs him, but he takes his time. She is moving around under the water. Her eyes are closed again. Her mouth is open. The water slips against her skin. Harry sits on the edge of the bath and removes his boots. She rises out of the bath, and puts her arms around him from behind, unbuttoning his shirt, and loosening his pants.

'Big strong soldier man,' she says. 'Give it to me.'

He stands and his dungarees fall to his ankles. She places

her wet hands on his hips and slips them under his smalls, slowly sliding around to the front. His body is as hard as iron. She is rubbing hers wetly against him, kissing him gently all over his back. He turns to embrace her. Her mouth is open, wanting him.

A car door slams and Buster barks a warning. A few minutes later Louisa edges through the passage carrying half a dozen plastic bags or more.

'Bloody hell, Louisa,' says Harry. 'You haven't gone and bought more clothes, have you?'

'Oh,' says Louisa. 'There's a sale on.'

'It really beats me how you can buy so much in such a short period of time.'

'It's just one of my many talents,' says Louisa. 'Not so long ago you were encouraging me to go out shopping. Don't you remember?'

'Whatever makes you happy.'

'Fine, then.'

She is going through an extended shopping phase. Spring has arrived and Louisa needs new clothes.

'I'm trying to reinvent myself,' she says to Harry. It isn't working. When she stands in front of the full-length mirror, she is the same.

'I've lost my spark,' she says. 'I used to have a spark.' Harry fails to contradict her, so she buys more clothes in an attempt to get it back. Clothes spill from the wardrobe and from the top of her bedside cupboard. The dirty-clothes basket is full, the clean-clothes basket, the dryer and the clothesline are full. In the walk-in robe her clothes are squeezing Harry's out of existence. Though he has holes in his underpants he refuses to purchase anything for himself. She has noticed that the more she shops, the less he does. She is currently testing this theory.

Harry doesn't seem to get the point. He tells her he has considered becoming a cross-dresser to use up some of her excess. But her maxi would be his mini, and he tells her he would not want to look ridiculous in drag. She tells him it sounds as if he has thought about cross-dressing quite a bit. So he does the manly thing to prove that he hasn't. He throws her new clothes into the washing machine and turns it on the hot cycle, ruining them. He would apparently prefer she spent their money on alcohol. He says that at least alcohol does not take up space for long, and makes both of them feel better before it makes them feel worse. He says bugger it, it doesn't do any harm. They have no one to worry about but themselves.

She hasn't given up on the challenge of trying to appear attractive. She reveals the truth gradually, like someone doing a presentation, shaves her legs and emerges in her new clothes as if she has had them for ages. Harry tells her that he does not find her any more attractive in her new clothes, just neater. 'That's a rotten thing to say,' she says and walks out. 'Men like women to look nice but it's supposed to happen magically and without any visible effort,' she calls out from the kitchen. She could walk around with nothing on. That would show him. Bits everywhere.

Later Harry apologises in his way. He puts the kettle on and makes her a cup of tea. 'The blue is nice,' he says. 'Blue looks good on you.' He is not so insensitive that he doesn't see when she's feeling hurt.

It's different for him when he ventures out. He goes for a reason. She's at work and he's home cooking up a stew. Halfway through the process he discovers that they've run out of his favourite sauce. More importantly, it's his special ingredient. He turns off the gas and ducks down to the local shop, but they've run out, so he ventures further afield to the Gateway Shopping Centre. The school holidays have started and there are kids everywhere. He soon finds himself distracted, disoriented and wandering. On the second circuit of the complex he finds himself drawn towards a display of fitness equipment attended by a salesman. He makes eye contact and realises it is the young bloke who occasionally parks out the front of their house. The man introduces himself and gives Harry his card. Harry reads it aloud.

'Mason Humble,' he reads. 'Manager, Fitness Fundamentals. Mason Humble. That name sounds vaguely familiar.'

'I was named after my father. The footballer. That could be where you've heard the name.'

'I guess so.'

'Do you have any equipment yourself?' Humble asks.

Harry has allowed his gaze to stop on a set of weights.

'I'm not really in a position to buy anything at the moment,' he says. 'But I'd like to get a decent set of weights at some stage. Good for keeping the bones strong. You need to think about these things as you get older.' Harry laughs loudly to cue him to the appropriate response.

'You've got a way to go yet,' he says.

'I try to keep fit.'

'Yes, that's good,' says Humble. 'And you are lucky today because this set of weights is the last one I have in this line, and it's been discontinued, so it's heavily discounted. There's nothing at all wrong with them but people these days seem to want something a bit more modern looking, so I'll tell you what. You're a decent sort of man, I can see that. Make me an offer.'

'Twenty bucks,' says Harry, being ridiculous.

'Done. They're worth a lot more, but since you've been so nice about me parking under your tree.' He is smirking as he packages up the gear.

'Oh that's you?' says Harry. 'Well no worries.'

'I like to take a drive at lunchtime but there's nowhere to park around here. I tell you, mate, it gets so you start to hate the sight of shopping centres after a while. I actually trained as a fitness instructor before I got stuck with this crap.'

'Fair enough.'

'You don't know of anything going do you?'

'No, sorry, mate.'

'No worries. I ask around. You never know, I might start up my own business.'

'Yeah, fair enough.'

Later, at home, Harry unpacks the weights and takes them outside to give himself room and fresh air. As he raises and lowers them he imagines he can feel himself getting stronger. He is standing by the bath, fully clothed, pumping iron. Carole rises out of the water like a nymph. The soapy water shines on her naked body.

'Oh, you are my big strong man,' she says. 'Big strong cave man.'

'Oh yes,' he says as he watches his biceps bulge and flatten. 'Oh yes, you can.'

He is smiling as he turns to find Louisa has arrived home and is standing at the back door watching him. She is holding yet another two shopping bags.

'You've bought yourself some weights,' she says, stating the obvious, in a blatant attempt to legitimise her own purchases.

'Twenty bucks,' he says.

'Well, just make sure you don't go hurting yourself,' she says. 'I don't want to have to try and get you out from under those things.'

CHAPTER FIFTEEN

Harry's laugh plays around in the back room. He is on the phone to someone he likes. He hangs up, emerges from the room and puts the kettle on.

'Want a coffee?' he asks.

'Okay.'

'Guess who that was?'

'Who?'

'Gordon. They want to catch up for lunch now that it's warming up.'

'Oh, I didn't realise he was back. Why didn't Carole ring?' she says.

'You women,' he says. 'You're never satisfied.'

It is a nice day. They take advantage of the sun, move outside, and sit side by side on the garden swing with their coffees. A crow has landed in the big tree in the backyard and is calling out. A willie wagtail chases him off but he comes back before flying off. Under Buddha's watchful presence, small lizards move across the stone wall and disappear into crevices. Louisa feels a sudden surge of desire for Harry. Life pulses through her somewhat erratically. Her spark comes and goes.

They are both in a good mood today. Last night they

celebrated as the country voted in a new government. Louisa reflects on humans as primates, not quite as noble as gorillas. A younger silverback has ousted the older one. There is new blood and a sense of renewed hope and optimism in the troupe.

Buddha's face is gentle and his smile is genuine. Things will change. Things will stay the same.

The middle of another week already. Every time the bell sounds at the local primary school, it reminds Harry of the air-raid sirens from the movies he has seen of the London bombings during World War Two.

The school sirens are more predictable – he'd set his watch, if he could find it. They signal the status of the oval that adjoins the school and mark his day into helpful segments, providing structure and external motivation.

The siren whines and, shortly afterwards, silence replaces the clamour of high-pitched voices. This promised reprieve from curious eyes through the playground fence is a signal for Harry to put on his ancient sneakers and head down to the reserve. It was marked out for football practice during winter, but more recently the lines for athletics have been refreshed, with measured lanes for running circling the oval.

Since the promise of a secret meeting with Carole has become more probable, Harry has decided to step up his exercise regime. When he was in Nashos he was so fit that he felt as if he could run forever. The laps were a meditation, and he fell into a rhythm that felt like gliding, the strength of his muscles rendering him almost weightless, his feet barely touching the surface of the ground. He could see how people could get addicted, marathon runners and so forth, running to the point of becoming skeletal, their eyes and cheeks sunken like famine victims, unable to quit until their bodies did. He has never been like that as far as he recalls, but he used to be fit and strong, and he liked the way he felt, as if he could have conquered the world and all the gorgeous women in it.

Now he starts off slowly, shuffling more than running, his knees and his ankles hurting, and his muscles tense and unyielding. This is temporary. He knows that once his body warms up he will be able to move more freely. Buster is with him, sniffing the goal posts and lifting his leg to leave his messages. He runs ahead and back, and across Harry's path, grinning and threatening to trip him up.

'Get out of the way, Buster!' Harry yells at him.

It takes unnecessary effort to scold him and Harry feels mildly put out, but he soon falls into the old rhythm and begins to enjoy the cool of the early south-westerly against his face. He visualises his calf and thigh muscles contracting and strengthening with every step, his arms pumping him forwards as he laps the oval for the first time. Not too bad for an old codger. He slows to a shuffle again and then a walk, holding his side where a stitch has started to develop. Buster circles back and slows to a trot by his side.

Harry finds himself thinking about the child at Carole and Gordon's place. What was Carole playing at, asking them around while she had the kid there? He shouldn't read too much into it, but he has a sneaking suspicion that Louisa has been talking to Carole about his history, and that Carole is trying her own brand of therapy on him. Women love to talk endlessly about their relationships. Apparently.

Mind you, Louisa hasn't talked to him much about Tom since the day he died, or what happened with her ex – not that he's invited it. He knows some of the old guys that came back from Vietnam and he knows that sometimes it's best to let it be. You don't know what you're playing with when you stir things up. People will talk to you when they're good and ready and anything else you try to get out of them is just morbid curiosity.

He is thinking too much. He starts to jog again and then to speed up, squeezing the thoughts out through his screwed-up eyes, out the sides of his head, leaving them behind. He begins to sprint, willing his body to work its hardest, until it is his body and nothing else that consumes him. He runs like that, pushing himself until he stumbles to ground. He kneels there panting and attending to the rhythm of his heartbeat until the siren sounds again to send him home.

They have arranged to meet Carole and Gordon for lunch at a winery in the Swan Valley. Harry chooses the venue and instructs Louisa, who describes it to Carole over the phone. Consequently Carole and Gordon have gone to one section of the winery and Louisa and Harry to the other. They have all been sitting there waiting for the others for some time when Carole takes the initiative to call Louisa on her mobile phone.

'Where are you?' she says.

'Where are you?'

'We're sitting outside where the hotel part is, near the bar. Where are you?'

'At the cafe.'

'Come over. It's nice here.'

'Hang on.'

Louisa puts her hand over the phone and relays the situation, but Harry has already signalled that he wants to stay where he is. Gordon is probably saying the same thing.

'It's lovely here,' says Louisa. 'We're outside too.'

'We're just having a beer,' says Carole.

'We're having a wine. The food looks good.'

'Just so long as there's alcohol.'

'It's a winery.'

'Do they have beer there?' asks Carole. 'Gordon's got a taste for it now.'

'Yes,' says Louisa, mouthing the question to Harry and taking a punt while he checks the menu.

Carole gives way and soon they are all sitting together.

The day sparkles. Light sunshine filters through shade created by a loose layer of vine leaves over and through the treated-pine pergola. The small wooden table rocks on uneven red-brick paving. Louisa finds an old electricity bill in her bag and folds it for Harry to place under the shortest leg. He ignores her outstretched hand.

'Why don't you do it?' he says.

'I'll do it,' says Gordon.

'We could move,' says Carole.

They stay.

Harry has already moved himself and Louisa to the table with the moulded plastic seats rather than one of those with the more aesthetically pleasing wooden chairs that Louisa chose while he was in the toilet. She has given up trying to predict what he will choose as optimal seating, because he always changes position two or three times. This happens even when he initially chooses the seating himself.

There is a backyard feel to the place, with some spider webs scattered around and no tablecloths on the slatted tables. Pretty soon everyone feels able to relax over a house red, and talk as freely as they would at home. A loud party is going on at the table next to them, comprised of what appears to be three or four generations of a large family. It is in the process of winding up. The restaurant manager carries out the birthday cake as Gordon and Carole arrive.

'Now that takes the cake!' says Gordon. They all laugh. Emboldened by Gordon and their age past caring, they join in the birthday song and applause, but skip the speeches. Apart from the party, there is only one other couple, who are halfway through their meal. They eat in silence and leave quickly.

Harry, Louisa, Carole and Gordon relax into the comfort and familiarity of the weathered plastic chairs and prepare for a long lunch.

'It's great about Labor getting in,' says Louisa.

'Grape?' says Harry, pointing upwards to the vine coming through the pergola and winking at Carole. Louisa rolls her eyes for Carole's benefit. 'Ha, ha,' she says, but Carole strangely abandons their old sisterhood solidarity and humours Harry.

'Don't mind if I do,' she says, smiling into his eyes.

'That's a grape shame. I can't seem to reach them,' says Harry, winking again, and Carole laughs and takes a swig of wine.

'They're not ripe anyway,' says Louisa.

'Oh that's just sour grapes,' says Carole and they both laugh again.

Louisa and Gordon exchange a look.

'I don't think –' says Louisa, as Gordon cuts across her.

'It looks like the prime minister is going to lose his seat. I don't think that's happened before to a prime minister, has it?'

Nobody knows for sure.

'Incredible, isn't it?' says Carole.

'Another drink,' says Harry, pouring himself another.

'I guess they usually get themselves into safer seats,' says Louisa. 'But it's hard to tell what a safe seat is these days. Amazing all right.'

'I think it's gr ...' says Carole, choking on her wine, and she and Harry get the giggles.

'I'm a bit worried about the guy who's running for my mother's electorate,' says Louisa. 'What's his name again? Anyway, looks like he might just dip out. The Libs seem to have loaded that seat with retirement villages for decades. Nobody gives out how-to-vote cards for any of the other parties it seems. That's according to my mother. They take them down to vote and give them the cards they want them to have. But my mother still has her wits about her. She noticed and protested. They said, what do you want to vote for them for? Sort of implying that she doesn't know her own mind. I mean, she's not stupid. She's just old.'

'Is that right?' says Gordon.

'I don't know for sure,' says Louisa. 'Don't quote me.'

Gordon and Louisa talk about the election while the others sit quietly, but soon there's nothing more to say about it, so the conversation moves on.

Carole and Gordon have recently returned from Scotland where Gordon was born and where Carole has discovered the graves of some of her own forebears. Everybody talks about ancestors while Louisa drinks wine from the carafe and also from a bottle that Carole has ordered. Gordon and Harry soon discover some uncomfortable ancient history. They work out that it's possible that Harry's ancestors slaughtered Gordon's. Or perhaps it is the other way around. Louisa has had two or three glasses of wine by this time so her syntax is fuzzy, and everybody else is talking fast and over the top of one another. The warm feeling, in any case, is not spoiled by this new knowledge. Everyone seems to be floating along in a pleasant alcoholic haze.

Carole says, 'I've got a good idea. Why don't we all go to Scotland together? We could check out all the ancestors. We might even find out that we're related.' She directs all of this at Harry, and then adds, somewhat suggestively. 'I've always thought there was something familiar about you.'

'Yes, that would be um, *grape*,' says Louisa.

It's as if she hasn't spoken.

'I've always thought there was something overly familiar about you,' Harry says to Carole.

'Overly?' says Carole, coyly. 'Not overly, surely?'

'Stop that flirting, you two. Another drink?' says Gordon to Louisa, pouring one as he asks.

'So who actually killed who?' asks Louisa, but nobody responds. 'I mean the ancestors,' she says. She has been wondering vaguely why people thought or think that you can put one atrocity right by causing another. 'I don't have any ancestors that I know about,' she says. No one is interested in this, but she blunders on anyway. 'So I feel particularly virtuous. Nobody that I know of has been killed.'

Carole, Gordon and Harry all look uncomfortable.

'Oh,' she says, 'I'm a bit drunk I think.'

'Never mind,' says Harry, and he places his hand protectively over the top of her hand. Carole drapes her hand over Gordon's forearm.

'I've saved just enough room for sweets,' Carole says. 'Anyone else?'

'Me too,' says Louisa.

'I'll go and get the dessert menu,' says Harry. 'I need a stretch anyway.'

'I need the loo,' says Carole, and she goes too, leaving Louisa and Gordon sitting there. They talk about something or other and Gordon attempts to refill the glasses.

'Oops, we've run out,' he says.

'Coffee time,' says Carole as she returns to the table.

Over coffee they begin to sober up and the conversation winds down to a point of reflective silence. Harry and Carole seem to have lost interest in one another.

They all go for a walk to look at arts and crafts in an old-fashioned gingham-curtained and overstocked craft shop on the site of the winery. Louisa lingers over a golf-playing frog but doesn't want Carole to think that she is attracted to it, so makes a comical expression that she hides from the shop lady. Carole draws her attention to a Buddha water feature with an inbuilt light. Louisa shows Carole a picture of her own Buddha under the rosebush; it is the wallpaper on her mobile phone.

Carole and Gordon haven't been to Harry and Louisa's place for some time so Carole hasn't seen Louisa's Buddha. She generously appears to be impressed by the statue, and they talk of their dreams of owning B&Bs, becoming artists and planting trees to ultimately save the earth from global warming. The men stand awkwardly, trying not to listen to what they describe as Louisa and Carole's 'secret women's business'. Harry is starting to sober up. He talks to Gordon generally about politics and football.

Carole and Louisa discuss their arrangements to catch up again with a mutual, but lapsed, friend, and they can try to recapture a feeling they had when they were younger and more optimistic about the future, before Harry and Gordon. After Victor. Before Tom. They have made plans to see Rhianna. They haven't met as a group of three for some years. Perhaps it will be better, deeper and authentic in a different way from when they were all young and lovely, and looking forward to life's uncertainties.

It is time to go. Gordon and Harry shake hands and everyone hugs and kisses the women. Harry says he is feeling fit to drive, so he takes the keys. He listens to jazz on the way home while Louisa tries not to fall asleep. When they get home, Buster is caught napping on the couch. He struggles off too late, wags his tail and tries not to look guilty. Louisa tells him to relax.

Harry says he is pooped. He staggers out to water the garden. The dog goes berserk as usual, jumping up at the water and trying to catch it in his mouth. Harry curses him as usual. Louisa potters around then comes outside to watch, to untangle the kinks from the hose for Harry, and feel a part of it all.

Another day is acknowledged and, as the dog loses interest and settles down, and Louisa notices that Harry rubs Buddha's good luck tummy as if there is something he is wishing for.

CHAPTER SIXTEEN

Harry is in the habit of browsing through the job section of the local paper. Nothing appeals enough to make a change. But one morning Louisa is hanging about without any work on, and he is worrying more than usual about their finances, when an advertisement captures his attention. It's something he could conceivably do, so he decides that it doesn't hurt to make an enquiry. The money looks good to him, the casual hours promise flexibility, and more importantly the job is out and about.

He is really only fantasising about it when he closes the door behind himself and makes the call. He speaks quietly. He is placed on hold. He hears Louisa pick up her keys and leave the house. As the front door closes, someone from Human Resources takes his call.

'Hello?' A woman has picked up.

'Hello? Yes, I'm calling about a job you advertised.'

'Which one?' There is a hint of exasperation in her voice.

'Oh it's the um, hang on a minute, ah, could you hold on a minute? I've just lost the page here.'

It's a good start. She already thinks he's an idiot. At least he can tell Louisa about it. At least he can say he tried.

'I'll put you through to John Doe,' says the woman. Is she kidding?

'John Done,' says the man at the other end.

'Oh, like Ken Done,' says Harry, 'pronounced like "stone", not, um, "fun".'

The man laughs obligingly. 'Yes,' he says. 'I've heard that one before.'

'I suppose you have,' says Harry, but he doubts it.

'No worries,' says the man. 'You're asking about the job we advertised in *The Gazette* this week, are you?' He sounds overly friendly.

'Yes. I really just rang on the spur of the moment.' Harry is apologising for wasting their time, but John Doe chooses not to pick up on it.

'Could you email your resume through this morning?'

'I'm sorry?'

'Or fax it.'

'I don't have one. I've been working for myself for the last ten years or so. I could throw one together, I suppose.' Because he lacks any sort of resume, he doesn't think they'll take him seriously, but he hasn't counted on the dearth of suitable people for the job market in the booming Western Australian economy. His timing is perfect. Or not – he thought he was making a tentative inquiry and he finds himself being dragged in, arms and legs flailing, like a bug sucked into a vacuum cleaner.

'Running your own business requires a lot of ability,' says John Doe. 'The position needs someone with that sort of initiative.'

This John seems like a reasonable kind of bloke, Harry decides.

'Yes, I have been running my own business, but when I saw the ad I also thought, I did major in chemistry,' he says, enjoying the opportunity to revisit this early achievement. 'That seemed to fit what you were after. But I have to admit, it was a long time ago, about twenty years or so.'

More like twenty-five, or just over.

'So I'm getting on for my late forties.' And a little bit more.

'A chemistry degree?'

'Yes.'

'And you're used to taking initiative, being a self-starter, taking responsibility for yourself?'

'Sure, of course.'

'Married?'

'Mm.'

'Not that it's an issue of course, just curious. These young ones are all over the place these days, unsettled. You sound exactly like the sort of person we need.' Harry's heart sinks. 'We can go through the rest of your experience later. I can see you about eleven, no, half-past. If things turn out the way I think they might, when could you start?'

'Next week probably,' says Harry automatically. Later he will decide that he responded while he was in shock. What was he thinking? There used to be zero chance of getting a job once you were pushing fifty. What's happened in the last few years? The world's gone mad. People have lost sight of what's really important. They don't know who they are any more. They even call themselves names that sound like 'John Doe'.

After he hangs up, Harry sits by the phone, stunned. How is it possible that on a day that started normally, he suddenly finds himself with a job interview? He tosses up whether to go or not, but the man has been so decent, and trusting of him, and of his potentially Oscar-winning performance on the phone, that it would feel bad to stand him up. He decides it wouldn't hurt to see where it leads. He changes into something more presentable. He goes. He can always turn the job down if they offer it to him. He can tell them when they ring back that he's been offered something else.

'The job's yours!' says Doe. He looks so pleased at the offer he's making that Harry feels compelled to return his handshake with a similar level of enthusiasm. Before he knows it, Harry has agreed to a medical that afternoon, and a Monday start.

The medical turns out to be a formality, apart from the drug test, which he will pass. Alcohol and coffee are his drugs of choice. He gave up on smokes and recreational dope years ago. The deal is done. Harry has a regular job.

He doesn't know what to feel, but this is something new and mildly exciting and he feels like telling someone. He won't tell Louisa yet. He needs time to think. He might still pull out. No harm done.

He tries out the news on Buster, but the dog is typically self-interested and pays no attention. He waits politely but anxiously for his turn to speak, then asks for a throw of the ball. So Harry tells Buddha, who is predictably enigmatic and leaves him to discover the truth for himself. Harry makes himself a cup of tea, stands outside, and gazes out at the scattering of treetops that spread across the suburb beyond the back fence. He notices the not-too-distant hum of traffic from the freeway, of people involved in their lives with places to go and things to do. He decides to call his mother.

'Come over and tell me all about it,' she says. 'That's great news, Harry.'

This is the point at which he knows that he will give it a go. He'll tell Louisa when he gets home. She'll be pleased, encouraging, but careful not to pressure him.

He has a sudden urge to do something nice for her, to give her something. Some romance. Some flowers. A bit further down the track when he gets his first pay cheque, they'll have a night out. She can get dressed up.

He'll make an effort.

Harry negotiates the steep driveway and parks under the old lilac tree. His mother comes out to meet him and gives him an awkward hug. They have never been given much to displays of affection.

'Well done, son,' she says. 'What does Louisa think?'

'I haven't told her yet. She's out. I just found out myself.'

'I'm honoured then.'

'Don't let it go to your head,' says Harry.

She has made a batch of cupcakes in the time since she spoke with him on the phone, and him getting there.

'You shouldn't have,' he says, taking one and disposing of it in two bites.

'Looks like I should have made more.'

'Why didn't you?'

She gives him a playful punch on the arm.

'Sit down then,' she says. 'Don't stand around looking untidy.'

He studies her as she goes about making tea. She's slightly built and as energetic as ever she was. Possibly more so. She seemed to find a new lease of life after his father passed away. He can't remember if she's just turned seventy-five, or seventy-six. She climbs on a step to reach a packet of biscuits on the top pantry shelf.

'Let me do that, Mum,' says Harry, getting up. 'You'll hurt yourself.'

'Don't be ridiculous,' she says. 'You know what they say: use it or lose it.'

'You'll lose something all right, if you keep being so stubborn.'

She arranges the biscuits on a fancy china plate, and places them next to the rapidly diminishing cupcakes. They sip their tea. She is watching his face closely, making him uncomfortable. She puts her hand over his.

'I'm very proud of you, you know Harry. Not just this, I mean. It takes courage to keep going. Life.'

'Yes, okay, thanks.' He wishes she wouldn't. She deserves something in return. 'Me too. Of you.'

'That's my boy!' she says. 'Now come and see what I've done to the garden since you were last here. Bring your tea. You can tell me all about the new job.'

Harry arrives home with ten red roses and a bottle of mid-range bubbly. He dislikes bubbly so this is some concession. His enthusiasm rivals that of a teenage boy on the verge of his first licensed drive. He recalls the feeling. He is a bit of a lad again. There is a definite spring in his step. There might be sex later. His mood must be infectious. Louisa seems excited too.

'Guess how much they're going to pay me?' he says.

'How much?'

'More than I get now,' he says. 'I start Monday.' He kisses Louisa on the mouth. She takes the roses from him, looking flustered.

'They're beautiful,' she gushes. 'I'll put them in water.' They have their own home-grown roses, but tend not to pick them. 'Red roses,' she says meaningfully, bouncing her eyebrows playfully and tucking a strand of hair behind her left ear.

'Sniff them,' he tells her. 'They smell.'

'Beautiful,' she says. 'Where did you get them?'

'From Mum's. I got this myself.' He indicates the wine. 'Mum gave us some walnuts too. There's nothing wrong with them. They get stuck under her plate, so she said we might as well have them.'

'Oh, that's nice of her,' Louisa says. She picks up the bubbly, coyly. 'So this is a celebration for the new job.'

'Yes. Then we might have a little lie-down, eh?'

'Ooh!'

The job is for a drug-testing contractor for an occupational health and safety company. Harry's degree in chemistry is ancient and has barely been used, so they will give him some on-the-job training, and put him on roster to send him out in the middle of the night whenever there is a workplace fatality. He will be given a pager. He'll like that, he tells her, walking around with a pager on his belt, playing the part.

The job pays quite well with penalty rates and on-call fees, he tells her. Now that he's a proper working man, he might start to demand more of her, if she knows what he means. Promises, promises, she says to that.

They leave their wine and have their lie-down first. Afterwards, Harry falls asleep, snoring loudly. Louisa makes soup for dinner. She hopes he'll be all right. She wonders about the changes ahead. She decides not to think too much about it.

After an hour Harry won't be woken; he barely struggles out after three. 'Bugger!' he says. 'The day's gone.'

'Glass of bubbly?' she calls out, too loudly. She is on about her third. She is standing alone outside watching the sky change. The colours are reflected in her glass of wine.

'Oh, why not?' he says, drains the bottle into a mug, and comes out to join her. He stands by her with his legs apart, a real man, mug of wine in one hand, his other arm around her shoulders.

'Bloody beautiful,' he says of the intensifying sunset.

'You know you,' she says. 'You're all class.'

'Sometimes I feel like I'm floating through life,' she tells him one morning, 'like I'm half asleep.'

'Floating's better than sinking.'

'I guess so.'

Something strange seems to have happened all of a sudden. Maybe it's the news of Harry's job, or the gift of roses, or the return of their sex life after an unusually long hiatus. Or maybe she's kidding herself. What does it matter what's causing it? Something feels like a new start. It could be a false spring, but she's feeling more optimistic. This comes with a freshness of perception she hasn't had for some time. In the last few days it's as if she is being shown wonderful things. She could force her old calmness back, but the idea of some sort of heightened reality stays in her mind, leading her to speculate on the possibility of a higher purpose. Everything happens for a reason. The Truth about everything is on the tip of her tongue. She looks for signs.

In the afternoon she is driving along a familiar stretch of road when she sees a snake from the corner of her eye. It appears to her first as silver, then black as she turns her head to see it properly. She takes her foot off the accelerator so that she doesn't run it over, and it moves off to the side, disappearing into the brush lining this section of road. Against a perfect sky two pelicans play over the familiar territory of the lake. She feels her heart slow and wonders why, at this moment of all moments, she is recapturing the ability to see beauty. It is something that she remembers from when she was small, but somewhere along the line of her life it fell away. She wonders if she will take out her paints today so that she can study the way that the light falls on objects, so that she can break this phenomenon down into its component parts and see what is really there.

The last few nights she has been sleeping without dreams. She goes to bed at night, wakes refreshed in the morning, and it seems no time at all has passed. This has done something to the way she sees things, clearing her vision. Birds, snakes, trees moving against the sky – everything seems remarkable.

When she returns home, Harry is wheeling and dealing on the phone in the study. He has the door closed and Louisa puts her finger to her lips to warn the dog not to bark and thus destroy the illusion of an office-based phone call for the person on the other end of the line. He has started the new job but he continues to maintain the trickle of work from the business. He has a foot in both camps.

He laughs. Now he sounds as if he's making a social call. His voice sounds as relaxed and comfortable as a politician settling in for another term, although she can't make out the words. She is about to go through the back door when she sees that there is a bobtail goanna guarding the threshold. She uses the alternative exit and moves around the side to get a better look. Its head turns slowly towards her. It extends its blue tongue in warning and hisses. Louisa feels doubly blessed today.

At five-forty pm the phone rings and an upbeat and friendly man named Nicholas has some fantastic news. He is able to offer her a wonderful vacation package in exchange for her mortal soul.

'What did you say?'

But he continues with his spiel as if she hasn't spoken. She hears only every second or third word because the phone is tethered next to the radio, and Harry has the sound turned up so that he can listen to 'Strike up the Band' above the barking, as he waters the garden and washes away the day's grime from Buddha. Louisa thanks Nicholas for his kind offer but says that she must decline. Nicholas points out that life can't be all work and no play. Louisa wonders how he knows so much about her and why he is using her first name. Nicholas sounds surprised when Louisa also uses his first name. After an exchange of banter he wishes her well, counts his gains, cuts his losses and exits the line before she is forced to hang up on him. A holiday would be nice, but she will not be pressured into it.

Louisa goes to the front door and looks out through the flywire. The man in the van with the mobile phone is back, parked under the tree in front of the house. This time he looks up and catches her staring at him. She lifts her hand in greeting. He gives her half a wave, half a smile, and drives off.

'You're nobody,' she tells herself. 'Just some guy.'

CHAPTER SEVENTEEN

After the high comes the low. Louisa is sitting on the lounge room floor in the corner with the light out. She is hunched over a cushion that she holds against her midriff. She hasn't bothered to dress or brush her hair. Harry is out.

The past has been waiting for her to drop her guard. It bursts in from the wings, plants itself centre stage, and prepares to play its part. She is powerless to do anything but watch as the drama plays itself out, yet again.

Meredith is colouring in at the kiddies' table. This is the idea that remains, that she is protected in a small sectioned-off place in the corner of the room. Tommy seems to be wailing, but the sound is elusive. It might be coming from Louisa herself. It could be a series of different events. Meredith is in one time zone and Louisa and Tom are caught in another with Victor. Someone is grabbing onto Victor's arm. A hand catches Tom and sweeps him through the air. He falls onto the couch and stays crumpled there, but he is processing and learning. Victor doesn't seem to notice, or else it's how he wants it.

She struggles but can't remember Meri at all, as if she has been put aside and forgotten. Louisa can't remember where she has left her. She feels a familiar sense of rising panic. The chair by the children's table is lying on the floor, the pencils scattered, one rolling towards the edge of the table. Meredith has disappeared.

Victor has been drinking all day and Louisa hears him saying once again that he will put them out of their misery. Uncharacteristically she retaliates, saying if he were a better person, that would put them out of their misery. If he would just fuck off and leave them all alone, that would put them out of their misery. Victor gives her a demonstration of what he is talking about, but stops short of killing her. He's giving her every chance to improve herself. He's teaching her.

Did you tell me to fuck off? He keeps saying it to the rhythm of his punches. It has become his mantra. Did you just tell me to fuck off? Did you say fuck off? Did you just tell me to fuck off? She's somewhere outside of this, watching as the scene plays out. This thing in a pile on the floor, this heap of old rags, is neither animal nor human. It deserves what it gets. He's doing it a kind of homage. He explains patiently as he continues his discipline: You're nothing, nothing without me, my darling little girl. Less than nothing. You told me to fuck off. He is speaking almost kindly, confusing her. This is for your own good. You're nothing without me. A woman is lying on the floor with dark fluid pooling around her. She is not right somehow. She is some sort of disease and he is the valiant doctor bringing her under control at his own cost.

The children are – where? Somewhere. Someone has taken them in hand temporarily and is looking after them. Later she tells herself the lie that they've survived to grow beyond Victor's influence. But she knows in the back of her mind that something has been left behind: a germ that proliferates in Tom's mind when he reaches puberty and destroys him. Victor gets off, apparently unscathed and unchanged. These things must be remembered. Louisa feels the gravity of her role as oral historian, telling Lucy, and Harry when he will listen, not having to talk about it to Carole because she doesn't need to be told; she was there. Were the children with Carole that day?

In hospital Louisa emerges from oblivion into fluorescent light. She remembers feeling bitterly disappointed. Now she knows that her continued existence has been needed at the most basic level because she will hold the past in her body as proof of things that shouldn't be ignored. Perhaps this is the meaning of her suffering. At some stage the police appear to interview her at her bedside and she makes up a story to satisfy them. When she gets home, people who used to be quite friendly avoid her, even when she speaks directly to them. At school the children lose friends.

Despite his promises, Victor has failed to put her out of her misery. He manages that feat with another woman, just over a decade later. Louisa follows the story in the papers. A woman has been found dead in his home. An autopsy is done, and there is an inquiry into the death. Victor might be charged following a coronial inquiry. She worries that they will call her as a witness to establish a pattern of domestic violence, but she needn't worry. Everyone and everything seems to have colluded. There is an open finding. The inquiry is wrapped up and Victor moves interstate, to Sydney.

The papers make a small meal of it at the time, a brief sensation, a member of the establishment caught up in something like that. Then the story becomes more sympathetic. It turns out that the woman has something of a history. The story sells until more important things take precedence. There are wars, and people cheating on social security, or turning down perfectly good jobs. Something about breast implants.

Louisa has gone back into her shell. Harry tries to keep upbeat but it's hard with her like this.

'Don't go getting paranoid on me again,' he jokes.

'No,' she says. 'No, I'm not.'

'Really?' he says.

'Oh Harry! It's just memories. I can't keep pushing them away forever. It's probably not even healthy to forget everything. You don't mean to tell me you never think of the past? Really?'

'Of course I do,' he says. He resists telling her about how he tries to keep himself more upbeat. A short silence. Louisa fills the space he leaves for her.

'Anyway, I suppose it's time I did some work. The house doesn't clean itself.'

Harry puts the kettle on, and as he waits for it to boil, becomes aware that he is thinking about Bella. He wonders how often this happens without him even realising.

They both need to go out. Today. Right now. They need to touch base with some normal people. The neighbours are normal people.

He decides to reverse an earlier decision and take up an invitation for a get-together extended by Brian, to play darts and drink beer in his sizeable shed. They've been over once or twice before, not long after that first Christmas they were here. It was well fitted out then, but recently Harry was given the grand tour after ducking across the road to borrow a pump. These days Brian has an impressive array of trophies and pennants for his wins at darts tournaments, all displayed above a workbench that runs along the entire length of the shed.

The shed is equipped with every tool imaginable, plus a generously proportioned flat-screen TV mounted above the bench on the wall – Harry imagines it to be perpetually set on the sports channel. Brian has collected an impressive range of comfortable chairs, a sofa bed, a bar fridge, and a deluxe dartboard that forms the focal point of the set-up opposite the security-controlled roller door. And there's still room for fold-out tables for the food.

Harry tries to keep his plan casual, low-key.

'You should come over later,' he tells Louisa. 'The women are bringing plates around six-thirty or seven.'

'Just the women?'

'I'm happy to throw something together,' he says. She ignores this.

'What are they bringing?' It's the sort of thing that always seems to make her panic.

He reassures. 'Nothing much. Just a plate of something. Chips and dips.'

'Oh Harry,' she says, 'It'll be more than chips and dips. I don't know. I've got something on.'

'What?'

'Something.'

'Anyway, I won't stay long,' he says. 'Just long enough to humiliate myself with my lack of darting and drinking prowess.'

'I don't mind. Stay as long as you want.'

'Yeah,' he says. 'You don't have to decide now. See how you feel. I'm sure it'll be fine either way.'

'I'm impressed,' she says, avoiding the point. 'You're really fitting in around here lately aren't you? I still feel a bit strange.'

'I always thought you felt a bit strange,' he says, catching her in his arms, and tickling her. She wriggles out.

'Very funny.'

'I thought so.'

She's still smiling, humouring him, being kind in spite of her low mood. Sometimes he wishes she wouldn't do that. Sometimes he wishes she'd be a bit more honest about what she feels about him, not verbose, just straight down the line. She could drop the act once in a while. She could say, 'Harry, talk me into it.'

'You *should* come,' he says. 'It'll be nice. It would be nice to have you there.'

'Really?' she says. 'I might come over. I'll see.'

'I'll come back in a while, then we can go back together if you feel like it.'

'Okay.'

He decides he's on a mission, to get them both out. They've

both been dwelling on things that can't be changed. Building new experiences, that's the key. Yes, they need to get out more. They need to socialise.

Harry grabs a sixpack out of the fridge, and turns back to Louisa.

'Come,' he says. 'It'll do you good.'

'I might come,' she says, and though her voice lacks commitment, she adds, 'I don't suppose it matters what I bring really.'

'Course it doesn't,' he says. 'They're good people. They don't judge.'

'I'll see how I feel.'

'No, don't do that,' he says. 'Just come on over. Or like I said, I'll come back in a while, and then you can come.'

'Okay,' she says. 'I'll see.'

Harry leaves the house. Bella is lingering in his thoughts. He drops the six-pack at Brian's, makes some excuse to duck back to the house, and takes a walk around the oval to deal with it before he has too many drinks under his belt and starts getting maudlin.

Something happened to him after Bella was born. He has been permanently altered by the fact of her existence. It's no less real than some sort of physical change in him.

A stone hits you on the head and you keep the scar; you fall off your bike and you skin your knee. Your body shows all the dents as evidence of the life you've lived. Bella is imprinted on him, as he must have been for his own father, or might have been but for the old man's alcoholic disease. How is it that the two things go together? He has a flash – himself as a boy.

His mother always dressed him neatly and made sure he combed his hair. She kept the house immaculate. She stuck it out with his father until Harry and his sister left home, and then some.

Harry is thinking about degrees of separation, how pain

spreads exponentially, accelerating as it affects more and more people, spreading outwards until everything is taken over. Before you know it the whole world is miserable and kidding itself that it's how it has to be. He couldn't be responsible for the world, but he could be responsible for what he did. That's why he drove his wife and daughter out. Yasamine thought it was her idea, but really it was his. Everything came clear that day.

One day he saw himself as if he was standing on the outside. It was like a rehearsal, a story that hadn't been written yet, something like that. He saw himself *push* Yasamine. He saw blood. He saw marks his hands left on her arms, felt his rising anger and his horror at his inability to hold back. He was sickened by how easy it had been, by how quickly it had happened, before he had time to think. He saw where the situation could lead, in spite of his best intentions, in spite of his determination not to go down that path, and from the bedroom he thought he heard the baby crying, his daughter learning that he was not to be trusted.

Harry has been circling the oval with his head down. He looks up to see a woman and a small girl walking towards him. The woman is carrying a plastic shopping bag and the girl is pushing a small pink pram. He stops and watches them. The woman glances at him suspiciously as they approach, and puts herself between her child and Harry as they pass. He smiles and nods, but she doesn't catch his eye.

'This is ridiculous,' Harry says to himself. He puts it away and cuts back to Brian's to sink a few beers.

By the time that Harry gets back to the shed, the party is in full swing. No one seems to notice his late arrival. There are no worries about formality here – the neighbours who make up the gathering drift in and out, as do their kids who span the various stages of childhood, adolescence and young adulthood. People in this neighbourhood have started their families early, but they seem to have got the formula right.

Their offspring look to be pretty well-adjusted. They're not in any hurry to leave home. There is plenty of rough banter accompanied by laughter, a common language of what it is that constitutes acceptable humour. It's hard-hitting, but never nasty. Life's not easy, but with loud enough laughter you can get through just about anything.

One or two of the women have already turned up with food and are passing comment on the dart competition. Brian is winning, predictably, but no one seems to mind.

Louisa has fallen asleep in front of the television. She is drifting away from a small island in the middle of an ocean. It is one of those cartoon islands with a single palm tree and a castaway. Tom stands on the shore looking out to sea, getting smaller, but he is never quite lost from view. If she looks away the after-image remains and if she directs her attention there she can see him smiling and waving. She closes her eyes now and she can see him, but it comes to her with a grip of pain. She opens her eyes.

Time has done nothing to diminish the pain in her body, but even pain serves its purpose. It binds her like a steel cage, keeping her together. She closes her eyes again, prepared this time. Tom is a castaway and her boat seems to have stopped at a set distance with his small figure on the shore, and she is bobbing about at sea, stuck, with no way of getting back or going on.

After she wakes it takes her a while to get her bearings. There is a documentary on the television about parasites infecting crickets. It is disturbing and fascinating at the same time. It has just finished when Harry breezes in, full of good cheer and encouragement to come on over.

This is the kind of life she could have had if she'd made different choices, if she'd been a different sort of person. The men play darts. The women pass comment or sit around discussing their kids' schooling, their new job, their philosophies on life and the inevitable demise of society. Other people. They drink beer or wine. One drinks only water.

Brian's wife Lorraine wants to talk about the people who lived in the house before Harry and Louisa moved in.

'They were a young couple,' she says. 'Too young really. Not great gardeners. So the place was starting to bring down the property values a bit. Still, I reckon they should have been out having a good time, travelling or something. It was inevitable that they'd split up in the end really, which they did, and then she took off. But I've seen him still hanging around occasionally. He's not a bad guy. He's quite sweet really, but I don't know that he's over it after all this time. He always has that look, you know, sort of hangdog. He's probably not quite the full quid, if you know what I mean, I mean smart enough, but a bit unbalanced. And some people really hang onto things way past their use-by date, don't they?'

'What would you consider to be a reasonable use-by date then, Lorraine?' Louisa asks acidly.

Her tone cuts through the general chatter, and attracts a couple of sideways glances. Lorraine laughs.

'Fair enough,' she says blushing. 'I've never really paid much attention to some of those use-by dates anyway. Where do they get them from anyway? I mean, like they say, how long is a piece of string?'

'Yeah, I've always wondered that,' Harry chips in from just behind them where he has arrived with a drink in hand for Louisa. He winks. 'Just long enough to hang yourself apparently.'

CHAPTER EIGHTEEN

Christmas is coming and with Harry's new job Louisa wonders if things will be different next year. They mark the passing of another year by taking out the old Christmas tree and the ancient angel whose thinning cottonwool hair is pleasing to them both, and Harry spends a day putting coloured lights around the outside of the house. When darkness falls he walks across to the park to see how they look from there. He will spend the next day adjusting them to maximise the festive effect for passers-by.

Each year he adds something new to the collection. This year he tells her that he is thinking of something big, like a sleigh for the roof. Louisa worries – she doesn't want him falling – but the idea is strangely appealing. She imagines herself, Harry and Buster flying through the night sky on Santa's sleigh. Tom could sit up front, just like he wanted to when he was a little boy.

That first Christmas after the great escape, as she calls it, they were at Simon and Rhianna's place, and Simon had decorated the entire house with lights for the children. Every year after that, Meri and Tom would beg for lights and Louisa would oblige. Somewhere along the line they grew out of it, but by that time Louisa realised that the lights were for her as much as the children. The few years without them seemed strangely empty.

The Christmas after Tom died she asked Harry to put up lights again, and she still keeps the practice for Tom, she says, as a kind of vigil. She likes to think that he is watching and that the opportunity hasn't passed. He always wanted a sleigh on the roof but when she was on her own with the kids they never got one, because it always seemed too hard.

'Get it,' she now tells Harry. 'We can figure out how to put it up there later.'

'It's not too much?'

'I don't think so.'

'Not too kitsch?'

'No. No, not at all.'

She finds it hard to tell these days. They have noticed their growing predilection for bric-a-brac with each year that passes. Perhaps it's something to do with moving to the outer suburbs. Some people have started putting gnomes in their gardens again. They say it's retro. She finds it strangely comforting. If she'd had grandchildren she would have amused them with her funny china ornaments. When they got older they could speak disparagingly but affectionately about their nanna and her stuff. She could have had bits and pieces from the two-dollar shop, tap-dancing dogs and spinning monkeys. She doesn't have grandchildren, but she has Harry, and he humours her. Together they have the dog, but Buster has little appreciation for the purely ornamental.

A few years ago, Louisa bought Harry a singing fish, when they were appearing everywhere, and she imagined Tom as a little boy, playing with it. Or Meredith. The thought hurts.

'Deal with it,' she says.

'What?' says Harry.

'What do you think of this parrot?' she asks him, showing him a page in the catalogue she has been flicking through. 'It says here that it says ten different things – affirmations to start your day off right.'

'No, Louisa.'

'There's nothing wrong with it. It's popular culture.'

'That *is* a bit much.'

'It'll cheer you up.'

'The fish is enough for me. We'll get him some new batteries for the barbecue.'

They are gearing up to have people over this year. The singing fish will feature as a talking point when things get too serious or quiet, or if someone starts talking politics or religion, because of the odd mix. The old man who walks his dog in the park. Carole and Gordon. His mother, and Louisa's. Her boss.

Later Louisa notices Harry lingering over the picture of the parrot. She keeps her Christmas list on the right-hand television surround-sound speaker under the saxophone-playing frog. She writes the parrot down on her list followed by a question mark in brackets which she uses when she doesn't feel confident enough to fully commit to a question mark.

At the end of the day Harry throws out the junk mail along with the page featuring the circled parrot, and she deadheads the roses. They sit, drink beer and watch Buddha and their newly acquired solar light as darkness falls, in an effort to catch the exact moment that it switches on.

They go inside prematurely and miss it.

Louisa has one more session booked with Lucy before Christmas. It's always a difficult time for her. She wants to talk about pleasant things, but Lucy has set the agenda.

Louisa notices something here: a subtle change in Lucy's expression. She has seen it before and wonders about it. There is something in Lucy's own history. She allows her gaze to drift to the happy family picture that Lucy keeps on her bookcase. A younger version of Lucy is surrounded by three children and no husband. Her gaze drifts to Lucy's fourth finger. She wears an elaborately decorated wedding ring. Lucy notices Louisa's attention and clasps her hands together.

'Take your time,' Lucy says.

'Yes all right.'

'I'm listening.'

'You're interested in the very first time? It's hard, Lucy, because these things don't seem quite so defined. I mean, of course there was a first time that he hit me, but somehow there seemed to be a kind of logic to it. A progression.'

'That's interesting. Can you explain that a bit more?'

'I'm not sure. I was shocked, I suppose, and angry, but not surprised somehow. I mean somehow in my own mind I had separated the sexual – um – behaviour from just raw violence, I suppose, because I think that there were certain social attitudes at that time about not getting yourself into certain situations. Which I had. I was young of course, but still. And also the assumption, which I bought, I must have bought, about domestic violence: that it only happened to other people of a certain class, and then if the woman nagged or provoked the man in some way I suppose. But as it turned out, that wasn't actually true.'

'No.'

'At least I couldn't think of anything I'd done, although something had been brewing for a few days. So I wasn't really surprised as such, but I was shocked, if that makes sense. I was shocked not only that it happened, but at the way it seemed to be almost inevitable.'

Louisa feels compelled to protect her midriff, but this is as much to guard her from what Lucy must think, as it is from the memory of the winding punch that sent her to her knees before that first real onslaught.

Lucy sits. Louisa collects her thoughts.

'And then there was the overpowering force of my own feelings. I hated him. Such an awful thing, and unusual for me. I don't tend to hate people. But I was angry: I'd never been so angry. I started fantasising about getting revenge. I thought – I thought he has to go to sleep sometime, and then we'll see. Then we'll see.'

'You thought of attacking him?'

'I wanted to kill him. That's terrible, isn't it? Yes.'

'Why didn't you?'

'What?'

'Why didn't you?'

'Are you serious? You're not serious are you?'

'Self-defence. He might have killed you.'

'Well yes, there's that. I don't believe in hurting people.'

'And yet ...?' Lucy is persistent. She stares directly into Louisa's eyes.

'Oh well, you know. You have these impulses, you think these extreme thoughts in the heat of the moment, and I think with all the adrenaline rushing through the body you don't realise how badly he has hurt you. After he calmed down, the next day he seemed so terribly sorry. And then someone had called the police and they came when Victor was at work and asked if I wanted to press charges, but I felt they were just going through the motions really, talking down to me, and giving me the hint that it might do more harm than good. What was the point? To be honest, I felt ashamed, as if I should never have got myself into that situation in the first place. I kept searching through my actions for a reason. Sometimes I could sound a bit blunt. Tactless. I thought that could be it. You trust people to let you express yourself without getting offended. I used to anyway, before that.'

'You have a right to speak honestly. Yes.'

'Yes. But people do tend to blame the woman.'

'Not always.'

'No? People judge you. You probably judge me, don't you, deep down?'

'I don't at all.' But there is uncertainty in her voice. Lucy on the back foot.

Louisa is annoyed at her now. It's time to move on. It's not fair that Lucy should pry: there's a fine line, and some things are too private, even for therapy. Nevertheless she feels compelled to explain herself.

'I did think of retaliating, of course. But part of me was thinking about my baby, and who would take care of her if something happened to me. That was before Tom was born, of course. So in the cold light of day it wouldn't do. Those thoughts are fuelled by emotion, and by the time I was actually capable of doing anything I didn't have the emotional power any more. Anyway, I'm not like that. I wouldn't ever hurt a fly really. But that was the scariest thing of all: being so angry.'

'Why didn't you leave, Louisa?'

'It's not that easy. People deserve a chance.'

'Well, yes. So did you.'

'Yes, but he wasn't as emotionally strong. I thought. Physically, yes. And I do believe in giving people a chance. I didn't know if it was just a one-off. I suppose I told myself it was a one-off. I suppose I'd already been backed into a corner and he was my whole world by then. I couldn't see the bigger picture any more. He and Meredith were my world. Also divorce wasn't a big thing then. I mean, not many people did it. No-fault had come in, but still. My family had always been quite conservative, I suppose.'

'Were you frightened for Meredith's future?'

'Well no, not really then, because I thought it wouldn't happen again. I thought he was genuinely sorry and that he'd exercise restraint next time he got frustrated about work or, or whatever.'

'Can you talk a bit about Meredith?'

Louisa feels her face tightening. She glares. Lucy persists.

'What about your daughter?'

'I don't know. What would you have done, Lucy? He probably would have killed us if we'd left. I didn't want to die. Not then. I didn't want anything to happen to my baby. What would you do if it was you?' Louisa hears the sarcasm in her own voice.

'Honestly? I don't know what I would have done. I don't know. He put you in a terrible situation. Just awful. He took enough from you, Louisa. Don't let him take any more.'

Louisa crosses her arms. Lucy presses on.

'I just feel that there's something stopping you from getting close to your daughter. That's all. I could speculate that you're punishing yourself, but I don't know. You probably do, at some level, which is why you're not reaching out more.'

'I do. I don't think she's interested.'

'I don't think that can be right.'

'I'm not sure what you mean.'

'It's just a feeling. I'm concerned. I feel we're not finishing on a very good note.'

'That's okay. It's Christmas after all.'

'Are you going to be all right?'

'Sure.'

'You're a good person, Louisa. I'm on call over the break. If you need to talk.'

'Okay. Thanks.'

As Louisa leaves she wonders again whether this therapy is making things worse. She really feels terrible now. Why would she think Lucy has the answers any more than she does? She's just a woman. What makes her think that anyone has the answers? All she wants is to go home and have a good laugh with Harry.

CHAPTER NINETEEN

At South Beach Cafe the furniture is cemented to the ground to make it impossible to steal. Carole, Louisa and Rhianna sit around the immovable table like the old friends that they were, and to the untrained eye might appear as solid and as difficult to shift.

Carole, who prefers everything out in the open, is determined to make the most of the meeting by ensuring that their common history isn't ignored, but Louisa and Rhianna resist. There is still something blocking progress. Louisa tries to ignore it, but feels it enclosing her, frustrating movement in all directions. Her habit is to pretend that it isn't there.

It is not good for her to live like this. She needs her friends. She tries to identify where the cooling of the friendship occurred. There was no single dramatic incident, but something has happened progressively.

When she was younger she was more forward-looking: after she left Victor, when he had found other distractions and faded from their lives, and also before him. In those days it seemed that there was still the possibility of better times ahead. She and her friends helped each other out and grew closer as a result, drawing up and replenishing each other's strength. Later, when she needed it most, in the years after Tom as her daughter became progressively more remote, Louisa was too worn out and too overwhelmed to ask for help or offer it. For whatever reason, the dynamic had changed and they all drifted apart.

Then one day, she wondered, and perhaps the others did too, what they were doing. It happened for her one evening as the sun was sinking from a cloudless sky into the ocean. She, Harry and Buster were watching together, wishing for a skerrick of cloud to catch the afterglow. Her thoughts had been drifting but a coincidental combination of thoughts came together in synchronicity. She felt a sense of longing for things lost: the warmth of old friendships. She began to see more of Carole, and sought Rhianna out again. She and Harry minded Rhianna and Simon's old dog when they went away, and they looked after Buster from time to time.

But that sort of contact is a different, diminished sort of connection. It is too fleeting and distracted, too polite, too pleasant, dropping off and picking up the dogs, talk of practicalities, quantities of food and emergency phone numbers. They never really talked the way they used to.

But three women, old friends meeting for lunch, has potential. So today they meet hoping to create something new. Or she does. Everyone remembers the past differently. Carole is pleased that they are all together again. Rhianna is giving nothing away but seems open to whatever happens. For the first time in a long time they really see each other. In the harsh outdoor light with shadows cast from the cafe shelter and the blue reflections from the painted tables, Louisa notices how old the others have become, and how changed. She'd seem that way to them too, she guesses. The women smile and appear relaxed, but their eyes expose their history, the difficult and unnecessary detours their lives have taken. Rhianna has never had children. She would have made a good mother. Louisa thinks that perhaps Rhianna resents her for having children and making such a mess of it. She looks closely for signs of this, but can't identify anything in her eyes, except kindness.

They talk and smile, and try too hard to recapture the relationship they once had. The years have banished it, and it won't come back. Instead of talking over the top of one another in their excitement to share, they smile pleasantly, protecting their gains and losses.

'Louisa said you'd been to Scotland again,' Rhianna is saying to Carole.

'I've been three times,' Carole says. 'We're planning to go back in March for about six months. Gordon's sister is going to Spain and wants someone to stay in her house so we said we'd go. It's going to be fantastic. There's a small studio room in the backyard where she said I can do my sculpture, and Gordon has long service leave. I can take leave on half-pay and then leave without pay, so I'm going to do it. Bugger it! You're only young once!'

'That's fantastic!' says Rhianna, as Louisa nods. 'It's about time you did something for yourself.'

'What are you going to do with your house?' asks Louisa.

'I don't know. I was thinking I might rent it out, but I don't want to take a risk with it. You never know who you're going to get, do you? Would one of you like to stay in it? You could have a holiday of your own. We'll need someone to look after Percy. There's a good cat-boarding place up in the hills, but I think he'd be more settled in his own home.'

'Have you still got him?' says Rhianna, amazed. 'How old is he?'

'Eighteen. He's got a couple more years in him.'

Last time she saw him, Louisa noticed that Percy had started dribbling, but he is very special because he belonged to Carole's daughter.

'Moggies last longer than pedigrees I suppose,' Louisa says.

'Yes. So what about it? House-sitting.' Carole sticks to

her agenda. She's angling to close the deal. It's made her the successful businesswoman that she is.

Louisa can't imagine anyone feeling particularly comfortable there. Carole is obsessed with having everything just so. What would happen if she were to break something? She might feel compelled to break something.

'You know that Buddha water feature with the light that we saw at the winery that day?' says Carole. 'I bought it. You could sit and meditate out the back. You could have Harry over, as if he was your lover. You know it's very private out there, except for the sound of the chooks next door, but you get used to them. I don't know if they are allowed to keep chooks in the metro area; do you? I wanted to complain, but Gordon wouldn't let me. He reckons it makes him feel like he is living in the country.'

'I don't know,' says Louisa. 'I'd have to think about it. It might be nice having my own space for a while, but I don't know about Harry. He might get used to living on his own. Or what if I did?'

'What if you did?' says Carole.

'You used to be more adventurous when we were younger,' Rhianna says.

'Why don't you move in then?' says Louisa.

'Because I don't want to,' says Rhianna, with a hint of her old liveliness. This gives Louisa some hope. Something of their old relationship might be salvaged.

'It's an interesting idea,' says Louisa. 'Can I think about it?'

'Sure,' says Carole. 'I want to sort something out soon, so can you get back to me by next week sometime?'

Louisa agrees to do this after she has talked it over with Harry. She wonders whether some distance might make the heart grow fonder or more remote. She wonders, for some reason that she doesn't analyse, about that man in the white van. Perhaps he is homeless. Perhaps he is driving around parking under people's trees so that he feels he has some roots.

No pun intended. She smiles to herself. Pun intended. Perhaps he would like to house-sit Carole and Gordon's house. Perhaps he is a nice young American man with good manners. Perhaps he is escaping some sort of situation.

After they hug and go their separate ways, Louisa drives slowly home with her window open, the radio turned off and her hair blowing into knots. When she arrives home, Harry is out. She makes herself a cup of tea and takes it outside to sit on the swing and think about what has transpired.

She wonders about the commitment of keeping up with old friends, that level of intimacy that women have. She provisionally decides that it isn't good to force anything. You can't go back, can you?

Then she thinks about Tom, and is suddenly angry at him for choosing the wrong path and for putting her and Meri and everyone through so much pain. 'It's too bad,' she says to him. 'I know you were young, but what on earth were you thinking? Why couldn't you just exercise a bit of self-control? What made you think you had no responsibility for the life you were given?'

The opportunity more or less falls into their laps. Gordon has had to fly back to Scotland because his mother is ill, so Harry has arranged to meet Carole at her place. When he gets there she takes a while to answer the bell.

'Who is it?' she eventually asks through the closed door.

'It's me, Harry,' he says, feeling foolish. Who did she think it was?

She opens the door. She is wearing a pair of dark blue pyjamas made out of some sort of silky material. Her hair, which she normally keeps tied up, is hanging loose. She looks younger, more approachable, less businesslike than normal.

'Oh Harry,' she says, 'just making sure. There's something wrong with the peephole. Come on through.'

She is wearing a familiar perfume. Harry has a

flashback – Yasamine dressed in a smooth black dress. She was wearing the locket he gave her for her birthday. He just fastened the clasp of the chain, and his fingers stopped to play with the fine silk of her skin. He wound his arms around her from behind and buried his face in her hair. He feels the sensation of it now on his cheeks. He shakes the thought away. He is here, now, in Carole's house, and not with his wife.

He is more nervous than he had expected. It's not the first time he's done something like this, but he hasn't been with anyone else since he moved in with Louisa, and her best friend is high stakes. The foreplay is over. This is the real deal.

He smiles, raises his eyebrows, and hands her the flowers he's bought from a roadside stall that is permanently set up around the corner from his house. The flower-seller is surly and never says more than two words, so there's no chance of it getting back to Louisa. If it did he'd say they were for his mother. The flowers are all pungent smells and bright colours, and the oversized bunch is wrapped in purple and red paper. One orange daisy thing is hanging its head as if its neck is broken.

Carole relieves him of the flowers and puts them on the hall stand beneath the pictures of her grandchildren.

'How thoughtful.'

She kisses his cheek, lingering there and slowly working her way around to his ear. Her perfume is heavy but not suffocating. His ear is cold where she has licked it. When she turns to get him a drink, his hand automatically goes up to wipe his cheek.

'Here's something I prepared earlier,' she says, handing him the drink.

'Thanks.'

'Don't mention it,' she says. She leads him into the sitting room and sits on the couch. 'Come and sit down.' She pats the seat next to her.

Harry sits, takes the glass from her hand and puts it on the table at his side, slopping a little over the rim and his hand as he does so. Carole takes his hand and licks the spilt drink from his fingers. It feels strange and Harry has the urge to laugh, but he controls himself.

'Sweet,' she says. 'Intoxicating.' She is leaning over him. He can see down her pyjama top. Her nipples are erect. He feels himself getting hard. It feels good to be hot, and he finds it reassuring that he is responding as easily as he is.

'Keep it up,' he says, half to himself.

'Couldn't have put it better myself,' says Carole. 'I'd better wipe that up off the table before it marks,' she says, grabbing a handful of tissues.

'Sorry,' he says.

'Don't worry about it.' She mops it up, leaning over him. Her pyjamas are silk and slide around on her body without making sparks: none of that cheap polyester stuff that Louisa wears. 'I don't want you to worry one bit,' she says.

'I wasn't,' he says, taking her wrist. He kisses her, a long, deep, slow kiss. She has just cleaned her teeth and is wearing some sort of flavoured lipstick. 'You taste nice,' he says.

'So do you.' She pushes him down so that he is only half lying on the couch, with his legs angled down to the floor, and climbs on top of him. 'I like it on top,' she says. 'I like to feel strong and powerful. I like to take control. All you need to do is what I tell you to.'

'Great,' he says. 'I like a woman who knows her own mind.'

She unties her complicated pyjama top without Harry seeing how. She has the body of a younger woman, at variance with her face. Harry vaguely wonders if she's had some sort of cosmetic surgery. Gordon has plenty of money and is generous enough, he thinks, and Carole's got a good job too. Between the two of them they'd be doing all right.

Carole starts to undo his shirt, kissing his neck and his chest as she goes down on his body. 'Mm, nice chest,' she says. 'What else do we have down here? What's this here?'

'I think that's pretty obvious,' he says. He cups his hands over her breasts, but the position is awkward and he lets go. She goes down on him now, licking and sucking.

He is uncomfortable, not enjoying it as much as he should. He clears his throat. 'Do you have a bed?' he says after a moment. 'It's just that my back is killing me.'

'Oh come on,' says Carole. 'Don't be an old man.' She keeps playing with him, kissing him, teasing him with her tongue.

'Well as far as that goes you're hardly sixteen yourself, are you?' Harry snaps this more than he intends to. His back has started to hurt quite badly and the pain is shooting down his left leg.

She stops and sits up. He adjusts his position and the pain subsides a bit.

'What?' she says.

'You're not, are you?' he says, still irritably adjusting his position underneath her. 'Anyway that's what beds are for. More room to manoeuvre.' He winks at her to relieve the tension.

Carole recoils slightly. She is reconsidering. 'It's upstairs,' she says, but there is an edge to her voice now. Then she laughs. 'Sometimes I forget,' she says as she climbs off him and stands up. 'You're right. We're not as young as we used to be. Gordon prefers the bed too. Come on.'

'You're only as young as the woman you feel,' says Harry automatically. He uses this line with Louisa all the time and she always smiles, but Carole doesn't get the joke. Too bad! He is annoyed that she has brought Gordon into the picture. There should be some sort of unspoken rule about that.

He is still lying halfway off the couch and he asks her for some help to get up. She grabs hold of his arms and pulls him sharply.

'Ow! Take it easy.' His erection has fallen away completely. Bugger. He's not as reliable as he used to be, but it's understandable under the circumstances.

'Sorry,' she says. She sounds resentful, petulant, childish.

'It's okay. I'll do it myself.' He eases himself off the couch until he twists around onto his knees, and leans forwards into the seat-back. He stays there a while, head down, backside facing outwards.

'Nice,' says Carole.

She doesn't stay to watch, or to help further. She clears the glasses and Harry hears her rinse them and put them in the dishwasher. When she comes back into the room, he has made it to his feet but is having difficulty straightening up.

'I need a moment,' he says.

'How do you feel about this?' She has tied her hair up.

'Not great,' he says.

'Me neither,' she says.

'I think I've put my back out. Can I take a raincheck? To tell the truth I haven't been feeling the best lately.'

'I'll have to get back to you on that.'

'Well,' he says.

'Well.'

'I'll see myself out then,' he says.

'Suit yourself.'

Okay, thinks Harry, I will.

'We'll catch up,' he offers. 'Soon.'

'Of course. Give Louisa my love.'

'Very funny.'

As he drives home he is feeling humiliated and annoyed with himself. What was he thinking? She's hardly his type: all feminist hard edges and neurosis. He knows, he knows from past experience that there is a reason why people don't sleep with their wives' friends or with workmates. You have to keep seeing them, and maintaining a pretended innocence. It's all so exhausting and, besides, he's not a hundred per cent convinced that he can trust Carole not to tell Gordon, or Louisa for that matter.

Plus he likes Gordon, he really does, and he doesn't want

to lose their recently burgeoning friendship. He doesn't like to think how finding out about this would hurt and humiliate him, and for what? He feels like an idiot. He'll kick himself if he loses Gordon's good opinion. These days, friends are few and far between.

Louisa isn't in when he gets home but the dog greets him, sniffs at his groin then wanders out the back. 'Oh, come on!' he protests. 'Et tu, Buster?'

But it's fair comment. Before Louisa gets home he will have a shower and pop his clothes in the wash. Just to be on the safe side.

CHAPTER TWENTY

Louisa has decided not to take up Carole's offer of the house. She'll stay with Harry. Last night he seemed a bit down about the idea. He seems to be struggling with some sort of existential angst.

She lends him her favourite book by Deepak Chopra, so that he can start the New Year on a new foot. She thinks that Deepak will be good for him, but after flicking through he tosses the book aside.

'Why do you get this crap?' he says. 'Why make the man any richer than he already is?'

'I guess so. Oh well, it doesn't matter.' She is embarrassed by her credulity and his disparagement, and finds herself back-pedalling. 'I remember seeing him years ago and being impressed, but I was younger. He said something about not having to age and it seemed to make sense back then. I don't know, somehow it doesn't now. Make sense. Not all. Of course I did age, so it didn't actually work. I think he thinks human beings are deluded.'

'Yeah, well that's hardly new. Anyway you wouldn't want to take that to its logical conclusion.'

'What do you mean?' she says, but he just shakes his head.

Today he can't even be bothered taking his own conclusions to their logical conclusions.

Louisa knows that Harry has had another unsuccessful year of buying tickets in raffles with the aim of winning a decent car. She leaves Deepak Chopra and asks Harry about whether he has planned his New Year's resolutions yet, but his eyes glaze over. He stares into space for a prolonged period before advising her that the calendar is arbitrary and that it is his birthday, and not the New Year, that is the time for admitting another year has passed.

Christmas has come and gone, and with it the traditional exchange of goods and services. She bought him a nice watch that he picked out, and he responded with a pretty stone-look birdbath. The gifts were exchanged prior to Christmas because Harry needed the watch for his new job and he needed Louisa's help to get the birdbath out of the boot and placed in a strategic position for birdwatching. They have placed it among the impinging greenery beneath the giant flowerless yellow rosebush that has grown too tall for Louisa to prune, and have sat for extended periods on the garden swing waiting in vain for the birds to come, but although Harry has put out seed and freshened up the water, not a soul has visited. A couple of weeks have gone by since they placed it there, and there has been nothing. A neighbour across the road has a birdbath which is never vacant. Harry and Louisa have discussed the various possible reasons for their birdlessness. The failure of the birdbath has reinforced Harry's belief that his entire life is destined to be nothing but a series of disappointments.

When darkness comes, the leftover Christmas lights decorate the barren space of the waiting bath, reflecting off stagnant water. Harry and Louisa have made the best of it, showing it off to those who visited around the Christmas season, have used it as a conversation piece, and sold the possibility of tender moments, rather than experienced the moments themselves.

By day the weather has been hot and the bath has dried out. Harry has filled it again and put out more birdseed. Louisa has attended from time to time, standing on the bottom garden step so that she is just a couple of heads higher than the pedestal.

On the day before New Year she has barely positioned herself there when a yellow and black striped wasp falls into the water in front of her. It floats there, hardly moving, its tail slowly bending backwards and forwards, twice, and then nothing. Another buzzing by her ear: a second wasp flies close to her face, hovers, peels off and disappears. It looks as if this one has killed the other.

Louisa takes a dead gum leaf from the ground and scoops the body from the water, taking care not to wet it any more than she can help. The wasp lies motionless in its leaf coffin. Louisa places it gently on the ground and moves back inside to watch for a while from the window, but there are still no birds.

Then, on New Year's Day, when she has just about given up, Louisa rises early and is shown something beautiful. She beckons Harry and he stumbles out just in time to see a kingfisher guarding the stone-edged pond with its mate watching on from the branches of the overhanging yellow rose. The kingfisher turns its head and looks with interest at the two of them. Harry stands quite still, just ahead of Louisa, who is looking at Harry. The dog is stretched out on the lawn, oblivious.

Harry stands there for a long time, saying nothing. Then he turns to Louisa and smiles. He moves to her side, puts his arm around her shoulders, and kisses her gently on the top of her head.

'Seeing that,' he says, 'gives me hope for the future.'

It's later in the day and they are having a quiet drink or two on the garden swing under the back patio. The dog sleeps at their feet.

'What about your New Year's resolutions?' she asks him after the second wine kicks in. 'Have you got any?'

He says, 'I told you.'

'Oh yes. It's not your birthday is it?'

She takes another swig. It is barely midday, but New Year's Day and nobody is working. She is saving her headache for tomorrow.

He says, 'What about you?'

'Mine is to look after myself. Simple.'

'Fair enough.' He is relaxed too. He speaks freely. 'Yasamine used to make New Year's resolutions. She never kept them.'

Louisa takes up the cue.

'You don't talk about her, Harry. You should. We should know more about each other so we can be closer. I'd like that.'

'Maybe.' He takes a moment, looking at her, which is unusual. 'Your hair looks nice today,' he says.

'Truth or truth?' she says. 'You know, it's a kids' game.'

'What?'

'You pick one. You ask me to tell you the truth or I ask you to tell me. The truth.'

'Never heard of it. I thought it was supposed to be something else. Dare or something.'

'I didn't want to give you a choice. It's my way of saying I'd like to have a conversation. I thought you might not be daring enough to listen.'

'What's that supposed to mean? I listen.'

'No.'

'Yes.'

'Okay then, I want to tell you something. I dare you not to walk out in the middle of it.'

'As if,' he says, smirking, but he looks trapped. He pours himself another drink. 'Go on then.'

'Okay. How do I start? I was a nurse, you know,' she says.

'I know that. Is that it?'

'Not a proper nurse, a nurse's aide they used to call us, when I first started work after school. They trained us in the hospitals, on the floor, and with brief blocks of time for intensive study in between. I left school early, at fifteen, just because I could. The deal was I got a job where I could continue my education in a way, so that seemed to fit the bill. Actually we didn't get all that much help to start with. We were thrown in the deep end. As soon as you put a uniform on, people expected so much of you, as if you were magically transformed from a kid into someone competent and worldly. Well I wasn't. I was only fifteen and I felt all at sea, scared really I suppose, and I was naive. Of course I was bloody naive. Some men have a bit of a thing about nurses, I suppose because they see people at their most human – naked, ill, not sanitised, you know – and men see that as some sort of sexual thing. Or it could be just the uniform. Old men were forever grabbing at you when you got close to the bed, propositioning you. Some were surprisingly strong. We'd have to clean up shit and blood and wash people. Cope with their suffering and the smell of all that. We'd even have to cause suffering in order to help people heal sometimes. I've sometimes thought about that – that it was better to suffer myself than to have to see someone else suffer. I'm kidding myself. It was always about not giving in to that desire to strike back. Some people are shits. Sometimes I would identify so strongly with a person that I would actually feel pain as they were describing it, or expressing it. I think I'm stronger than some people. But then I wonder if I'm not. I feel pain, I'm very sensitive to pain. I don't like it at all. So I'm not a masochist or anything, I'm not saying that. It's just that I'd hate to be the cause of someone else's suffering and if I can save them from that, I will, even at my own expense, because I can take it, you see.'

Harry doesn't speak or react, so she ploughs on. It doesn't

matter. He could be asleep, but she feels she wants to talk.

'Victor had a bit of thing about nurses, because he had seen the truth about human beings as well, having seen people killed in the war, and killed people. He did, as I later found out: he killed people – young families. What would that do to a person, to have to do that? Can a soldier say no, I'm not doing that, and offer himself instead? And we have to remember, they're only young too. What sort of pressure are they under to do what they're told, and what does all that training trigger in them? You should know, Harry, from your basic training, even if you didn't end up going. I suppose it all depends on what he sees there in front of him. There's so much confusion. He killed children, Harry.'

'That's war.' He is listening.

'I know.'

'Collateral damage.'

'That's a horrible euphemism. I don't believe in that crap, but he couldn't tell. Anyway, what did I know? They could have been Vietcong. The Vietcong were very small, weren't they, since they were able to fit into those underground tunnels and everything. There was a lot of confusion in the heat of the moment. Still they were people, that's the point really, isn't it? Our troops were in their country.'

'The South wanted us there. We were trying to help.'

'But children. It's horrible.' Louisa allows herself to see it clearly for the first time. She is overcome with horror, nausea.

'So what he did is that he brought the war home with him. He brought it into the family that we would have, that karma. It was like that was what he had *become*. I'm not saying it happens to everyone, but with Victor ... that's what it was. That might explain it. What I can't understand is what we'd done to deserve it. My children didn't do anything to deserve it. Anyway, the truth he saw was that physical truth, that we're all just meat when it comes down to it. If that's what you think then it would be easy wouldn't it? To kill? If instead of seeing something as precious as life, all you're seeing is meat. But that's such a cop-out isn't it? And such a terrifying thought. Maybe it's a mindset surgeons have to get into, or how could they cope? Once I was allowed to look in on an operation, and this nurse was assisting, and she had to stay with someone who was in the middle of brain surgery with the top of her head off, while everybody else went off to have morning tea. Or afternoon tea. It was such a long operation and they needed a break so that they could keep concentrating, I suppose. Then the anaesthetist had to duck out to the toilet. He told her to keep an eye on the patient, keep the blood pressure cuff pumped up to a certain point, and then this nurse had to duck out herself, so she asked me to hold the fort for a minute. See that was the uniform again, wasn't it? Thinking I was more competent than I really was. I knew something by then; not much. I might have been sixteen. The patient started to stir while they were out, with her brain open and exposed like that. Nowadays I think they do some brain surgery with the patient awake anyway. Still that's not the point. But it makes you wonder about what we are, when you can see a person's insides. It's obscene, but fascinating at the same time.'

She glances at Harry. He's not looking at her, but attentive just the same.

'She was okay. Nothing bad happened. Not that you hear what happens to them once they leave the recovery room.'

'Is that what you wanted to talk about?'

'No, something else. I'm getting to it.'

'Yes, okay.'

'The first time he picked me up from my parents' place, our first date, and I was still only fifteen then, just before my sixteenth birthday. He was about ten years older, twenty-five, and so much older because of having seen active service, so I was a bit overawed. We were meeting some of his friends, colleagues I suppose you'd call them, for a meal and I was dressed up to the nines and feeling a bit inadequate because they were all professional people, mostly lawyers with their private-school girlfriends who were mostly at uni, and what I was doing didn't fall into that category of course: quite a bit below. Plus young men in those days were so cynical and patronising towards women. Anyway it was a very expensive restaurant and everyone was talking about this and that, but I was having trouble holding my own so I was becoming more and more withdrawn, and I couldn't tell what Victor was thinking because he wasn't giving much away, but he was drinking more than the others. So every time he looked away, I'd take a swig out of his glass to sort of slow him down because he was driving me home. I was drinking my own as well – technically I shouldn't have been drinking at all, but I looked older all dressed up – and after a while he said, and he seemed to be in good humour, they all liked him – he said, I'd better get this chicken home to bed, and everyone seemed to laugh at that, the men anyway, but I think I got some sort of feeling of disapproval from the women. So instead of going straight home, he said we'd go somewhere and park so that I could sober up because I wouldn't want my parents to see me in that state, which seemed reasonable because Dad would have been ropeable, and I was thinking that he was a decent sort of bloke but I was thinking I probably wouldn't see him again – just put it down to experience. Because I felt out of my depth really.'

'I can see where this is heading.'

'Of course you can.'

Harry sinks his head into his hands and pushes his hair back. 'Okay,' he says. She has dared him to stay, so he stays.

'Anyway of course now I know that he knew exactly what he was doing, but I'd been brought up to think it was all about women leading men on and men not being able to control themselves, so it was up to the woman to not let them get into that situation in the first place. Plus there was this thing that women said no when they really meant yes, but they were just being coy, cock-teasers, which was the worst thing to be. And women were somehow more mature than men, which is probably true in some cases.'

'Sure.'

'We drove straight to this place in the bush – he must have known exactly where he was going because we didn't drive around at all. I was feeling weird and I might have fallen asleep for a minute, but the next thing I knew he was on top of me and there was this searing pain, I was frightened and I think I was saying no, please stop, it hurts, you're hurting me. I was thinking it. My voice was trapped in my throat. But he wouldn't stop and I was trying to push against his chest to get him off, but he was too strong. I hadn't had sex before, I was a virgin, and I didn't know what to expect, if this was normal or not for the first time.'

'Oh, Lou ...'

'Anyway, Harry, he wouldn't stop so I started kicking out at his car and I had high heels on and that made him stop all right because he was scared I was going to damage his car, so he said, 'Shit Louisa, there's no need for that,' and he stopped and was quite nasty and told me to straighten myself up because I looked like a slut, and then he drove me home after that. He more or less pushed me out of the car and said he'd pick me up the next day at about eight o'clock. The next evening.'

'What?'

'I went inside. I had a long shower. A long, long shower to wash him off me and out of me, and I felt so, so ashamed and humiliated. And the next day he came and he picked me up as if nothing had happened, and I went. I went, and he took me there again, to the same place, and this time I just gave in. And so it seemed that the logical thing after that was to get married. I heard you could get married at sixteen with your parents' permission, and they could see where it was heading so they didn't hesitate, and anyway well my parents seemed so happy and proud about their daughter going up in the world and everything. And in a funny kind of way I did for a while there.'

She can't look at him but senses his discomfort.

'I know it was wrong to go on with it. It felt like I didn't have a choice in the matter. I was very young,' she says. 'It wouldn't happen again. Shit, I'd run a mile these days. I can't believe I was so naive. What are you thinking?'

Harry stands up and stretches his back. 'I need to take the dog for a walk,' he says.

'Is that all?'

'I don't know what you want from me, Louisa,' he says. 'You can't change the past. I mean it's not as if I can do anything about it, any more than you can. Life sucks sometimes. It really does. How old were you? Sixteen?' He rubs the back of his head. 'All right, I hate it that the bastard did that to you, but what can I do about it now? Do you want me to go after him? I would have if you were my daughter, but now, well now there's just too much water under the bridge, isn't there? You didn't do anything wrong, just ...'

'Just what?'

'Just that the messages were all mixed up back then? Free love, and all that. Besides, he knew exactly what he was doing. You probably didn't. I don't know what else to say. Life isn't fair.'

'No, I suppose not. People can make it fair though, can't they Harry?'

'Maybe. I'm going for a walk. Why don't you come with me?'

Louisa considers this for a moment. Sometimes movement is just about putting one foot in front of the other.

'Okay,' she ventures.

He reaches out to offer a hug, but she ignores the gesture and he drops his arms. 'I want to say something, Louisa. I just don't know what you want.'

'Yes,' she says, turning away to seek out her walking shoes. 'That's all right. Don't worry. It's an old story. I just thought you should know.'

CHAPTER TWENTY-ONE

They have been pretending the conversation never took place. Harry puts it down to the wine talking. But he vaguely understands that she expected more from him. He arrives home with flowers, which he presents to her rather self-consciously.

'Your favourite colours. Purple and yellow.'

'What's the occasion? You haven't been having an affair have you?' she says, but her tone clearly implies that she doesn't entertain the idea. He feels vaguely insulted and wonders how she'd react if he told her about Carole. He is tempted but it wouldn't be doing anybody any favours to dump on her just to test a reaction, though it would clear his conscience at least. She probably wouldn't care anyway, and it wouldn't matter if she didn't. They'd have a laugh about it.

She is staring at the flowers in his hand, but is miles away. He is on the verge of telling her to wake up when Buster rushes to the door barking. When he checks at the door, no one is there. The dog is losing his faculties, hearing things and chasing ghosts. When Harry turns back, Louisa is putting the flowers in a vase, moving efficiently.

'Thanks Harry,' she says. 'It was thoughtful of you.'

When he was in one of his final years of high school, Tom had to do a still life. He procrastinated, saying that everything involving fruit, flowers and fabric had already been done, but Louisa insisted he make a start, telling him that even the mundane could be made interesting. Wasn't that the whole point of the exercise? To escape her insistence, he rode his bike away to see what he could find, and stopped at a roadside memorial where a boy had crashed into a tree. Someone had been there recently, so Tom picked up the flowers they'd left. It was a bouquet of yellow chrysanthemums and purple statice.

'Happy Mother's Day,' he joked when he got home with them hanging, windswept and wilting, on his handlebars.

'Why thank you, dear, they're lovely,' she said, joining him in the joke. When he told her what the joke was, she went cold.

'Take them back.' Her voice came out in a whisper, and he drew back. She modified her tone, pleading with him. 'Those flowers are for someone's loved one. You can't do things to add to their pain like that. You can't, Tom.'

He began to giggle, struggling for control, but he'd already lost it. She caught his laughter at her own stupidity and her self-righteous front dissolved before him. She was naive. She didn't know how teenage boys thought or felt. They were deep and mysterious. They were incredibly superficial. Who was this child of hers? She half laughed with him, even as she scolded. He stopped laughing then. He didn't want connection. He wanted separation.

'They're for my still life,' he said. 'I have to do a still life, so I'm going to do something kind of dead, get it?'

'You can't keep them. Come on, we're taking them back.'

She made him get into the car and drove him to the memorial where she replaced the flowers, smoothing them down as best she could. She made him bow his head and apologise to the spirit of the boy before they went to the nearby roadside flower-seller from whom the flowers had probably been bought. She chose a similar bunch for her son.

'It's not the same,' he said. 'I preferred the look of the others. They were falling apart. That's the whole point, Mother.' His voice was querulous with frustration and defeat. 'It's not as if he'd care. He's dead.'

'Yes, but it's not all about him,' she'd said harshly.

'It's his life. No, it's his death.'

'Not really, it isn't. Wait a couple of days, Tom. Leave the flowers outside. You'll get the effect you want.' He said he couldn't wait, the assignment was due.

Later he took the bunch outside and smashed it against a steel down-post on the carport until he got the effect he wanted. Each time he hit it against the post he expelled a small sound, a little cry.

'That's better,' he said when he came in. 'Now I have something more interesting. If I had the dude to put with them, it would be perfect.'

She was preparing dinner when he came to her side and hugged her. He was already a head taller than she was, growing into a man.

'I love you, Mum.' That was the last time she can remember him saying it.

'I love you too. Go and wash your hands.'

Harry's not sure about Louisa's response to his gift of flowers. Some things he just doesn't get. He still misses things. They seem trivial, but they turn out to be important. Like all the little things that must have led up to the incident with Yasamine.

One day he found her sobbing in the bathroom.

'What's up?' he asked impatiently.

'Nothing.' Still crying.

'Shit, Yasamine!' he said. 'It's obviously not nothing. You complain that I never talk to you and now when I show a bit of concern you shut me out. What's wrong?'

'Nothing!' She tried to push him hard out of the bathroom and he reacted automatically. He pushed back and she fell and hit her head on the ceramic basin as she went down. Blood everywhere.

It's what happens with head wounds. They always look a lot worse than they are. At least her sobbing had stopped, out of surprise, he supposed, or disbelief. He'd never done anything like that before. As history showed, he never would again. He grabbed a towel to stop the bleeding but as he came towards her she held up her arms to protect herself.

'Please don't hurt me, Harry,' she whimpered.

He was shocked by those words, but more by the way she held up her arms, covering her head in some sort of instinctual protective action. Her action had set off a flash of his father's face, red, shouting obscenities, the back of his thick hand sweeping down. The picture in his mind was from one of the many times he'd tried to stop the old man from getting to his mother, offering himself up in her place. He must have been a skinny little kid when he started doing that, and then went on doing it all through primary school.

Now with Yasamine he just stands there, a towel dangling from his hand and his mind stopped in its tracks. He is frozen to the spot, with a sickeningly familiar weakness spreading through his body.

'What?' he says to her. He can hardly get the word out. It comes out as a sort of whisper. 'What did you say?' It's a question, not a threat.

'Please,' she says. 'Please, Harry. I can't help it.' She speaks with difficulty, her words tumbling out, one or two at a time, between gulps of air. 'Please don't hurt me.'

'I wouldn't. Yas, I wouldn't hurt you. I didn't mean to – I'm sorry.' He stretches out his arm and hands her the towel. He notices his hand shaking. He feels like crap. 'Here, your head is bleeding.' She takes the towel.

Looking back now, that was a turning point. Or the turning point might have been when he left her crouched there on the bathroom floor, walking out, closing the door behind him, closing all the doors behind him. He took the car, squealed the tyres, drove around the block twice, three times, came back. As he walked in, she had just hung up the phone. The towel was wrapped around her head like a turban and some of the blood had seeped through, exaggerated by the whiteness of the towel.

'Who was that?' he asked, but she ignored him, twisted away and busied herself in the kitchen. Then Bella started crying from her bedroom.

'The baby's woken up,' she said sharply. 'Can you get her?' It was the old Yasamine, strong, confident and slightly sarcastic. 'And when you've done that,' she continued, 'you can clean up that bloody mess you left in the bathroom.'

It's been years since she could bring herself to watch the video. The quality of the film is grainy and the colours aren't quite right. It's strange, Louisa thinks, to see herself as another person. Nothing of this young woman remains. It is as if she has been taken over by another soul, another body, and yet there are sense memories being stirred as she watches this person who is nominally herself.

This Louisa, in her crocheted wedding dress, is actually beautiful, no more than fifty kilograms, young, smiling and uncertain. She wears a circle of flowers on her head, and her hair is long and shining. Victor is disturbingly young too, younger than she ever thought he had been, handsome, and strangely nervous. There is vulnerability about him as he awkwardly guides her around the room in the bridal waltz. The strains of music are barely audible, but she remembers his unremarkable choice: 'The Last Waltz'. She had nodded agreement, as she continued to do throughout their marriage. And yet there was hope present on that day, or if there wasn't, a lie had been captured on film.

Louisa rewinds to the speeches. Victor is the first to stand. 'On behalf of my wife and myself,' he says. Everyone applauds and there are some wolf-whistles from a group of his university friends. 'I would like to thank everyone for witnessing this auspicious occasion. Ain't she a beauty?' he says, raising his glass in Louisa's direction. 'But seriously, ladies and gentlemen, a marriage is no small undertaking. A marriage is forever, an unbreakable commitment buried in an institution that has stood the test of time. But then, who wants to live in an institution?' There is general laughter. The camera pans to Louisa. Her smile is present, if a little tight. 'I jest,' says Victor. 'You're stuck with me, girlie,' he says, and people laugh. 'I'd also like to thank the folks, Terry and Margaret, for taking me into their family so warmly.' His voice falters on the last word. It seems to Louisa that he's not so certain. 'Especially as my own couldn't be here today. As expected.' He raises his glass. 'Margaret and Terry,' he says.

It's like watching people who have already passed away. Some of them have. She switches over to the television. The announcer forecasts unsettled weather. There's a heatwave on the way.

Instead of avoiding the heat, Louisa enters into it, walking through the house to the backyard as if she is pushing her body through silt. She sinks into the synthetic cushions on the garden swing and her eyes fall on the rosemary bush, her mind as close to blank as it can get. There is no sun. The day is softly lit and the colours seem to be glowing with some sort of radioactive light. It would be easy to paint on a day like this because the light and the heat make everything seem strange, creating clearer vision, resisting interpretation. Today the rosemary bush is beautiful with muted grey and blue blocks of colour that could be mixed on a palate, placed on paper in rough form, and hung on a wall.

The leaves on the big yellow rosebush hang limply. As her eyes focus, Louisa discovers that there is a flower there. One deep yellow blossom appears before her eyes. At first the rest of the bush seems devoid of new life, but the longer Louisa looks the more she sees. Buds appear on the bush; little yellow light bulbs switch on in her brain. Her body is so heavy that it is hard to move. She doesn't want to move. Her mind doesn't seem able to take control.

Yesterday Harry said he saw a wasp taking a drink from the birdbath. It stretched its slender body down to the surface of the water and took a long drink. But today absence becomes the focus of attention. Everything is under shelter, hiding. Only mad dogs and Louisa go out in the mid-morning heat. The dog stays briefly and then goes back inside. Louisa still can't bring herself to move. Her eyes fall on Buddha. His eyes are half closed. Everything happens around him in imperceptibly slow motion. His thoughts travel at the speed of light. He sees the future. He sees right through.

Later that day Louisa will drive past a roadside memorial that has been neglected for some time. A small group will be placing flowers, one bent over, one standing. Two will be kneeling. An old white sedan will be parked further up the road. An anniversary.

She walks in and tells Harry about what she saw, and how she thought about it all the way home. She says that from now on she's decided to stop over-thinking everything and take it at face value. She's simply going to let herself see something but try not to build a story around it. The stories are too sad, and anyway she could be right off the mark. It's like everything, she tells Harry. It's not to be taken to heart. She wipes her eyes.

Harry concedes that Louisa makes a valid point. If people didn't think so much they wouldn't spend all their time worrying about what was going to happen, and they'd enjoy life more.

Harry prefers not to listen to the news just before bed because it keeps him awake. He switches channels but instead of news he gets a documentary. He lies awake thinking of everything, and of how he couldn't protect his daughter even if she wanted him to. He feels so weak in the face of it all. Louisa is lying awake next to him, staring into the darkness. He can feel her thinking. He can hear her breathing monotonously, in and out. What if he were to put a pillow over her face? What then? He feels uneasy, disturbed by the strange thoughts that emerge and subside in his overactive brain. It's a terrible thought. Sickening. He thinks of lying in bed alone, the sheet cold beside him, the terrible feeling of being utterly alone. He has been watching too much television, too much violence, too much that's way over the top.

Everything is exaggerated these days, super-sized they call it, as if everything isn't already big enough. He's just watched a documentary about a super-volcano under Yellowstone Park, which would cause global chaos if it went off. A regular-sized volcano is bad enough. Also he read somewhere that Greenland is becoming green again and that if its glaciers all fall into the sea, sea levels will rise dramatically, killing millions and displacing millions more. What else?

Now he remembers reading somewhere that men are becoming infertile and could be redundant someday. He could have seen it in a movie.

He thinks about the polar icecap that is melting, endangering polar bears, and all the currents that regulate the world's temperature that will cease flowing if too much ice melts into the sea, plunging the earth into another ice age, and the fact that, apparently, it's just a matter of time before another asteroid hits.

As if that's not enough, someone has noticed that once sharks are wiped out, plankton eaters will proliferate and eat all the plankton, which will put even more carbon into the atmosphere. Not that it will matter, because of nuclear proliferation.

Plus he's just been given another bloody speeding ticket. How many points is that? Sometimes he wishes he was an animal without all the complications of living as a human. Sometimes he wishes he didn't know so much.

Louisa says she wouldn't mind being an orang-utan. Or a parrot. He'd like to be a pelican, but too many of them get caught up in fishing lines these days. Not that orang-utans are any better off.

He thinks of food shortages, people dying in cyclones, tsunamis and earthquakes, acts of heroism, corruption, cowardice and procrastination, the way governments prevaricate, the way people in high places keep behaving as if the laws of nature can be negotiated, the way good people try to help, while scammers scam, and fundamentalists see everything in black and white. There are songs on the radio that encourage every man to act for himself, as if he is more important than the rest of the species, as if reason never existed, as if mateship, the diggers and, yes, even chivalry towards women and plain good manners never existed. Old men are bashed in their homes by young men and even girls these days, wanting money that they haven't earned, for drugs they don't need. War medals are stolen. Grandmothers are raped.

Meanwhile he and Louisa keep getting older, less certain, shakier, weaker, like all the other old codgers. Their friends refuse to grow up. Carole puts the whole future of her friendship with Louisa – not to mention his with his old mate Gordon – on the line by having a fling to see if she can still get a man. And what about him, what he's done to Louisa? What if she finds out, what then? No, nothing happened. Not really. He feels sick, feverish. He tosses and turns.

CHAPTER TWENTY-TWO

On Australia Day Louisa is driving towards the freeway, heading out on her weekly visit to her mother's. Ahead, a red and white jet hangs motionless, suspended in blue sky. A jeep speeds past her, flying an Australian flag from its antenna, window down, radio blaring some sort of heavy metal music. It is still hot. A section of road in front of her glistens, a haze rising above it and distorting the traffic that has gone before.

Louisa wonders if she exists. She wonders if she is asleep. She doesn't know whether she wants to wake up or not. She has created the boundaries to her own world. She knows every nook and cranny. What would be waiting for her if she awoke?

She winds the window up to allow the air conditioner to work, to block out the outside and to lock herself in. She turns up the opera that she has recently placed in her multi-disc CD player. Madame Butterfly is singing 'One Fine Day'. She feels her heart fill. Tears prickle her eyes but discipline themselves before they are substantial enough to fall, dry up, draw back. She examines her thoughts. There is nothing there but Madame Butterfly and the knowledge of things to come. There will be disappointment, the disillusion of love diminished to human proportions, rendered fragile; a clinging to the transcendent;

loss; finally harakiri. The opera seduces with music and sad stories. Suicide seduces because it seems romantic, feels like a final solution, provides instant gratification, promises an end to suffering. The promised ending hangs in eternity.

At the beach, Louisa lies on her back on a towel and pretends to sleep beneath her sunglasses as Harry bodysurfs the relentless waves. Louisa is running a commentary inside her head, talking to Lucy. She places the two of them at a kitchen table, as if they are two old friends chatting over coffee. Lucy has just been telling her something about her life – some indiscreet love affair. Then Lucy asks Louisa about the day it happened.

The trouble, Lucy, is this. When something terrible happens you don't believe it. Not because you haven't been warned, and not because you haven't seen it coming, but when you hear something as terrible as that, you don't believe it. You immediately decide to think that there must be some kind of mistake. So you hear the news but you dismiss it, as if someone is playing some sort of tasteless joke on you, but never mind: people are ignorant so you'll forgive them. They can't hurt you. Life will go on as usual. There is this sort of period where you float along as if nothing has changed and you feel a bit of anxiety as you're waiting for confirmation of that good news, and you'll all have a good laugh about it, or obviously not if someone else has suffered misfortune, of course not, but the odds are against it being you. Most people survive to maturity, to old age, don't they? It's what you expect. And you're kind of middle-class, and bad things happen to people who have been unfortunate, people who have had bad starts. They did, my kids: they had a difficult start in life, but I'd made it all right and somehow you don't think of yourself in that way. So it's always someone else who has the bad luck. You don't think this consciously, don't believe it when you use your reason, but it's down there somewhere in your view of the world. In my view of the world. So I dismissed it of course. People get mixed up. They fail in their communications all the time. Things get mixed up. Messages and so on, people should be friends but they say the wrong thing and the next you know you are at odds with them. But when I heard the news I said, no, they've obviously made a mistake, but it's okay. People are only human. People make mistakes. They aren't saying it to hurt you deliberately, so there you go. It's all very silly really, isn't it?

But as it turns out it's shock that has stopped your thinking, as if you can change a truth just by not seeing it. You can't make things right with some sort of trick of the mind. When it hits you, it blows you out of the water and there you stay, lying on the jetty gasping for breath and suffering, hoping for rescue or death, but neither comes and nobody cares really. They don't even see you there.

So the question that I've been trying to solve but can't seem to, Lucy, is this – what can you do? What can you do?

Louisa feels ice against her body, then the sting of sand on her arm. Harry spreads his towel and lies beside her, his thigh cool and damp, resting next to hers.

'This is the life,' he says.

CHAPTER TWENTY-THREE

When Rhianna calls it is about five pm on a Saturday. She has two spare tickets for a concert that night and wonders if Louisa and Harry are free. Louisa is, but Harry says he isn't. He needs a good two weeks' notice to psych up for an outing like that and, besides, he is very picky about where he goes. Louisa suggests Carole, who is still sufficiently impulsive to pick up an offer at the drop of a hat. Rhianna thinks it a good idea and Simon calls out to say that he likes being surrounded by women, when Rhianna checks with him, her hand off the mouthpiece. She says she'll ring back and let Louisa know the final count.

Half an hour later she calls back. Gordon is working and Carole is keen because she is missing the busy entertainment life she got used to when she was travelling. She is bringing a mystery guest and an extra ticket. They arrange to meet at Rhianna's and then go for a meal at the Old Shanghai because the show doesn't get started until about nine or nine-thirty. The support act is a local jazz band containing two members of the original line-up of Harry's band. When Louisa relates this to Harry he says he is half sorry he didn't say yes, but is hardly convincing.

'You should come,' she says, but she knows he won't, because he is in his track pants with his slippers on, and is looking forward to a night in front of the television.

Rhianna and Simon live in a semi-detached in Fremantle. Louisa arrives early, well before Carole, who invariably manages to be late. Rhianna is ready, wearing a flowing outfit, mauve with sparkling features. She is tall and slight and her long hair is piled casually on top of her head. She possesses what Louisa thinks of as regal bearing, that intangible sense of inborn class, something that those of more humble beginnings, like Louisa, struggle to meet. Rhianna's mother is a retired doctor from southern India; her deceased father was an English public servant. Simon is peaches-and-cream English and the same height as his wife, but his once fair hair is now almost grey. He could pass for a member of the British royal family for his apparent goodwill, his awkwardness and his usually impeccable, but occasionally foot-in-the-mouth manners. He puts aside the book he has been reading when Louisa follows Rhianna into the house, and gets up to make tea for them all. He reminds himself of how Louisa takes it, milk and no sugar, and brings out a packet of biscuits. Louisa eats. Rhianna declines. These are old friends from the old days. Louisa feels as if she is slipping back in time, as if Meri might be hanging off the back of her chair wanting her attention, as if Tom could walk around the corner any minute.

'It's a shame Harry couldn't make it,' Simon is saying to her. 'It was short notice, but let him know I'd love to catch up. He's such a character – he makes me laugh. We could do dinner next week. What do you think? Saturday night? Pencil it in your diary and check with Harry.'

'Yes. Wonderful,' she says. 'I'll write it in ink.'

Carole arrives with someone. Louisa is momentarily taken aback. She becomes conscious of her own breathing. Carole introduces the man who could be Brad from the white van, but says that his name is Chas, some sort of corruption of

Charles, Louisa supposes. He looks to be in his late twenties or thereabouts. He has a small scar on his left temple and deep-set eyes. Carole has brought him along to introduce him. He will be staying in her house while she and Gordon are away in Scotland. She tells Rhianna and Louisa that she hopes they will keep an eye on him for her, and winks in an exaggerated fashion at Chas as she says this. She has her arm linked in his. They are obviously sleeping together. Chas takes it all in good humour.

'What sort of work do you do?' Simon asks him. Rhianna looks slightly embarrassed. It's not the sort of question people usually ask these days.

'I'm an actor,' he says, 'but I do a bit of modelling on the side. It's more lucrative, and there's more regular work.' He's very sure of himself. The answer is well-rehearsed. He might have struggled with the question previously.

Louisa shakes hands with him and looks directly into his eyes, seeking a sign of recognition. It doesn't come.

'So where did you two meet?' she asks Carole later.

'I've taken up life drawing,' says Carole. 'Wednesdays. I'm going to miss it when I'm away.'

'I bet,' says Rhianna.

'Was he modelling?' asks Louisa, 'or one of the artists?'

'What do you think?'

As Louisa gets to know more about Chas through the evening, as she is able to watch the way in which he carries his body and turns his head, she realises that he couldn't possibly be the van man at all. He is nothing like him. For one thing he's older than he looks – around forty, he tells them. Also, he smiles too much. And Carole is barking up the wrong tree because he's obviously not into her at all. He seems more interested in Simon. It has been a case of mistaken identity all round.

At the back of his mind Harry can't help feeling nervous about Louisa and Carole catching up. Carole won't deliberately say anything, but she could let something slip. He'd deal with it. He's been on the other side of the fence, and he's had to deal with it.

He'd thought that he'd never put a high store on fidelity, but when he found the letter in the kitchen drawer, he wasn't able to take it in. Some guy had written to Yasamine. It was an old love letter, he supposed, from before they met. Undated. But the address on the envelope didn't add up. There was some problem connecting their current address and the contents of the letter in Harry's mind. It was their address. They had moved there after Bella was born.

Yasamine walked in and grabbed the letter off him, straight out of his hand.

'What's this?' he said, but she didn't answer straight away.

Then she said, 'You can't talk.'

'Shit Yasamine,' he shouted. 'What the fuck?'

'What do you care?' she'd said and wrenched her arm free. He must have grabbed it. There was a red mark on her forearm. She saw him looking at it and her hand went to it, rubbing. 'You're such a hypocrite.'

'Fucking bitch,' he'd said, or words to that effect.

He left the house for the rest of the day, but that night he came back and fucked her stupid. She went for it too, told him she loved him, that she was sorry, asked for his forgiveness. He should have asked for hers. He knew what it felt like then, being cheated on. He knew what he'd done to her.

After that they didn't mention it again. The letter was gone next time he looked and he didn't find any others when he turned the house upside down.

'No, Harry,' she said. 'I said I'd give it a chance and I will. For Bella's sake, and ours.'

But he got complacent again and slipped into old habits. Other women. Drink. Late nights with the guys. He sabotaged himself really. He couldn't admit it at the time. She did well to stick it out as long as she did.

It was another two years before she bundled up Bella for the last time and walked out of his life for good. He told himself he didn't care. He was relieved in fact.

Two months later she was already shacked up with someone else. Was it the same bloke? Does it matter? That's what he thinks now. Somewhere along the line it stopped mattering.

CHAPTER TWENTY-FOUR

'Everything counts,' says Harry. 'Every single thing you do.'

Louisa is about to elaborate on his behalf, but Harry talks over the top of her.

'Whatever you do today causes what happens in the future,' he says. 'Just imagine,' he says, 'if you knew how to work it out, you'd be able to run your life exactly how you wanted.'

He's been drinking, of course. It always brings out the philosopher in him. He and Louisa are sitting in Simon and Rhianna's lounge room, Carole is ignoring him from the other corner of the room, and Gordon has just gone back into the kitchen to forage for more food.

'What do you want that you don't have?' Louisa asks him.

'Is there any of the red left?' says Harry pushing his glass forwards, but he has had enough and everyone ignores him. 'Anyway, it's too late now,' says Harry.

'Are you referring to anything in particular, or everything in general?' asks Simon grinning.

'About what?' says Harry.

'Do you have anything in mind? Can you give a specific example?' Simon says. Still grinning.

'Can I give a specific sample?' says Harry. He starts to undo his fly. Louisa stops him.

'It's his new job,' she says laughing, trying to bail him out. 'He has no shame.'

'Never did have.'

'How's the new job going?' Simon again.

'Not so new any more,' says Harry. 'It's coming up to about four months now. Time I threw it in.'

'I thought you were starting to like it,' says Louisa.

'So you actually have to watch men pee?' says Simon.

'Pee?' says Harry. 'Yeah, I have to watch them piss in a jar, and make sure I stand back a bit to stop from getting sprayed. It's no different to standing at a urinal, except in this case you're supposed to look. It's not all I do. I don't particularly like it, Simon, but you know, you get used to it. There are probably worse things to do for a living. Can't think of anything off-hand.'

'It surprises me that you would do a job like that.'

'Why? I've got nothing to hide.'

'Yes, but that's interesting what you were saying about the future,' says Rhianna. 'How could you actually do it? You'd have to know what you wanted. You almost need to try out your life first and then go back and do it all again properly.'

'What was that?' Harry looks nonplussed, as if he has stumbled into the wrong conversation.

'You know what you were saying earlier.'

'You can't expect me to remember what I said two minutes ago at this stage of the evening,' says Harry.

'I always think that we need to start with our children,' said Louisa.

'Well that's hardly rocket science, is it, Louisa?' says Harry. 'Where does that leave people like us? Any of us. Our generation stuffed up big-time didn't we?'

'That sounds like rain,' says Carole.

Rhianna goes to the window, pulls the curtain to one side, and looks out.

'Yes,' she says. 'The weather's been strange lately hasn't it?

You'll need to be careful on the drive home. The road will be slippery.'

'They'll need a coffee first,' says Simon. 'I'll make it.'

'Not for me. It'll keep me awake,' says Harry.

'Anyway,' said Simon, 'I don't know so much. I've been very impressed by some of the young ones I've come across lately. It's life, isn't it? Every generation must feel like they've failed in some way, but on the whole – if you look at even a few hundred years ago in Great Britain for example – people are becoming less tolerant of brutality.'

'Notwithstanding all the massacres over the last hundred years, you mean?' says Rhianna.

'Oh all right you, touché. Now, coffee?'

'I'll be doing the driving,' said Louisa. 'Thanks, Simon. I'd love one.'

'Good,' says Harry. 'That's settled then. Now where's the rest of that red?'

'Just say whatever comes into your mind,' says Lucy.

Louisa has come to enjoy these sessions. They're like the kind of psychotherapy you see in the movies. She lies down on the couch and closes her eyes. There is something that has been going through her mind, and she wouldn't mind trying it out on Lucy.

She rattles on, working it out as she speaks.

'I'm thinking about what happens between a man and a woman. The man somehow takes the woman over, like some sort of alien creature. I don't mean literally – it's just an expression. Anyway, when he leaves her, something of him remains. I mean something that ... that *changes* her somehow: her body, her soul, the person that she is.' Louisa opens her eyes and looks across at Lucy to see whether she agrees with, or even understands, what she is trying to say. Lucy is writing something down. She realises it doesn't matter what Lucy thinks, relaxes back, closes her eyes, and continues. 'And it's fine. It helps them to bond in most cases. But in some cases she is destroyed by him.'

'Go on.'

'I'm not sure what I'm trying to say exactly.'

'Well, try. Sometimes it's good to think aloud.'

'I don't know.'

Lucy hesitates fractionally. 'Could you ...' She sighs heavily. 'Could you give me some sort of an instance then, Louisa?'

Louisa thinks hard, but it is not about the example. It is about whether she dare go on. Where will this lead her? Lucy seems unsympathetic: irritated with her, even. What does it matter? She continues.

'I saw this documentary on the TV once, about a parasite that infects crickets and makes them behave in odd ways. See, normally a cricket will never go near water. But when they're infected with this parasite, this worm, it makes them seek out water, and then they jump in and drown, sacrificing themselves for the sake of the parasite. They filmed it, over and over again, infected crickets jumping into a swimming pool. There was footage of this worm crawling out from the cricket and into the water where it completes its lifecycle. Then when they studied the cricket's brain – they have one, believe or not – they found it had twice as many brain cells. See the worm had somehow converted the DNA or mimicked it or something. So the parasite actually changed the way the host thought.'

'Interesting.'

'I think this is what happened with Victor and me, because I've been trying to work out why I stayed when I could have gone, when I should have gone. And I'm thinking sex, and I have no evidence for this, but now I'm thinking that sex changes a woman somehow. You literally have this man – this man's DNA – entering your body and I'm wondering if it does something to you to make you see things from his point of view, even when your logic is saying, no, this is wrong, but you are driven somehow to your own destruction. You go towards the danger instead of away from it, and the more sex you have, the more you go towards it, because he's becoming part of you, changing you into something else. And there's still this kind of faint echo of your true self struggling, seeing your children, his children, suffering, and yet because they're part of him too, they are approaching when they should be retreating, and when you try to do something about it they don't join with you necessarily. Do you see what I'm saying?'

'So how is it that you finally were able to leave?' Has Lucy been listening to her? Louisa gives her the benefit of the doubt.

'I don't know. I don't know. I guess he didn't have all the strength. I suppose there's something of the woman that enters the man too. Do you think that's possible? That he changes too?'

'He might. What do you think?'

'I don't know. It's different, but there came a time where he started to lose his power over me, the sick attraction. Sometimes when that happens men get frightened or angry – don't they? – and they do terrible, terrible things. They don't care about what happens to them; they just think, well if I can't have her, no one can. But not with Victor – I don't think my hold over him was that strong. Thank goodness. Because he'd been with other women all along. And I hated that too. Isn't that strange? It was a push–pull thing. I tried to believe it was love, but really it was some sort of parasite in my brain, confusing me. Driving me towards his environment even though it was toxic to me, you see, to me and the kids. It wasn't till I got away and my mind and body eventually cleared of him – and it took a while – it wasn't until then that I could see it and why I felt sick with shame, for what I'd done to myself, and to them.' She clears her throat, breaking her own spell. 'But sometimes you just have to suck it up and get on with it, don't you?'

Lucy flushes. 'You don't have to suck it up!'

'What then?'

The therapist takes a moment to respond.

'I mean ... it's good to reclaim your life, but if you're talking about sucking up shame, why should you? Why should you! No, Louisa. You did the best you could, the best anyone could, in the circumstances. If I get frustrated at times, it's just that I wish you could see that.'

CHAPTER TWENTY-FIVE

The first appointment Louisa has double booked so she calls to reschedule her routine two-yearly mammogram. The next time she can go is a fortnight later, and after that she has a trip away for work. A day after she gets back, there is a letter asking her to ring the clinic. The letter says:

> *Please telephone regarding your recent breast screening mammogram.*
>
> *One of our Breast Assessment Nurses has attempted to contact you by telephone, without success. It is our policy not to leave messages on answering machines without your permission, or with friends, so we would ask you to contact us as soon as convenient. It is not uncommon for women to be contacted.*

The last sentence strikes Louisa as funny, as does the capitalisation of 'Breast Assessment Nurses' as though that is the official job title. Perhaps it is. She notices herself feeling light-headed, but puts on her professional voice when she rings.

'I've just received a letter asking me to telephone one of your nurses following my mammogram.'

'Sure,' says the voice on the other end. It is a kind voice. Tactful. 'Could I have your name and address please?'

Louisa gives it.

'And your date of birth?'

Louisa gives it. The nurse introduces herself. Louisa doesn't take in the name.

The nurse tells Louisa that they need to get some clearer pictures because of something on the left showing up on the mammogram, possibly a cyst, and on the right extending under the armpit, a thickening of glandular tissue, and that they will need to make an appointment for further tests.

'Is there anything you'd like to ask?' the nurse asks.

'No, that's fine,' says Louisa.

'The first appointment we have is in two weeks' time at eight am,' says the nurse apologetically. 'I'll book you in then.'

'Is there a later time?' asks Louisa. 'The traffic is bad in the mornings.'

'Our last appointment is nine-thirty,' the nurse says. 'I'll book you in at nine-fifteen because you've got both breasts. You'll need to bring a book and some lunch because you'll be here all day. You'll get most of your results on the spot. You are most welcome to bring a girlfriend with you if you want,' says the nurse.

Louisa wonders about that. Who could she bring? When Harry gets home she tells him about it and asks him if he can drop her off, or stay for a while then go away and come back and pick her up.

'Of course,' he says.

'It's probably nothing. It is not uncommon for women to be contacted.' Her tone of voice makes it a joke.

'Is that so?' he says.

Next day she drives to work with the opera turned up. When she gets there she thinks about resigning from her job.

Life is too short, she thinks. I've always wanted to do art and open a B&B.

That night she goes to bed early and sits staring into the wall with the light on. Harry comes in and pats her arm.

'Give me a hug?' she says.

So he holds her close until she breaks away.

'You'll be all right, Lou,' he says. 'You'll be fine.'

CHAPTER TWENTY-SIX

'I don't like getting attached to things,' says Harry, with some irritation. 'As soon as you get attached to things you lose them.'

He is looking for his glasses, but has the feeling that there is something else that he has misplaced, something that he can't quite put his finger on. He thinks of baby Bella. He thinks of Yasamine watching him play. Yasamine with Louisa's face. The two merge.

Harry feels like crap this morning. He's got an unfinished job that he keeps shoving to the background, and has opened his computer to an annoying email from one of his clients. He realises that he was able to read this, so he must have had his glasses on then. He's looked all around the desk in case they've fallen on the floor, but they aren't anywhere to be found.

'Have you seen my glasses?' he calls out to Louisa. He makes the question into something of an accusation.

'Where did you last have them?'

'If I knew that I'd know where to find them,' he says.

'Well, retrace your steps,' she says, but he can't be bothered, so she comes out of the bedroom and starts looking around. She walks outside and comes back with the glasses in her hand.

'How did they get out there?' says Harry.

'You must have gone outside for something. They were on top of the bin.'

It's a mystery, as if she has a sixth sense about his things. Then Harry remembers that he went outside to give Buster a biscuit, but he doesn't say anything.

'What would I do without you?' he says.

'You'd be all right,' she says. 'Men always find someone.'

It is hard to be with people all the time. The only place where Louisa can be alone is in her car, but it is a glass box, and people can look in. She feels as if she is on display all the time. It's Bentham's panopticon, or Snow White's coffin. She's no Snow White, although when she was a girl she dreamed of being pure like that, innocent and desirable.

Now she can't see the appeal. She decides that she doesn't need it. She doesn't want it. If she loses a breast or two what does it matter, as long as she is alive and well.

In the newsagency her eye is drawn to all the beautiful young women smiling out from magazines, wearing little, exposed to public view, simultaneously desired, envied, ridiculed for a presumed lack of depth and intelligence, underestimated, overestimated, constantly on display, nothing to hide, breasts out. What does that kind of public life feel like? She thinks of orang-utans, and how she read somewhere that they get stressed when they're looked at all the time. So must people; or perhaps something else happens to them, to their souls.

Somebody emailed her to say that the man who told her about Bentham's panopticon died last week. He is closed up in a wooden box now, alone at last, no one looking in. He used to sit next to her at work in another life, and they'd steal moments in their busy days to talk about philosophy and their dreams.

One day she would be a painter, but she was worried that she had no talent for it. One day he would start his own business, but right now he needed security. He was married with two or three kids. He loved his wife. He was a funny guy too – always laughing and joking around. But the office where they worked was open-plan, and their manager humourless, so they had to be careful to look like they were discussing work matters when they were really talking ideas.

One day he told her about the panopticon, a prisoner surveillance system, and how people who were used to being watched kept on behaving as though they were being watched even when they weren't. From then she had a name for what she had been feeling all those years. The word gave her control. Her mind made her feel watched even when she wasn't, filling in the gaps. Her mind could change and leave her more space to think.

That was after Victor and before Harry. Now Harry expands to fill the space available. She no longer feels watched. It's one of the benefits of growing older. Even so, it is hard to find her space. At home she can't be alone because Harry's music, or football commentary, or the television, is on, even when he is not in the room. She goes into a room, any room, and Harry or the dog follows her. They are territorial. Or needy. She says as much and that she will go away for a few days to have some time to herself.

But Harry beats her to it. He has a friend with a house near the beach. He needs someone to mind his dog while he travels. Harry takes Buster and leaves early one morning, angry at Louisa for reading him wrong, he says, for accusing him of restricting her when she is the one who restricts him. For a change she sleeps in. When she gets up she notices that the bedroom is in need of a good sorting. She takes a bundle of plastic bags from the bag that holds all the bags and throws them on the bed.

I have too many clothes, she thinks. Too many clothes cluttering up the place. She begins to sort them out but it is time-consuming and tedious. It's time I started to live more simply, she decides. So she picks out seven outfits, one for each day of the week, and then she takes the rest of the mess and shoves it into plastic bags. Then she takes a whole lot of other stuff, and shoves that into plastic bags too.

There's still too much clutter, she thinks. So she starts to sort through Harry's stuff. He'll never miss it, she decides, shoving most of it into plastic bags. Louisa chuckles aloud. She feels like a naughty child, testing the limits of her power or their relationship.

Louisa decides that it's time Harry faced his fear. It's time she faced her own fear as well.

At the Jurien Bay beach shack, Harry indulges himself with fish and chips, beer and the game on the television. Later on, they'll go for a nice long walk, just him and the dog. They might meet a mysterious and beautiful woman walking in the other direction with her golden retriever. Harry will spot her from a long way off. Buster will run on ahead and make friends with her dog. Maybe he'll mount her. The dog. Harry will apologise. They'll laugh and she'll look suitably embarrassed. They'll get talking and she'll invite him back for dinner. 'Bring Buster with you,' she'll say. 'No, really. I'd be disappointed if you didn't.' He'll go down to the bottle shop and get a nice bottle of wine.

Harry smiles and cracks another tinny. The dog lies on the couch. Here Buster can go and do what he likes. He can sit at the table and sleep in the bed, watch television with Harry, the two of them stretched out on the couch until three am, and piss on the patio for all Louisa knows. Freedom knows only the limits of Buster's imagination and Harry's indulgence.

She is probably spending time with her friends, having them round while he's away. He can't understand how she can see her friends so often and still have anything left to talk about. Obviously they don't. The focus was all on him that night at Simon and Rhianna's. He made a fool of himself, but it serves them all right. It serves her right. She knows – he's told her – that he feels like he is having frequent contact if he sees his friends twice a year.

Yes, she's either home alone or seeing her friends yet again, probably seeing Carole. Why worry? Carole won't say anything. She won't want a rift between herself and Louisa, and she'll have some other guy in tow by now anyway. Not the gay guy, some other guy. Gordon knows and turns a blind eye. Best to just forget anything happened, put it behind him. Good old Gordon.

Besides, if worse comes to worst it wouldn't be too bad living his life like this, just him and the dog, a six-pack of beer and the game on TV. Except that Gilchrist has just missed a chance.

'What's wrong with you?' he yells at the television. The box sits there and takes it, but Buster diplomatically leaves the room.

'Oh now that's just great, isn't it?' says Harry. 'Now my dog is leaving me.'

Two days later Harry is home and he and Louisa are arguing over his missing stuff. 'How could you throw out my blue and white polo top?' he says. 'There was nothing wrong with it.'

'It had a big oil stain on it,' she says. 'Honestly, Harry.'

'It wasn't yours to chuck out,' he says. 'It's like stealing.'

The phone rings. Louisa listens for a moment and then slams down the phone.

'I've had enough!' she screams. 'I've had enough of calls from people I don't know trying to sell me things I don't want, and I've had enough of people crowding my life, and I've had enough of being taken for granted and treated like I don't exist until I do something, and then I think that the only way I am ever going to exist for anyone is when I cease to exist!'

The worm has turned. Harry is backing off in the direction of the car keys. He has the urge to laugh, but manages to control himself. Better get out of here, he thinks. Give her time to cool down. She anticipates his movements and inserts herself between him and the keys.

'What do you think I am?' she screams at him. 'What do you think I am?'

'I don't know what you're talking about,' he says.

This is not strictly true. He has an idea. They've been coasting along for years. She's been there in the background, like the old furniture that he brought with him when they amalgamated their households. Everything has mixed in together very nicely, Louisa included, as though it has always been there and always will. She's a familiar object but he recognises with some surprise she would leave something of a gap if she were gone. It's something he hasn't seen coming. You don't really know that things have changed until they have. One day you realise you're living a different life. You're a different person.

Louisa is crying. He panics and does the wrong thing. He pats her arm in a formal show of sympathy, while maintaining a safe distance. It doesn't work. She jerks away. He tries another tack.

'Shit, Louisa,' he says. 'Pull yourself together. You can do better than that.'

'How the fuck would you know?' she says, but her voice is jerky. 'You don't know who I am. I don't,' and at this point she tries to say something but whatever she is thinking has started a new bout of tears. 'I don't –' she says, but whatever it is that she doesn't do, or think, remains a mystery.

'Say it,' he says, but she can't. He is feeling agitated, unsure of which way to go. 'Look, look what about me?'

'What?' says Louisa.

'It's not fair on me.'

She's always been a sucker for fairness. But she moves away from him, to the other side of the room, breathing heavily, picks up a mug that is sitting on the bench top and throws it at him. It misses and smashes on the tiled floor behind him, spilling a residue of cold coffee amongst the shattered pieces.

He stands there for a moment in shock or surprise.

'Why did you do that?' he says, but now her arms hang limply by her sides. She is crying again, silently, her face strangely impassive, as if she is in shock. She doesn't answer. She goes for the broom, the clean-up, and he sees that her hands are shaking.

'No,' he says. 'No, Louisa. Let me do that.' He takes the broom from her hands, leans it against the wall, and puts his arms around her. She shudders her sobs into his shoulder for minutes before she is able to speak.

'Sorry. Sorry,' she whispers into him.

'No Lou, don't say that,' he says. 'I'm sorry. I just don't know what to do sometimes, that's all. You're my girl. We're an item. Aren't we?'

CHAPTER TWENTY-SEVEN

'Do you think I'm in denial?' Louisa asks Harry.

'Do you know what the definition of denial is?' he says, and she knows what he will say. 'A river in Egypt.'

'Yes, funny,' she says. 'I knew you were going to say that. I must be a bit psychic.'

He goes back to reading the paper.

'We could go out,' she says.

'I've got stuff to do today. How about tomorrow?'

'I'm already going out tomorrow,' she says. 'I told Carole I'd catch up for morning tea.'

'Oh yes,' he says. 'That's right.'

'I think I'll go and see my mother.' Louisa kisses him on the lips. It is Good Friday.

When she arrives she discovers that her mother is having a bad day. Louisa pulls out the chocolate that she bought as a gift for Easter Sunday. But her timing is wrong.

'Aren't you coming Sunday?'

'I thought you might like something to wake up to.'

'I don't like chocolate.'

'It doesn't matter. They're only small.' Louisa puts them on the kitchen bench.

'Do you want a cup of tea?' her mother asks.

'That would be nice. I'll make it.'

'No, I'll make it.'

'All right.'

They drink tea and eat a hot cross bun. There is nothing to talk about.

'Would you like to go for a drive?' Louisa asks.

'I'd like to get some flowers. I have nothing in my vases.'

'I thought people didn't get flowers on Good Friday,' Louisa says defensively, 'or I would have got you some.'

'People go away at Easter, they have parties, I don't see why I shouldn't have flowers,' she says.

But she brightens up once they are in the car. Louisa puts on some music that she might like. Her mother tries to sing along, first going too high and then, when her voice doesn't hold, too low.

'I could have been a singer once,' she says.

'Why don't we go up to Kings Park?' Louisa suggests, and her mother brightens up further.

As they drive through the city her mother reminisces about buildings, some gone and some still preserved, where she has worked. Time compresses in her memory. It seems like yesterday when she was a young woman working in the city. Some of the old buildings are still there, but the Barracks Arch has nothing behind it. It is just a façade.

'My cousin used to work there,' she says. 'But it's gone now. Why did they just leave the archway? Silly, isn't it? Where does the time go?'

She has remarked to Louisa on these things before. Louisa, in turn, finds herself responding as she has before. They drive slowly through the park. It is a typical blue-sky day and the park is lively with the usual mixture of tourists and locals. Louisa tries to see everything as if for the first time, like a tourist, or a child, but she can't. Too many thoughts, ideas, interpretations intervene. They stop for a coffee at one of the park's cafes. There are more lively people, colourful in their holiday clothes, children, a girl carrying a guitar, another with a digital movie camera, viewing life as it happens, on the small screen.

'Harry says that how you see life just depends on where you happen to be looking.'

Her mother searches for something to say. 'Harry's a nice man,' she says.

'Yes.'

'You were lucky to meet him. Lucky to meet each other.'

'Yes, I think so too.'

They sit in silence for a moment. Louisa can't remember her mother ever saying anything much about Harry before, good or bad.

'I'm so glad you got away from that other horrible man.'

'Victor?'

Louisa finds herself disorientated for an instant. She wonders where this has come from, after all these years.

'Of course Victor. There haven't been any others have there? I always felt that I should have stopped you marrying him.'

'Did you? Oh no, Mum. Don't say that.'

'I never did like him.'

'I thought you did.'

'No I didn't. A mother tries to be supportive of her daughter.'

'What about Dad?'

'He always thought he was a con man.'

'You're kidding.'

'No. You shouldn't have married him in the first place. You were a bit naive. It doesn't matter. You finally did the right thing, getting out. Still, two beautiful kids, well, yes, two beautiful kids.' Her mother is playing with the sugar packets, not looking at Louisa.

'Why didn't you say?'

She meets Louisa's eyes.

'You wouldn't have listened. You were always headstrong.'

'I might have.'

'Do you talk much to Meredith these days?'

'I ring her about once a fortnight or so, just to keep in touch. She's busy. We don't really talk.'

'No. She's your daughter. You should try. It's important.'

They drink their coffee.

'That's a nice tree,' says her mother. 'You could paint that.'

'It's a Silver Princess.'

'I know what it is.'

The cafe owner clears the table as soon as they have finished. He has been keeping an eye on them. It is the busy time of the day and tables are at a premium. It is a gentle hint to move along. He is friendly but firm, the perfect balance of tact and diplomacy. If only Louisa could achieve that.

'That was lovely,' says her mother, pre-empting the termination of their outing.

'Perfect weather,' says Louisa.

They drive slowly back and within five hundred metres of her mother's home Louisa stops at a roadside fruit and flower-seller.

'I'll buy you some honey,' her mother says.

'No, Mum. I don't want anything. I don't need anything.' Her mother wants to buy her things. What is so wrong with that? Louisa feels mean, edgy and ashamed. She tries to modify her refusal. 'The flowers look lovely. What do you think?'

Her mother buys flowers and seedless grapes and lingers to chat with the flower-seller.

'I'll just drop you off if that's okay,' Louisa tells her once they are back in the car.

'That's fine, dear,' she says.

Louisa helps her into the secure building and notices that she is, after all, in her eighties and doing pretty well. They hug and her mother greets a friend and fellow resident. She is still standing there chatting as Louisa drives off.

Louisa turns up the music that she had turned down at

some stage during the drive there. The disc in her car starts up in the middle of a Wagnerian number. It comes in with such a dramatic flourish that Louisa is taken by surprise and starts to laugh, and keeps bubbling laughter until she is all laughed out and forced to wipe her streaming face with her sleeve.

Harry feels that Louisa is being melodramatic, but he doesn't want to call her on it in case she turns on him. She'll be okay. Anyone can tell that just by looking at her. She's as fit as a horse and everyone in her family, as far as he knows, has lived their full quota and then some. Especially the women. If anyone is likely to die before their time it will be him. He's spent his whole life fantasising about dying young. It's a bit late for that now, but he'll be buggered if he'll let Louisa beat him to the post. Given that he is statistically more likely to die first, the least she could do is to cut him some slack, instead of being there in his face all the time. For all she knows he might not have much time left at all. He really hasn't been feeling too well at all lately.

There it is, in the back of his mind, that niggling doubt. Maybe she really does have 'the big C'. He does tend to worry. He's superstitious. He starts to build monuments out of little household items, shrines to keep Louisa from getting sick and dying. He builds a couple more to protect himself and the dog and his mother. And Bella.

It's what happens when you don't have religion, he decides. You end up creating your own. DIY religion. He knows what he's doing, but won't stop even so. It would be too much responsibility to bear if something went wrong.

He turns on the radio in the bedroom and in the back room and he turns on the television. The random mixture of all that sound around him makes him feel better. Louisa goes around after him, turning everything off. He goes around turning it on again.

CHAPTER TWENTY-EIGHT

'Carole and Gordon are going to see Loudon Wainright the Third,' says Louisa. 'They want to know if we want to go along. I'd like to go. I've always wanted to see him. I might not get another chance.' Louisa notices her voice rising in pitch. She pulls it back. 'It would be nice to go,' she says.

Harry looks up the cost of the tickets on the internet. His idea of expensive is different from Louisa's. He is hedging. Again she argues that she might not have the chance to go again. She jokingly tells him that she might as well milk her imminent death for all she can. He fails to respond. Out of habit or just plain stubbornness, he is non-committal, but everywhere she goes she finds that he has been creating pyramids of lemons and the little packets of sugar that she bought to take on picnics.

She lets a day go by and then asks again.

'I didn't say I didn't want to go,' he says, 'it's just that I'll be on call all that week. I might have to rush off in the middle of the show.' Louisa takes this as his way of saying they're not going, but an hour later he has checked out whether there are tickets left and becomes positively encouraging. Louisa finds this disturbing. He thinks I'm going to die. Yet another wave of panic sweeps over her.

She leaves a message on Carole's phone to say that they'll come if they can get tickets. Then she wonders if she wants to go after all. What is the point? Harry can use the money they've saved for food. Or booze. She tries to be cheerful but her timing is off and her joke falls flat. Harry barely raises a smile.

Her usual strategy is to barricade herself with information. She has already conducted extensive research on the internet, but new things are coming up all the time. People who are depressed are less likely to survive cancer than people who aren't. So she tries to be happy. Alcohol increases risk; the more alcohol the more risk. She won't give up drinking – it calms her nerves. It is best to be selective in following advice. Being fat increases the risk, but just because a person is a bit overweight doesn't mean anything. There are a lot of people who are a lot fatter than she is and don't have it. Still, she would like to be thinner for Loudon Wainright III. She might diet until then.

Over the next couple of weeks Harry and Louisa are unable to get tickets to go the concert. It is frustrating but somehow fitting.

'We're not meant to go. The universe is telling us not to go,' she tells him. He tells her not to be so silly. The universe is indifferent. He's not convincing. He doesn't seem all that keen. He seems to have gone off Carole and Gordon lately. Carole has been acting a bit weird around him too, ever since the day of the babysitting. Louisa wonders if he and Gordon have had a falling out, but she doesn't pry. She doesn't want to know.

The ticket agency refuses to sell the tickets online because of an intervening holiday. The usual outlet that they go to no longer operates. There is one at a university near another destination of Harry's, but as the students are on a study break, this too is closed.

Louisa leaves messages for Carole and Carole leaves messages for Louisa but they seem unable to connect directly. Nothing falls into place. In the end, Harry and Louisa decide to simply turn up at the venue and take pot luck on tickets being sold at the door.

They meet Carole and Gordon for a meal at the markets and then go round to the Fly by Night Musicians Club to check on the tickets. There are no door sales, so they all kiss, shake hands and go their separate ways.

Harry and Louisa go to a second-hand bookshop and she buys a book featuring photographs of philosophers. Later they wander back past the music venue and sit outside on the low brick wall at the back of the stage. They can hear Loudon clearly singing about sleeping with another man's wife and how to stop time. Now he is telling a story, but Louisa can't get the gist of it. He sounds nice though. Somehow sitting outside alone in the dark is more intimate than sitting inside amidst the crowd. She feels very close to Loudon and he doesn't even know she is there.

She puts her head on Harry's shoulder and feels like telling him that she loves him, but is afraid she will cry if she speaks at all, so she says nothing.

They walk to the car and drive home in silence.

Lucy tells Louisa that she might be suffering from generalised anxiety. She can't slow her mind down at night. She spends the early hours on the internet, seeking answers. She is becoming obsessed with ideas about time, finds a second-hand book in Fremantle called *A World Without Time* and buys it immediately. The dustcover describes a friendship between a mathematician called Gödel and Albert Einstein. Gödel and Einstein used to bounce ideas off one another.

As she lies in bed next to Harry with her eyes wide open, her mind is everywhere. She fantasises about bringing Tom back from the dead. She's going to change the course of history. Nothing is fixed. Everything can be changed. It's all about bouncing a whole lot of balls off the wall without dropping any. It takes work and practice. She remembers how she used to bounce a tennis ball off the brick wall at school in some sort of game that started easy, but became increasingly complicated with each stage that passed. It was used to establish a pecking order of competence among her peers; she always came to rest somewhere around the middle. Ideas of past and future bounce around in her head – two, three, four balls. She is throwing them against a brick wall at the back of the school but she keeps dropping them.

It's two am when she finally accepts that she can't sleep. She goes to the computer, seeking her answers there. Not long after World War Two, Gödel decided that time did not exist. The idea is seductive. What does it mean? What is its significance – that things just happen randomly? That nothing has any meaning? People are bits of matter bumping about and shooting off in different directions. Does nothing have any value at all? Her mind is spinning. Stop it, she says. Stop it, stop it, stop it.

She is going nowhere. She switches off the computer and turns to her photos. There is a black and white picture of her and Zoe as children in their Sunday School clothes: patent leather shoes, nylon dresses and straw hats. The light is strong and they are squinting into the camera. It mostly seemed a happy childhood. She remembers it that way.

She recalls herself as a small child standing on the train platform. She is waving goodbye to her mother, who is travelling to Perth for a break. She is holding her father's hand and Zoe is tossing pebbles onto the track. It feels as if the platform is moving off. Is their mother leaving them, or is it the other way round?

Louisa puts the computer away and climbs into bed beside Harry, her mind racing. She feels futile and demoralised as if she has achieved little and learned nothing. All that information and no answers at all. She gives up, turns her back into Harry's warmth, and waits for sleep.

In the morning the van is back and Tom sits behind the driver's wheel eating his lunch and listening to his iPod, bobbing his head up and down. Louisa's heart aches for him, just for the chance to say hello. She idly wonders if there has been a mistake. It wasn't Tom who died after all. She was distraught. She was mistaken. What was she thinking?

Then something happens. He opens the door, gets out, stretches his body to its full height, gets back into the van, and starts the engine. She sees that he is the wrong height, the wrong shape, the wrong everything. A wave of embarrassment washes over her and subsides. She is hollowed out.

CHAPTER TWENTY-NINE

When the pager goes off in the middle of the night, Harry is dreaming. Something is screaming, high-pitched, chasing him, but as he runs he finds himself becoming more and more furious. Just as he decides to stop, turn around, and fight, he wakes up, still angry, and discovers that the noise has transmuted into the pager alarm. He swears, and reaches out into the darkness to kill it.

The pager and his expletive have roused Louisa. He isn't good at this. It takes a moment to remember who he is and where he is and that he now has a job that requires him to drive somewhere in the middle of the night to take samples from other men. It turns out there has been an accident, a fatality, and the driver needs testing before he can have the counselling and be sent home. The sooner Harry can get there, the better.

He makes himself a coffee and Louisa comes out fully clothed.

'I'll drive you,' she says. She is already dressed, so there is no point arguing. She is used to waking up quickly, going to work early in the morning. He doesn't feel like arguing, and besides, he wouldn't mind the company.

'Okay,' he says.

They are speeding into town along a poorly lit section of the freeway when Harry spots him – a young man clinging to the railing of one of the overpasses. The scene might be ambiguous. Perhaps it is not what it seems. Louisa hasn't noticed, so it is up to him. It would be easy to talk himself out of making her stop. The man is probably trying some sort of prank and has everything under control. He will not thank Harry for interfering. He has seen people come to grief before, for trying to help where it's not needed. The bloke looks to be in real trouble. 'Stop the car, Louisa,' he says. 'Stop!'

She pulls abruptly into the emergency stopping lane and slams on the brakes. 'What? Oh, shit!'

The man has seen them. As Harry opens the car door he gets the impression that he is calling out, but the sound is carried away on the wind. Harry is calculating the fastest way to get up there. He has already started to run. He is fleetingly conscious of the pounding of his heart. He has that same feeling that he used to get when he was younger, running, gliding, his feet don't touch the ground, he is aware of nothing except this man in sharp focus as if he is viewing the image of him through a tube. This stranger is connected to Harry through the improbable circumstance of this new job and a middle-of-the-night call-out. This moment is everything. There is nothing else, just Harry running as if he is continuous with the man on the bridge suspended above him. He imagines himself looking down. The scene is surreal and distorted, and he is running, drawn out and stretched to breaking point. A stream holds him and is him, as he flows through time. He discovers that he is in two places at once.

'Stay here,' he is saying to Louisa.

'I'll come,' she is saying, 'just in case.'

Now there is no Louisa, just Harry and the man clinging to the outside of the railing, his legs flailing as he tries to find a foothold.

He seems to hear the man's voice, the words breaking up like a bad connection. Harry fills in the gaps, catching the feel rather than the detail. He wants help and Harry is there to provide it. It has all happened before. Harry recognises this situation, the exact sequence of events, and he knows that everything will be all right as long as he plays his part. He is overwhelmed with joy and excitement.

'Hang on, mate,' he calls out. 'Hang on.'

As Harry reaches him he gets the feeling that the man is almost ready to give in, but they work together and he manages to help the man pull himself up and over the railing to safety. It isn't easy. The man is no lightweight, but Harry feels stronger than usual. It occurs to him that if it hadn't been for all the running and weightlifting that he has been doing, he might not have been able to finish the job and the man would have fallen to his death.

The two men drop to the elevated metal footpath with their backs against the railing and sit exhausted and speechless, heads back and gasping for air, as Louisa gets to them. When Harry has caught his breath he takes a sideways look at the man. He has his head down now. He is clean-cut with dark hair and fair skin, flushed from the effort and the cold air. He is young, probably still in his teens, kind of innocent-looking. Louisa stands above them, looking down.

'It's cold,' she says to the kid, taking him gently by the elbow. 'Let's get you somewhere warm and safe.' This is a gently authoritative side of Louisa that Harry has hardly seen.

On the way to the hospital Harry sits with the young man in the back seat while Louisa drives. He takes his coat off and places it around the kid's shoulders to stop him shivering. Louisa turns up the heater.

'What's your name?' he asks the boy.

'Adam.'

'I'm Harry. That's Louisa.'

'Thanks,' says Adam. His body is shaking in an exaggerated manner, a delayed reaction to the shock.

'You okay, mate?' Harry asks and the guy nods. Harry searches for something useful to say. Louisa is driving, saying nothing. 'You'll get through this,' he says. 'You're going to get through it.'

When they get to Royal Perth Hospital, Harry phones work and explains the situation. No, he won't be able to attend, he's sorry. The kid hasn't got family here. He needs someone to stay with him. It's too bad, they'll just have to send the accident bloke home without the test or get someone else. Surely someone there can watch him wee into a bottle. Better than nothing. It can't be helped. He turns back to the kid and gives him an explanation. Gets him to crack a smile.

Louisa gives them space, sits further up and reads a magazine. They talk. The kid is into various kinds of music and had some mates that wanted to start a band, but it fell apart, just like his dad said it would. Harry encourages him, and tells him about his own experience. Louisa brings coffee. Hours go by. Some emergency waiting room. Unless someone's bleeding to death they don't get seen. Hospital staff drift in and out. Nobody seems to know what they are doing; nobody seems in a hurry or concerned, but Louisa later says that they are. It's an illusion of calm covering the real situation: ducks gliding on water, paddling like mad underneath. Harry's not so sure.

He goes to the desk, and kicks up a fuss. Finally they get a doctor to come and see the young fellow.

'Are you family?' he asks Harry.

'No.'

'Friend.'

'Uh, yeah.' The kid is shell-shocked but he shows the ghost of a smile. Out of his hearing, Harry gives the doctor the run-down on what happened. He thinks it might have been a suicide attempt, but that the kid changed his mind at the last moment. Thank God. He is admitted for observation.

Harry says goodbye, doesn't promise anything, and wishes him luck. Adam doesn't ask or expect anything. He shakes Harry's hand, and tries to give him his coat back. Harry tells him to keep it for now – he can get it back later.

One the way home Harry and Louisa are lost in their own thoughts. Louisa shivers suddenly, and Harry turns up the heater.

'I'm so proud of you, Harry,' she says. 'I didn't even see him there.'

CHAPTER THIRTY

Harry is in the backyard when the phone rings, playing with the dog. He just makes it to the phone before the answering machine cuts in.

'Hello?'

'Is this Harry?'

'Yes.'

'My son asked me to call, from the hospital. Adam.' It is the mother of the boy from the bridge. She sounds exuberant.

'Oh, yes. Yes, how is he?'

'He's doing so much better. They're keeping him in to monitor his medication, so that's a good thing. He said you took him to the hospital and you and your wife sat with him until he was seen. Four or five hours.'

'That long? Yes, it must have been about that.'

'We were away in Sydney you know or we would have come. We love our son. We love him so very much.'

'Of course.'

'He's had a long battle with a depressive illness.'

'Yes, I thought it might be something like that.'

'I don't know how to say it enough, but thank you. Thank

you so much. You have no idea what this means to us. To him. Thank God for people like you.'

Harry is feeling embarrassed by her effusion and the obvious emotion in her voice. He is surprisingly moved. He clears his throat and mumbles something.

'No worries.'

She is talking on, telling him the story of her son's life. Apparently Adam has been feeling down for a while and his psychiatrist had just put him on some sort of new tablets. Now he is back on his old medication which seems safer than the other stuff he was on. She blames the new stuff for this latest incident.

'God moves in mysterious ways,' she says. It's the second time she's mentioned God. Oh well, each to her own. 'Of all people, you were the right one to be there for him. He liked talking with you, talking about his music. It was very good of you. He said he felt a real sort of connection. His father hasn't been supportive of him doing anything artistic, but I think he's realising now. It's important to Adam. He doesn't have many friends.' Her voice is trailing away.

Harry wonders if he should offer to visit. His instinct is to back off, but where has that ever got him? What the hell? Besides the boy still has his jacket.

'I might pop in on him,' he says.

'Oh, would you?' she says, and the relief in her voice clinches the deal. 'That would mean so much, so much to him. He's getting moved to Alma Street at Fremantle Hospital, so if you ask at the front they'll tell you where to go. He'll be there for at least two more weeks. Oh, and we've had your coat dry-cleaned. I'll bring it to the hospital, or I could bring it round to your home if you'd prefer. I'll need your address.'

'Bring it to the hospital. I'll probably go the day after tomorrow then.'

'I won't let him know,' she says, leaving Harry an escape clause. Harry makes up his mind that he will go for sure.

'You can surprise him,' she says. 'God bless you Harry.' And she hangs up.

After Harry puts down the phone he returns to the backyard to find Buster stretched out in the long grass, soaking up the sun, a broken tennis ball lying discarded next to him. He rolls on his back for a tummy scratch. For the first time in a long time Harry realises that he is almost happy.

CHAPTER THIRTY-ONE

Louisa is ready to embrace the possibility of the illness, almost to the point of looking forward to it. She has thought it through, imagined it and observed its effects in others. She has known people who have had the diagnosis and coped well, many recovering and being stronger for the experience. She's heard of people claiming to have found meaning in illness and saying they have taken something positive from it, a joy of living that has changed their lives. Louisa tells herself, and whoever else is listening, that she is prepared to change her life regardless. She is unconvincing. She tries too hard. What if this is her time to see Tom again? This might be her time to see Tom again.

Imagining illness in the abstract is easier than going through with it. Some have died, bravely she supposes, more bravely than she would. She thinks of a friend. Barbara. Louisa took her a mango from the garden and later her husband found it on the hospice bedside table and fed it to her. At the funeral he said she ate with gusto. Would Harry feed her like that or would he abandon her? Some do. His instinct for beauty, or to protect himself from hurt, might be greater than his concern for her. Or he perhaps he doesn't care for himself. Why should he care for her then? Her mind is bouncing around.

Harry should have stayed a musician. He should have grabbed his chance with both hands. He should have seen where the music would take him. His saxophone is still sitting there and Louisa has never seen him pick it up. She doesn't know that part of him at all. She would have liked to have known him as a musician. One night when they had gone out for dinner together, they met Ziggy from the old line-up. 'The guy's a genius,' Ziggy said to Louisa. Then, 'Do you still have a blow? We should catch up,' to Harry. 'We're going through a bit of a revival. We've got a few gigs lined up and we could do with you. It would be great to have you back.' He gave Harry his card. Harry was thinking about it, Louisa could see that. But he didn't act. They never did catch up.

This musician side is a part of himself that he won't share with her. If he really is that good, that could be the meaning of her illness – to get him to play again. He could give her that gift. He could play for her. She could leave him with that. That could be the pay-off. His life could be changed for the better and he could start to be the person he really is. If he could cope with losing her he could benefit from her death, but would he cope? He probably thinks he would, but really?

Would she? She has been avoiding details, but now she fills them in. How would she deal with pain, loss of a breast, loss of her hair? She imagines herself in the shower, hair on the floor, a scarred hole where her breast used to be, her arm heavy, red and swollen. She tries to imagine the nausea, the light-headedness. She begins to feel ill. She stops.

No, she decides. I don't want it. I certainly don't want that.

On the day of her tests Harry is called in to work, so Louisa drives to the hospital by herself. When she arrives she is glad, because no one else has brought a friend. How would it look if she'd brought Harry? It would look as if she were expecting bad news. Bad news might inevitably follow.

The women are mostly around Louisa's age. One or two look younger, by quite a bit. That would be hard. At least she's had a good run. In some parts of the world, she would be considered a very old woman.

The breast clinic at the hospital is, appropriately enough, undergoing renovation. There is banging and drilling, and the walls are a patchwork of old and new. She has brought some old scans with her, and leaves them with a nurse. Later, over a tube of cold jelly, the doctor congratulates Louisa for her initiative.

'That's a very intelligent thing to do,' she says. 'That will save us some work.'

'Thanks,' says Louisa. She had just been following instructions after all. Maybe people aren't always as compliant as she is.

After the form-filling, the nurse takes her into a curtained cubicle and asks her to change.

'Remove your bra and your top and put this on,' she says, handing Louisa a floral one-size-fits-all. 'Then pop all your things in the basket.'

It is a small red shopping basket, the kind you pick up at the supermarket for ten items or fewer. Or is it twelve? Ten or twelve? The people behind you get annoyed and resort to shopper rage. Ten or twelve? She should remember. Different stores, different rules. Sometimes it's as few as three. Does a number of the same article count as one or many?

'Nice and cheerful,' the nurse says, referring to the top, and not to Louisa. 'When you are finished you can come out and sit on one of the chairs just outside. Bring your basket along with you.'

'Like Little Red Riding Hood,' says Louisa, and the nurse laughs.

'Yes, all you need is a red cape. Now, are you okay?' she says. 'Do you have everything you need?'

'Sure do,' says Louisa.

She changes and finds a seat near a woman older than her. The woman nodded at her on the way in. Louisa picks up a magazine and flicks through. She can feel that the other woman is nervous and wants to talk, so she puts the magazine down to make herself available.

'Hello,' says the woman. She has some sort of accent.

'Hello.'

'Is this your first time here?' says the woman.

'Yes,' says Louisa. 'I did have to go somewhere else once before though. It was fine. What about you?'

'No, my first time,' says the woman.

Louisa has the feeling that they are both going to be all right, but she says nothing. What if they're not? She smiles at the woman in what she hopes is a reassuring manner.

'Ah well,' says the woman and she sighs. 'Nothing you can do about it.'

'Yes, that's right,' says Louisa. 'But it is usually all right. I looked up the website, and apparently in most cases it turns out not to be cancer.'

She's prattling on without thinking. She shouldn't have said cancer. It sounds like a swearword here.

A woman emerges from a curtained cubicle, dressed in her own clothes. She has been crying. They wait for her to pass by and disappear into one of the other rooms, before speaking again.

'They said I could bring someone,' said the woman, 'but I thought I'd come on my own.'

'Do you have any children?' Louisa asks.

'Two,' says the woman, and she tells Louisa their ages.

'That's quite a gap,' says Louisa, thinking aloud, and then wishes she hadn't.

'Two of my children died,' the woman says.

She doesn't elaborate. She could be a refugee from one of those countries where they disappear people. Families have to carry on.

'Oh,' says Louisa. 'That's awful. I'm so sorry.'

The woman smiles and shakes her head. 'What can you do?' she says.

Sometimes it's better to say nothing. She could mention Tom, but it is so public, lined up on straight-backed chairs with hammering and drilling going on in the background and people pretending to read magazines.

Louisa wonders if the woman is half hoping that her result will be positive. Is she the only one here with mixed feelings? The woman is called into the privacy of the treatment room shortly afterwards.

'Here we go,' she says.

The woman emerges after a while. She is full of smiles and gives the thumbs up.

'I'm okay,' she says. 'I'm going home now. Good luck!'

'Thanks,' says Louisa.

A volunteer worker is taking orders for tea and coffee. The women order their cups of tea and mind each other's as one by one they are called in and come out, some to sit again and wait, and some to get dressed and go home. There is a connection by virtue of their potential situation, their gender, and the colour-coded pink and green floral uniform that they have been given on arrival. Everyone is looking casually cheerful and the atmosphere is one of waiting at the hairdressers, rather than at a clinic where the outcome could be years of difficult treatment, surgery and perhaps even death.

The woman opposite Louisa now is texting. A pretty young woman, who looks like she could be in her twenties, is devouring copies of women's magazines. A very large woman of about fifty, with socks rolled down around her ankles, shows off the novelty ring tone on her mobile phone. Everyone joins in the joke, until she is taken away.

Louisa is called in for another mammogram to compare with the one that has brought her here, and is sent out to sit again. She orders coffee. It arrives. She drinks it. People come and go. She waits. She takes a toilet break, comes back, flicks through a magazine, waits some more. Finally she is called in for an ultrasound. They have to examine both breasts, because they both show some sort of abnormality that needs further investigation. One looks like a cyst, but the other one is more suspicious.

'I'm not liking the look of that,' says the doctor. 'That looks like flecks of calcium. It's probably just a fibro adenoma, but we'll need to get a closer look.'

'I had a fibro adenoma before,' said Louisa. 'It could be the same one. I've got my previous scans there.'

This is when the doctor compliments her on her foresight. After that, things move quickly.

If I'd told them that in the first place I could have avoided all of this, Louisa thinks. I thought they already knew.

So they check and measure and decide that the fibro adenoma has stayed the same, and that the cyst is bigger, but that won't kill her.

'You're in the clear,' they tell her.

It is all something of an anti-climax, but, then again, anti-climaxes are underrated.

When Louisa walks from the hospital she is greeted by winter sunshine. Her day is free. She can do as she likes. She drives to a shopping centre, orders lunch at a coffee shop, and sits for a full hour reading yet another women's magazine before heading home to an empty house.

Louisa walks from room to room wanting something, but unsure as to what it is. She decides to ring Meredith, although she will be at work. It doesn't matter, she thinks, I'll leave a message that I rang.

The phone has barely engaged when Meredith picks it up, her voice heavy with flu.

'Mum?' She sounds surprised, even pleased, her defences down. 'Is there anything wrong?'

'No, darling. I just felt like giving you a call. Are you sick?'

'A bit of a cold, that's all.'

'Oh. Look after yourself. Go to the doctor.'

'What's happening?'

'Can't I just ring?'

'Of course you can. Was there anything else?'

Louisa tells her about the tests and the all-clear. There is silence at the other end of the phone. Meri says, 'You should have told me.'

'I didn't want to worry you.'

'I am your daughter, you know.'

This touches Louisa deeply and she finds it difficult to respond immediately.

'Actually, Mum,' says Meredith, 'I'm glad you rang today.' She hesitates and then she says, 'I've been thinking, we never really talk enough when you ring. I should ring you more. It would be nice to be able to just ring up and talk sometimes.'

'Really?' says Louisa, amazed. 'I'd like that.'

'I've been thinking a lot about Tom,' Meredith says. 'I don't know.'

Louisa waits but she doesn't elaborate. She realises that the ball is in her court. Her heart is beating erratically, warning her, but she plunges in anyway.

'I've been thinking too,' she says. 'I've been thinking of all the things I did wrong, not just what happened to Tom, to all of us, but how I should have been a better mum for you.'

'What are you talking about?'

'All the terrible things I put you through.'

'All the things you put us through? You didn't put us through anything. Well no more than most parents I guess; I don't know. Dad – he's another story. I'm not a kid any more. What things?'

'Leaving your father. What happened to Tom. I made so many mistakes. I could have done, should have done much better.'

'No, Mum.' Her voice sounds some frustration. 'No. You

know I loved him too. He was my baby brother. But he made his own choices. There were lots – *plenty* – of times when he could have made better decisions. He even talked about it. He knew the risks. But he didn't want to. We ... we all have to live our own lives. We all have to make our own decisions, otherwise what is the point of anything?'

She pauses here to give Louisa an opportunity to speak, but Louisa can't think for a moment. Finally she says, 'He was only a baby.'

Meredith almost scoffs. 'He was eighteen, Mum. Yes, he was young, but he grew up fast, just like me. He was old enough to be responsible for his decisions. He could have thought about what it would do to us, to his family. I could have my brother now. I'm sorry, but after what he did. Anyway, it's too late now. And as for Dad, leaving him was the best thing you ever did. What would our lives have been if you'd stayed? There's no way you could have stopped him. Neither could I. No one can make an alcoholic stop drinking. He has to choose that for himself. He would have just got worse. Actually he was getting worse. I thought if I was good enough he'd stop.'

'You?'

'Yes. I always thought it was my fault.'

'But you were a child.'

'I suppose so. It didn't feel like that back then. Then I used to pray you would leave him, and I felt so bad for wanting it. We've both got to stop this. Blaming ourselves, Tommy, even Dad. It's not healthy. It's not doing us any good.'

'No. You're right. I know you're right,' Louisa says. 'I haven't been thinking clearly.' She is speaking automatically.

There is a long silence at the other end of the phone. She knew it was too good to last.

'I should –'

'No, look Mum. I'm a grown woman now. I'm thirty. It's funny, isn't it? It doesn't seem to matter how old you are, it's hard to think of your parents as just ordinary people.'

'That's true.'

'I feel proud of how strong you are.'

'Really?' Louisa is barely able to respond. Her eyes fill.

'Yes. Anyway there's something really important now. I have news. Listen, I was going to ring you soon. I have been thinking of ringing you for a while, but I didn't want to until ...' Meri hesitates, searching for words. 'Until I was sure everything would be all right. I'm pregnant, Mum. We're thinking of coming back to live in WA. What do you think?'

Louisa's mind is racing. Her daughter's voice has taken on a tone of vulnerability that Louisa hasn't heard before. Louisa realises that she hasn't responded.

'Oh darling, that's wonderful. A baby? That's wonderful. *Yes*, come home. Of course I'll be there for you.'

'Really?' says Meredith. 'You are happy for me, aren't you, for me and Todd?'

'Of course I'm happy for you. I'm happy for me. It's just wonderful.'

'Thanks, Mum.'

'When?'

'I'm ten weeks,' she says. 'I was going to wait until the end of the first trimester to be sure, you know, but you rang. I wanted to tell you as soon as I found out.'

'When will you come over?'

'Todd says next year.'

'So long?' says Louisa disappointed. 'I'll come over there. Soon, as soon as I can.'

'We could talk some more.'

'Yes we should, we'll talk soon.'

'Okay. Talk to you soon.'

When she hangs up Louisa still can't quite decide what to do with the rest of the day. She feels strange, happy, scared. She could paint a portrait. She could do a mother with her baby, a Madonna, mixed media.

CHAPTER THIRTY-TWO

'This was really strange,' Louisa tells Lucy. 'I was dreaming about Tom. I kept trying to see his face but I couldn't. I woke up and I had to go straight to his picture to study it. I needed to memorise his expression. His expressions. It started to come back then. His tone of voice. The way he used to sing. He used to try to sing, but really he couldn't hold a tune. We joked he just had the one note, but it was a good one. He'd ham it up, you know. I can't remember the song. I kept trying. It'll come to me. In the middle of the night, probably.' She laughs.

'Do you want to talk about the dream?'

'Yes, I wrote it down. Wait a minute.' Louisa rummages and finds it in her bag. She reads it through before continuing. 'I could just read what I've written.'

'Okay.'

'It was about three o'clock. My writing is a bit hard to read at the best of times.'

'That's all right.'

'Okay then. I'll just read what I've written. *I know this is Tom but I can't see him because he won't turn around. He is bent over a table and there is someone else there – someone I don't know – but I don't get a good feeling about this. There are long blinds with vertical strips of material, blocking the light, and the room has an odd sort of smell, I can't place it, but familiar. Tom is doing something but he has his back to me so I can't see. I don't have a good feeling. There is a bag on the floor, like an overnight bag, open, and dog-eared school books, coloured pencils, and some coins spilling out onto the floor, and a syringe rolled up in a fifty dollar note. Nobody is taking any notice and the money seems pointless because the room they are in is dingy, and smells, and there is not a nice feeling.'* Louisa looks up. 'There is an anxious feeling but that could have been me.'

'Okay.'

Louisa hesitates before reading on.

'Then I wrote: *What does this mean? The floor gives way and they are all falling. I look for Tom but he is falling with his back to me. It might not be him. I keep trying to see the man's face, hoping it isn't him.'*

Louisa stops and looks up. 'That's it, Lucy. I woke up at that point. It was three o'clock, and I went to the study to get his picture. But it wasn't enough, so I tried to think about what he was doing at the time the picture was taken, and how he looked from the different angles. I tried to remember what he said on the day of that photo. I tried to remember who took it. I couldn't remember. I stayed there until it got light and Harry came out to give the dog its breakfast. He looked in on me and then he went back to bed. That would have been about six, six-thirty.'

'Are you waking often? Early in the morning?'

'Sometimes. Occasionally I sleep through. What do you think it means?'

'I don't know Louisa. Do you know – did Tom deal drugs?'

'No, of course not.'

'Are you sure?'

'Of course I'm sure. There was nothing like that. I think I might have been afraid that he had a drug debt. He had used heroin, I told you that before. I think it was only the one time, as far as I know. So you don't know what it means.'

'What does it mean to you?'

'I knew you'd say that. I mean I thought ...'

'You thought?'

'I was going to say I thought that was your job. How should I know what it means? If I knew I wouldn't ask you.'

'Oh really, Louisa! It's your mind, not mine. You need to do the work yourself. Go on, think. If you think it means something, what do you think that might be?'

'I've just remembered – I should have written this down but it was just in the background – there was smoke in the room. Not cigarette smoke, but black or grey smoke. What was that?'

'I don't know. I haven't studied dream interpretation. I've told you that. There's no one way of seeing something. And to be honest I'm not even sure that this is something we should be spending your time on. Some people do specialise in that, if you want to explore in more detail. I don't know how helpful it is, or if it makes things worse, continually mulling over everything. Yes, it can be helpful to process the events that brought you to this place, but there is a point where thinking about it becomes the problem itself.'

'Are you giving me the sack?'

'Of course not. I'm saying it's all right if you want to use other options. If coming to see me is helpful to you, all I can do, in this case, is facilitate. All I know to do is to ask what you get from the dream. What does the black smoke mean to you? What are your feelings about it?'

'Black smoke isn't good, is it?'

'Not usually, I suppose.'

'Not that any of this matters. It feels like I don't have much time left to see what I need to.'

Lucy stares at her. 'Can you explain what you mean by that?' she asks. 'Have you been thinking about suicide?'

'Oh no!' says Louisa, shocked by Lucy's bluntness, especially at this time, as if she's made no progress at all. 'I wouldn't do that. Not now. Not that. I'll be around for a while yet. It's just that I'm forgetting things. I'm afraid – I feel like everything is falling out of focus.'

'Like what?'

'After I talk to you, all of this, what I've talked about, goes through my mind. It starts to feel like a story, rather than something that really happened. Like it's something I can close up sometimes, and put on the bookshelf. Or take it out and read it, if I want. Sometimes it even feels like I'm making stuff up. Like it used to be real, but it has stopped being real somehow. Does that make sense? I mean, this dream could be part of the story. I could put it away.'

'Is that a bad thing, do you think, or is it okay?'

Louisa takes a moment to think about that. She is trying to be honest with herself.

'Yes, okay. I feel like it is. I feel sad about it, but it's okay.'

'Sure?'

'Yes. Although I'd like to be getting more sleep. I must still be trying to work something out. That's time, isn't it?' Louisa prepares to leave. 'Oh Lucy! Guess what?'

'What?'

'I should have told you about this straight away. This is what I really want to talk about. I'm going to be a nanna.'

'Whoa! Congratulations.'

Louisa smiles. 'I know! Yes. Thanks.'

'When did you find out?'

'A few days ago. I rang Meredith to talk about my test results, and we had a great talk. She's coming back here to live, she thinks. We'll be a family again.'

'And your test results?'

'Clear.'

'Clear?'

'Yes.' Louisa can't stop herself from grinning.

Lucy sits for a moment gazing at her with a big smile on her face. 'Can I give you a hug?'

'Go on then,' she says.

As Louisa cooks, she wills her mind to dwell on positive things. At first she focuses on her health, and then on Meredith and the baby, but she is afraid that she has more to lose now, so she pretends to herself that she doesn't care. She determines not to tempt fate. She refuses to be afraid for her daughter, the baby, and the future. She refuses to think too much about such uncertainty. Her eyes are stinging because she is chopping an onion. She finishes quickly, and scrapes it into the pan. A spatter of hot oil gets her on the arm and she pulls back quickly, drops the chopping board on the bench and runs her arm under the tap. Concentrate! Life takes effort, concentration, and a certain amount of risk.

It suddenly occurs to her that this could be why her mind goes to the past all the time, to the fait accompli: to Tom, who can be harmed no longer. Except that she is starting to suspect that it's not Tom that she is holding so close to her heart, but her own creation. She turns off the tap and mops her arm with the tea towel. Get real, Louisa, she tells herself. Who was he? What did he actually do? She searches for an answer. What about that incident with his father?

Tom went to see Victor when he was sixteen. He'd started passing the occasional comment about his father in recent years. Victor hadn't been there so it was inevitable that Tom would create an idealised picture of the man. The better Victor began to seem to him, the worse he viewed her.

At home there'd be arguments, adolescent tantrums. She'd had to deal with the day-to-day problems. She'd done everything, endured sleepless nights, borne the brunt of his teenage moodiness, borne the guilt. It wasn't fair that it should be her guilt alone.

This must have been in her mind when she finally relented and accepted that the meeting would go ahead. At first she'd tried to talk Tom out of it, but when he succeeded in tracking down the number she consoled herself with the thought that perhaps Victor had changed, or, if not, at least Tom would finally know the kind of man his father really was. He'd have to find out for himself some time.

Victor was sober, apparently, when Tom finally went.

'I don't believe it!' she said, unable to resist the cheap shot.

'Don't do that,' said Tom. 'You haven't seen him, like, forever. People do change you know, and anyway, you're hardly objective.'

'You don't know the half of it,' she said, wishing as she said it that she could stop herself, but she couldn't. She figured that if he was old enough to contact his father, he was old enough to know the truth. 'You have no idea what he put me through. He just about killed me once. I thought he was going to kill me. He was capable of … capable of anything.'

'I was there,' said Tom.

'You were six years old,' Louisa reminded him, but he said he saw more than she gave him credit for.

'I remember things,' he said. 'He wasn't the only one to blame for what happened.'

But when Louisa asked him what he remembered, he fell into silence. She could see the hurt working in his face. She felt sick, sorry she hadn't shut up. She saw him closing off. She struggled to rescue the situation.

'You're right, my love,' she conceded with some difficulty. 'There are always two sides to everything. More probably. People do bad things, but he is a person after all. That war did terrible things to the young soldiers – not just him. But don't forget, we were trying to survive too. He brought the war home with him.'

'So? What do you expect? They laid their lives on the line.'

'What, so we could lay ours on the line for him?'

'Maybe.'

'Then what's the point of it all?'

Tom shook his head, clenched his fist, and was about to walk out. It wasn't going the way she wanted.

'Look,' she said, 'it's true they weren't given the help they needed when they got back. So many of them were shell-shocked. Post-traumatic stress. More than that, they were met with protests. People just wanted the war to end. They wanted to bring the boys home. But when the soldiers returned they saw it as a slap in the face, as if people didn't appreciate what they'd been through. We probably didn't.'

Tom had turned back.

'That's an understatement.'

'Besides, he's your father, so there must be something good in him – the good bit that came to you.'

Tom wasn't really listening anymore.

'If you thought he was so bad, why didn't you stop me from going?'

Louisa said something lame and Tom gave her a look of disgust, almost hatred. He was young, she tells herself, halfway between a boy and a man. All adolescents have to move away from their mothers at some stage. It was natural. She was feeling something else, something that she couldn't control. She could feel him slipping away. She remembers the sudden feeling of dread that flooded her body.

'I love you, you know,' she said, but a part of her was still angry with him.

Tom looked embarrassed, and his next remark was bitter.

'You were right about one thing,' he said. 'He's a real arsehole.'

'I don't want to be right if it hurts you.'

'Then you're an idiot. Dad was right about that.'

He said it, but Louisa could see that, although he was angry, he was sorry that he had. She wanted to say that it was okay, that she understood, but she couldn't bring herself to voice the words.

Later that night Tom told her what had happened. His account was brief and detached, but at least he was talking to her and she saw that it was his way of trying to apologise. After a promising start, things turned. Tom had said something that Victor didn't like. He didn't elaborate on what that was, but it changed things. Victor poured himself a drink, and another, and then he told Tom that he'd turned out exactly the way he'd imagined. He said he was a bloody disgrace. Victor always did have a way with words. Tom put down the drink that his father had given him and said he'd better go, but Victor blocked his way and said that if he'd had his way, Tom wouldn't have been born, and that he was a namby-pamby pathetic excuse for a human being, just like his mother.

Louisa knows that Victor would have enjoyed saying that, hurting him deliberately, and getting back at her through her son, but Tom took it to heart. Victor was just getting started. He said he was glad that he'd washed his hands of him and that slut mother of his. He said that the only one of them with half a brain seemed to be his sister. Apparently Meredith had been in touch with him the year before, but she'd never mentioned it to Louisa. Then Victor said something unforgiveable. He said that Tom probably wasn't his son anyway and that he'd always suspected Louisa of playing around. Tom reported this one last, carefully watching her for a reaction that would tell him that his father was telling the truth.

'It's not true. Sometimes I wish it was. I wish it was true.'

'How can you say that?' said Tom. 'How can you say that?' He looked totally deflated. Then he walked out on her.

That was it. You can't unsay something. How could she wish half of him gone? Of course Tom was like Victor in many ways, but she refused to see it. She saw only the differences and turned away from the rest. She had committed the offence of not accepting Tom for who he was.

So there was the cold reason for Tom's death. There was the cause and there was the effect.

'I'm just so very tired,' says Louisa. 'I wish I could have a nice long sleep.'

'Yes. I know.'

'So.'

The counsellor and her client sit in silence. Ultimately Lucy speaks. 'What use is guilt?' Silence. 'What use is it? I'm asking.'

'I don't know.'

'Try. What use does it serve for you?'

'It's my responsibility.'

'To feel guilty?' Louisa nods. 'Responsibility is important to you?'

'Yes.'

'Responsibility for?'

'Tom's death. I deserve to be punished.' Louisa is crying now. Lucy passes her the box of tissues.

'Is it your responsibility to be miserable?'

'I guess.'

'What if you're wrong about that? What if the real responsibility that you have is to be happy? For Tom's sake, if not for your own.'

Louisa wipes her eyes, but says nothing. Lucy continues.

'You know Louisa, when I've listened to you I can't help thinking about your age. When you married Victor you were younger than Tom was when he died. Now days, you'd be considered a child. I mean, where does the responsibility for that lie?'

Louisa maintains her silence. Lucy tries again.

'Of course we affect our children, we're important in their lives, but it's not everything. They have their own minds, their own motivations, and their own experiences outside the home. Once they have grown up, it's none of our business, not really. We can't own what they do. That belongs to them. We can care, of course, and try to help, but we can't keep them. We can own our memories of them, but if that's our entire world, then what about your life here and now?'

'What do you mean?'

'Building strong relationships with the people that are here doesn't mean you can't still have a relationship with Tom, but if the relationship with Tom is so painful and persistent that it fills up your whole world, then where is the room for other people in your life? What about your responsibility to them? Just as importantly, to yourself?'

'I do. I try.'

'I know. All I'm saying is that I'm sure Tom knew that you loved him. He loved you too. If the shoe had been on the other foot and you'd taken your own life, would you want to see him continuing to suffer like you are? To put his life on hold? So would he want you to suffer the way you have? He just doesn't sound that vengeful to me.'

'Vengeful?'

'Yes.'

'Maybe I'm the one who's vengeful. Is that what I am?'

'That's interesting. Are you?'

'No. I don't think so.'

'Neither do I.'

'I know it's not all my fault.'

'Yes, that's right. It's not your fault Louisa. You didn't set out to hurt him.'

'He was just a boy.'

'Yes.'

'It's not his fault either.'

'No, it isn't his fault.' Lucy smiles and places her hand over Louisa's. 'I want to say something more, something personal, Louisa. Is that all right?'

'Of course.'

'I like you. I really do. I'm not sitting here in judgement. How can I? I can teach you some techniques for managing your stress or shifting your habits of thinking if you want to work on that, but I don't have any profound or miraculous answers. I wish I did, but I don't. All I can really do is be a witness, and if you like, to let you know what I think or what I've learned through the years that might be helpful. It might not be helpful. I could be wrong. I make mistakes. There are no guarantees, are there?'

'No.'

'Awful things happen. People do horrible things. I don't know why. Power seduces, I suppose. They're looking for short-term gain, or revenge. Or they just don't care. Life goes haywire. Or maybe it doesn't. It's life, not some sort of utopian ideal. We can't make it what it isn't, whether we want to or not. Believe me I've been down that track myself. It led to a dead end. Now all I do is to try to live in peace, and once something is beyond my control, I try to think about it differently, and not to suffer over my own suffering.'

'Your suffering?'

'Yes, I lost someone dear to me. It's really hard.'

'I'm sorry.'

Lucy nods.

Louisa says, 'I am getting better. I don't dwell as much as I did.'

'I know. I think you are too. I feel that you are starting to come back into the present. That being said, I want you to do something for me every morning when you wake up, until you come to see me next time. Will you do something for me?'

'Yes. What do you want?'

'You have a lot of different types of birds around where you live don't you?'

'Yes.'

'Every morning, as soon as you wake up, go into your garden for five minutes, on the clock, and listen to the birds. Count how many different calls you can hear.'

'You want me to count the birds?'

'That's right. Report back. I'd be interested to know.'

CHAPTER THIRTY-THREE

When Harry visits Adam in Fremantle, they walk to the hospital gardens, where Adam sneaks a cigarette. Adam tells him he's no stranger to this place and asks if Harry knows what it's like to feel so bad you want to die.

'I went through a bad patch when my first marriage broke up,' Harry says. 'I felt like topping myself, but I couldn't be bothered.'

Adam laughs. 'You're kidding, are you?'

'Yeah. But I had fantasies of ... never mind. Water under the bridge so to speak.'

'So how did you get through it?'

'I generally find exercise is the best thing,' says Harry. 'I feel okay most of the time now. That proves it works, eh? I do a bit of jogging and I've taken up weights lately.'

'Yeah, I should look after my health more,' says Adam staring at the cigarette in his hand. He throws it on the ground and grinds it out. He's dressed in jeans, a black T-shirt with a peace sign, and expensive-looking sneakers. 'They don't like us wearing pyjamas all day so they make us get dressed,' he says, 'I don't usually wear them anyway.'

They spend nearly the whole time talking music, and Harry

promises to bring his sax next time for a jam. He'll have to drag it out first and have a blow so he doesn't make a fool of himself, he says.

At some point they get to talking about whether Harry has any kids. He tells Adam about Bella and how he hasn't seen her since she was around four.

'I've thought about her a few times lately,' he says.

'Why don't you get in touch?'

'I wouldn't know how,' says Harry. 'She could be anywhere.'

'She'll probably be on Facebook or something.'

It hasn't occurred to Harry. The possibilities start to grow in his imagination.

'I don't know how to get on,' he says.

'I can show you.' They are back on the ward by this time. Adam gets out his laptop and signs him up on the spot. And there she is. A version of Yasamine, and himself he supposes, but better looking. Beautiful, in fact. His daughter.

'Look, you can send her a message,' says Adam. 'You just put it in there.'

'I'll think it through.'

'Fair enough.'

The time skids past and Harry feels great when he finally leaves with a promise to come back next day. He will keep this promise, is looking forward to it, and sees the possibility of a friendship developing. He pushes Bella out of his mind for the moment, focusing instead on Adam.

He'll get his sax out again to see if he can still play. He could even make an effort to catch up with some of his old friends. He has Ziggy's card from when he and Louisa bumped into him that night. Ziggy was just the same, a bit older. They were the best times, those summers. Great memories.

One hot evening late one January everyone was sitting on the front veranda of the old weatherboard house in East Vic Park. Yasamine told him she was pregnant and they invited friends over to celebrate, Harry's music buddies, their partners, and Yasamine's bridesmaid, a sullen woman who didn't really get into the spirit of things. A couple of the guys brought along their instruments for a jam. Yasamine was in a good mood, singing 'Fever' along with the old Peggy Lee standard. The guys indulged her request and complimented her on her voice, which indeed had a nice texture to it. She became self-conscious when everyone grew quiet, and she drifted off pitch. Harry found it endearing.

The music had gone well into the night. Harry remembers the improvised feel of their lives as they were back then. There was no worry if someone wanted to crash on the floor for the night, rather than drive home under the influence. Next day they usually went down to the cafe strip for an early lunch and sat there nursing a coffee or two well into the afternoon.

They were good, lazy times, and he remembers the neighbours, all fairly young and tolerant, coming across with bottles of wine to join in the small party. Nobody got very drunk, just relaxed, and they passed around a couple of joints. That was as far as anything went. They kept to their own partners. It wasn't the rock-and-roll lifestyle people imagine. They just liked the music. They liked messing around, experimenting, inventing.

He and Yasamine talked about how when the baby was born, if they felt like it they'd just take off on the road somewhere, head off to America, New Orleans, not be tied down by conventional expectations. It would be good for the kid, teach him to be flexible, adventurous. Then Bella was born. He loved her – of course, who wouldn't? If he is honest with himself there was also resentment.

It beats him how so much can change after you have a baby, and why you feel you have to follow the usual paths. Yasamine forgot all about New Orleans and just going where the mood took them. Then it turned out that Yasamine didn't really like jazz. Or even Madonna. Truth be known, she was a closet country music fan.

Dear Bella, I haven't used this so-called social networking thing before, so here goes. How are you? You might be wondering who I am and why I am writing to you. You won't remember me probably, and I don't know what your mother has said. Last time I saw you, you were just short of your fourth birthday. I remember you had beautiful long curly dark hair and your mother's dark eyes, and that people used to say that you had my mouth. (Let's hope not!) Anyway your old man is still alive and kicking. Yes, that's right, the original model that your mum got fed up with. She had every right, what with the way I was headed, but I turned out better than expected and I have a good job, and I'm not some old drunk. What about you? Are you married with kids? Am I a grandad? I wasn't going to get in touch – not that I didn't want to. I didn't think I had the right. I still don't know if it's right. I don't even know where you are. I met this young bloke recently – it's a long story and I won't bore you with details – he said I should be able to find you on the internet and bang! There you were. If you don't want to contact me that's fine: I won't bother you again and no hard feelings. No worries, but if you do want to give me a call sometime, I'll send my number. You can call but not one of those texts. I'm still getting the hang of that little screen so I might accidentally delete you. I hope your mother is well. Say hi for me if you want and tell her I'd be happy to hear from her, but don't feel obliged. Enough said. I hope to hear from you soon. All the best, Harry (your biological father) O'Keefe P.S. Do you still have Dolly Pink?

Harry writes his letter as a practice run, with no real intention of sending it. His finger twitches, he presses return, and the message disappears into cyberspace.

CHAPTER THIRTY-FOUR

Somehow now with the baby coming, and everything that has been stirred up by the other night's adventure on the bridge, Louisa feels a sense of urgency in getting herself straight.

'It's not easy,' she says.

'The more you avoid it, the more power you give it,' says Lucy.

'Tom used to say darkness has its own beauty.'

'What are you thinking about?'

'I'm thinking of the painting that Tom did, the day he brought the flowers home.'

'Can you describe it to me?'

'It was a picture of a car crash. There were flowers strewn across a car that had been twisted around a lamp post, and a young man's um blood-streaked hand hung from the broken passenger window. On the ground was a package tied up in brown paper and string, and another hand, a woman's hand, was reaching into the frame towards it. He used watercolour – it was all done in a delicate watercolour. He called it *Still Life*.'

'Still life?'

'Yes.'

'Whose hand do you think it was, the one reaching in?'

'I don't know. I've thought lately it was mine.'

'And the package?'

'Not what it must have meant to him when he painted it, obviously. This package of pain that I've been carrying around.'

'Why don't you ever play your saxophone anymore?' she asks Harry one day.

'I'm thinking of selling it,' he lies.

'That would be a terrible shame. I wish you would start playing again. I think you're just being stubborn.'

'Takes one to know one.'

Still, the exchange surprises Harry because of what he has been thinking and feeling lately. Whether he is still capable of playing. She definitely has some sort of sixth sense. She might even know about Carole, or suspect. Is she telling him it's okay, forgiveness is possible, that history doesn't have to weigh a person down as much as it does? She's letting him know that everybody makes mistakes, that nobody's perfect.

Something still holds him back from getting everything out in the open; about Carole, about why he doesn't play anymore, if only he knew himself, and about the changes that are happening to his heart. It's possible that some things just can't be said in so many words.

Louisa goes into his study, climbs up, pulls the case down from the top shelf, and places it on the kitchen bench. 'Anyway, suit yourself. I'm going out for a while as soon as I get changed,' she says.

'Where?'

'My new painting class. Remember? Lucy suggested it.'

'I get it,' says Harry, 'you think playing would be therapeutic for me.'

'It's not all about you, you know, Harry,' she says. 'But yes, I reckon it would.'

'Just checking,' he says. 'Sometimes I can be a grumpy old bastard.'

But she has already gone.

It is difficult to tell where the music is coming from. Snatches of sound move across cold dark air. Louisa winds her window down and turns the engine off. The sound is drifting out, originating from somewhere in the house, possibly the back room. Harry is playing, softly at first, but as her ear adjusts, Louisa can hear the notes greet one another, tentatively, and then as the closest of old friends. He is improvising, floating long, sad notes into the night. A melody is emerging; each note follows the one before like a story, vulnerable, erratically spaced and breaking like a voice, releasing years of feeling. The sound is not perfect. He might be losing his breath or perhaps the notes have congregated in irregular pockets throughout the house so that the music escapes in uneven rushes into the darkness. He is feeling his way, but the music is all the more moving for that.

Louisa sits in the car for a long time, on the brink of a discovery. What is it? Something that music can get at, but words cannot.

> *Hi Harry, Thanks for the message. I thought of looking you up, then I wondered why I should bother. It's not like you did. True I wanted to fill in gaps. Not when Dad was alive. I didn't want to hurt him. Don't get the wrong idea. He was the best father. The best. Even when my sisters were born he never once gave me the feeling that I was less important and I knew he loved me the same as them. Mum is devestated as you can imagine but my sisters both had their kids early so she has plenty to keep her busy, she's an awesome Nanna*

and Mum, but she gets arthritis and has to pace herself. I didn't know if I should tell her about this but she was alright with it only worried for me but I told her I'd be alright. Mum never talked about that part of my life and I never felt like I could ask her, she always says you can't keep looking back or you'll miss what's right in front of your nose. Since Dad died she forgot her own advise. I have lots of things to say and want some questions answered, which I think is probably the least you could do. Mum said not to open the can of worms but I make up my own mind about that. Send me your number. Or not. I can't promise anything. I hope you are having a good life and I might talk soon. Regards, Arabella Smith. I can't believe you remembered Dolly Pink.

CHAPTER THIRTY-FIVE

At the second meeting of the art class the teacher has brought in branches of bougainvillea, wet with spring rain, which she places on a blue velvet cloth. The moisture makes random spatters of dark spots on the already-dark material. Louisa feels ill when she looks at it, but she is determined not to turn away. Not this time.

At the end of class she stands back from the work and is startled to see that there is an explosion in what was intended to be a benign depiction of branches. Her eye travels across the canvas to the depths of the painting. Hidden in thick swirls of paint turned to mud, shapes emerge. An interplay of destruction and human matter slips in and out of visibility.

She is unsettled and fearful. She focuses, desperate to see bougainvillea, but her eye travels to the outer perimeter, where she has inadvertently painted layers of despair. Death is hidden in the greenery.

Louisa had a premonition, but the trouble with premonitions is that they can only be called such after the event. This one happened about a year before Tom died. He had asked her to film him as he tried out for an important belt in karate.

Through the camera she saw something, or an echo of

something, as if another time and her immediate impressions had become entangled. She recalls a sense of unreality. She remembers feeling sick. Still holding the camera to her face, she stumbled into one of the plastic chairs that had been placed around the perimeter and continued filming.

None of it made sense. For the first time since she could remember, everything had been good. She had a new love in Harry. Tom was happier than she had ever seen him. She fought to comprehend what was happening.

Afterwards when it was too late to do anything else, she played the images over and over, reviewing what the camera had caught that day – Tom's struggle and desperation to succeed. How in his exhaustion he fell down, tried to get up, fell down again. She was searching for a clue, but something was missing. She recalled how she'd felt driven to put the camera down and rescue him, to hold him and tell him that it was going to be all right, but it wasn't allowed. He would have found it humiliating. It was her need, not his.

Tom was achieving manhood and he wanted the proof, so she kept filming. She felt heavy with grief, though there was nothing yet to grieve. She remembers fighting back tears when his name was called.

'Thomas Bradley Peters. Congratulations.' They presented him with his new belt and hung a medal around his neck for his courage.

Later, when what had been foreseen finally occurred, it seemed like a rerun at first. Everything was familiar. Holographs surrounded her. She felt that she had to put her hand right through them to discover their true nature. She put out her hand and discovered their true nature.

At that moment she ceased to feel anything, but it was only a temporary reprieve. She hadn't escaped. As soon as she decided to go on living, the pain hit her like a king wave.

For a long, long time it was as if Louisa hung there uselessly in her own life, feeling nothing, watching from a distance as her apparently unnecessary life continued. It is how she imagined the last of a species might feel – the vestige of an age that had already passed.

There are snatches of memories. She remembers sitting at the funeral with the medal hung heavily around her own neck, her lips kissing the cold metal, her face burned with tears that wouldn't stop. She has an impression of Victor near the back door at the funeral as she turned to leave. She seems to remember the warmth of Harry's hand on her upper arm as he helped her into the car afterwards. Time must have passed. Meredith looked back at her as she walked away from the house after the tea and sandwiches that her mother had insisted on. Did she have something left to say? She didn't seem able to find the words. Meredith left with Todd a little over a year later, with no plans to return.

There is an early hot spell. A cricket has found its way into the bedroom and increases their irritation in the hours before exhaustion gives way to restless sleep. They take turns at rising and feeling their way through the dark house to the relative cool outside. There are no stars, just the indifferent glow of a moon on the wane. As the nights drag on, Louisa finds her dreams increase in number and intensity, but when she wakes she remembers them as more curious than troubling. Despite Lucy's reservations about discussing her dreams, she'll bring it up at her next session. It might suggest some sort of breakthrough – except that she is losing faith in the idea of breakthroughs. Breakthrough to what?

'I've been having more dreams,' she tells Lucy half-heartedly. 'It's been so hot hasn't it? The heat has been keeping me awake. Everyone. Harry too. Weird dreams. I think the kids used to get that when they overheated. Night terrors. They couldn't be comforted. They'd look at me like I was some sort of alien.'

'Do you want to talk about them?'

'I don't really. I just want to talk generally, and then I'm thinking that we could call it a day for now.' She hesitates. 'I feel I need to get on. We can't go on forever here, can we? I can always come back if I need to, can't I?'

'Sure, absolutely. That's a good thing Louisa. We can keep it as a casual arrangement, if you like.'

'I've been thinking about denial lately. It's one of those things you see in other people, but never recognise in yourself. I can't tell – am I motivated to forget, or am I motivated to remember? I wonder if you can forget something, if you can tell yourself another story so that it's almost as if it didn't happen? I've always felt as if there's some sort of barrier or wall inside my mind and on the other side there's this, this large room. And that room is dark, in darkness, but I can feel,' and here Louisa presses her hand hard to her chest, 'I can feel that there is something there. It's not empty. It's not an empty room.'

Her mouth is dry. She takes a sip of water.

Lucy says, 'What do you think it is?'

Louisa sits with her head down for a long time. 'It's Tom, of course, and what happened. Before that it was Victor. Before that, I don't know.'

'What are you feeling right now?'

'Oh ... loss. I suppose that covers it. A great big gaping ...' Louisa sighs heavily. 'I lost him, Lucy. Somewhere back there before – it happened before he died – but then when he did, afterwards, the door was closed, sealed. The door disappeared as if it had never been there in the first place, and there was no way for him to get back. I mean, no way of getting him back.'

Louisa drinks more water. It is indistinct, this feeling of disquiet, the inevitability of something about to happen. Darkness swirls before her. A shadow of a figure waits in the gloom drawing her closer. She recoils from whatever she is on the brink of seeing.

Forcing a smile she speaks quickly and by rote. 'But I feel like he's with me now. He's in a safe place. See, Lucy, I still feel him around me all the time, here, now, I do.' Her voice trails off.

The image forces its way into her mind: Tom sitting in the car, his hands on the wheel, his eyes dark, staring into an emptiness that must have been all he could make of the future. She tries to remember. She tries not to remember. She wants to place her hands gently over his, take them from the wheel, to lead him away from the danger. She wants to make everything all right again.

'How alone he'd become,' she says to herself. 'My poor child.'

'What are you thinking?' Lucy's voice is gentle.

'Oh,' says Louisa. 'Why did he do it? It's like something was started and he just kept going instead of stopping, just stopping there. If he just could have stopped, even at that point, we would have got through it. Things change all the time, don't they? We think we're in a black hole. Everything's moving so fast that all the light is swallowed up. We don't know if we're up or down. We don't know if time has stopped and we're going to be like this forever. I wonder if he felt like that. I don't know why he couldn't just stop and wait to see what happened. Stopping's the hard part for us human beings, isn't it? Putting the brakes on. Self-control.' She feels oddly detached. 'Once, a long time before, when the end couldn't possibly have been in his mind, when we were going past the spot, he said, that tree with the bougainvillea around it looks like it's on fire. That was a clue, wasn't it? I should have picked up on that.'

A thick band of silence stretches between them. Louisa dries her tears and blows her nose. 'In a way it was planned. He must have already known, as if he was in love with the idea of death, as if he was creating something predestined. But that's such rubbish. Such rubbish! Nothing is predestined. Everything is just what you make it. He was too young, just a kid with his life ahead of him, so much to do. I hate that he threw that away as if it was nothing. It wasn't … wasn't nothing. It isn't fair, is it?'

'No.'

'I feel so much shame. I'm implicated. I stayed with his father through more than I should, longer than others would probably, and my boy watched and learned. But he wasn't Victor. He felt for other people. There are consequences, Lucy. There is so much sadness.'

Lucy takes her hand, squeezes it reassuringly.

'There's no answer to it, I know,' says Louisa.

'It's complicated. It's really hard. You do the best you can. What else can you do?'

'I don't know.'

'Neither do I. I do believe Tom had to live his own life, and make his own decisions. Allowing another person freedom, which is their right, after all, involves some risk. And it takes an ability to surrender. It means giving up the desire to take control over what they do when you see them doing things you don't agree with. You can try to help, but … What can you do? All you can do is to go on living.'

'It's hard. It's hard to live and feel happy.'

'If you can, it would be a wonderful way to honour his life. And all those you love. Harry, and your daughter. And a new grandchild. A beautiful new grandchild. Life is incredible, isn't it?'

CHAPTER THIRTY-SIX

The first time Harry saw Louisa he was with his mother at a flower show. Louisa came around the corner and they nearly collided. It was an excuse to start a conversation. It could have gone either way. He remembers having the strangest feeling, as if he recognised her, as if he knew her from somewhere. She seemed familiar. He told her as much.

'I've got one of those faces,' she said. 'Generic. People think they know me all the time.'

'It's funny,' said Harry. 'I could have sworn we'd met.'

'We were just about to stop for a cup of tea,' his mother said. 'Why don't you join us?' It was all too fast. They should have talked more first. Harry was about to demur, embarrassed by his mother, when to his surprise Louisa agreed.

As he plays, blowing wistful notes into the afternoon, this is running through his mind. He is remembering how it was that day, his feeling of anticipation, as though he was starting something that had been planned a long time ago, as though it was inevitable that he and Louisa would be together, as if it was already mapped out and he was simply joining up the dots. He remembers thinking that she seemed more cultured than he had expected. What had he expected? Why had he expected anything?

Was his mother matchmaking? Probably. After they bumped into Louisa, the old girl made herself scarce on some excuse.

'I'll be back,' she said. 'You'll keep my boy company for a few minutes won't you, until I get back? I won't be long.'

She didn't wait for her to agree.

What first struck Harry was Louisa's hair – long, dark, and dramatically contrasting with her pale skin and blue eyes. Unusual. It was like a secret or a puzzle that kept him looking at her.

Then the more he looked, the more he felt that they would meet again, that there was something here that needed more time to resolve. Not passion, nothing so hot, but something persistent. The expression around her eyes made him feel strange: as if she were carrying an unresolved sadness that he felt he understood.

His mother took her time coming back. Louisa was making her moves to leave, pushing back her chair and gathering her packages, and Harry began to feel mild panic. He asked her out. She hesitated for so long that he was about to withdraw the offer and make a joke of it. Then she said yes.

'Great,' said Harry. 'Fantastic.'

Things moved quickly from there. He'd been seeing someone not long before, but nothing had come of it. Louisa had been on her own for some time. They wasted no time in moving in together. Passion grew quickly and it went deeper than he'd expected. It stayed that way until the business with Tom.

After Tom's death, the whole thing just about went belly-up. She backed off, closing herself off from him, from everyone, even herself. He respected that, the distance she needed, but it didn't mean he liked it. It hurt.

He realised too that despite themselves people get older. Men get older and sex is not as important or as easy as it was.

In the beginning they made love every day, but eventually they were too tired more often than not. It happens, Harry tells himself. There is just so much a person can take. He thought he'd made up his mind a while ago that they were both past it. He was wrong.

It is a strange thing. In the last few days he has started to look at her differently. Maybe it's something about all the paintings that she is bringing home, and that she is not at home as much. She looks somehow clearer too, more in focus to him, as if a veil is slipping.

He wonders if he has been getting complacent. For the first time he seriously entertains the idea that she might find out about his aborted affair with Carole, and decide to leave him. It makes him nervous. And strangely, since Bella's reply to his message he hasn't spent as much time thinking of Yasamine. Somehow he'd never pictured her as a grandmother. He can't get a clear picture of her any more. She probably looks old now, just like everybody else.

He's printed out Bella's letter to him and keeps it in his top pocket, transferring it from one polo top to the next as he changes. Louisa hasn't asked him about it. He'll talk to her, but not yet, not until he is clear. Every now and then he looks at that bit of the letter about Yasamine and the other bloke. Each time he puts the letter away, he finds his feelings have changed slightly.

It's sunny and cool, quieter than normal because it's a weekday, and they both have the day off. Louisa is watering the front garden. She's been taking it in turns with Harry, who is now inside, trying his hand at some rice and dhal.

A van pulls into the street and stops suddenly, a little way up. It's the young man who parks under their tree sometimes. Louisa stands her ground, watering, watching, and resenting his presence.

'Damn it,' she says. She drags the nozzle back to the tap, and turns the water off. Progress requires action. Life is short.

She is walking purposefully up the street, meeting his eye. He looks away, looks back, hesitates, caught out, winds the window down.

'Anything wrong?' he says.

'No. I just thought I'd come and introduce myself. I've seen you around a few times. We haven't actually met, have we?'

He shakes his head, says, 'You've got lots of trees out the front. They look like they've been there forever, but they haven't.'

'We like them,' she says.

'Sure.' He says, 'How long have you lived here?'

She tells him.

'Did anyone ever drop in who'd lived here before?' There's strain behind the question, overlaid by an attempt to sound casual.

'No,' she says. 'Nobody. Why?'

She waits for more, a story, but it doesn't eventuate. He looks deflated.

'Is it someone special?' she prompts.

At that his eyes star up and he looks as if he might tell, but instead says, 'I have to go.'

'Hey,' she says, to give him a chance to reconsider, but he has wound the window up and is starting the engine.

He drives off. Louisa watches him until he's almost out of sight. As she walks back to the house, Brian saunters up to meet her.

'Hey, Louise,' he says.

'Oh, hello Brian.'

'What were you doing talking to that guy?'

'Oh, you know, I've seen him hanging around. I just thought I'd introduce myself.'

'Yeah? He used to live in your house with his girlfriend.'

'No. Really?'

'Yeah. Funny guy. He used to lose it a bit from time to time.'

She did as well. She had a good set of lungs. You could hear her right across the road, going off her face at the poor bloke. One day he buried a dirty great lawnmower in the front yard!' Brian laughs, looking to her to share in the joke. She chuckles.

'Yeah,' she says. 'You were the one that told us about that. Harry dug it up.'

''Course he did. I remember now. I took it to the tip for you. Never did get to use up all those tip passes you gave us. Seems like we had more council pick-ups back then. I dunno, I just got more junk now.'

'Oh, well.'

'Yeah, he was a bit of a weird one. Nah, he was all right most of the time, but he pretty much kept to himself. Anyway I heard they split up after they moved out. Lorraine saw her down the shopping centre one day and got the whole story. Reckoned he'd been playing around. Ha! Trouble is he'd got caught! Nah, just kidding. She was off back to England. Pregnant apparently, but she didn't want him to know. You wouldn't tell Lorraine, but, if you didn't want it to get around, would you? She had some family over there, I suppose. Anyway, a while back we heard she'd come back. It can get bloody cold over there, I suppose.'

Brian looks up the street to where the van disappeared. 'Don't know what he's started hanging around for after all this time – like a dog sniffing out his old patch. Beats me.'

'It's been a long time,' she says. 'We've been here coming up for ten years now.'

'Yeah, well, you know, some people cling on to things don't they?'

Brian hangs there, looking as if he is wondering how to take his leave.

'Yeah, strange all right,' she says.

'Yeah.'

Louisa says, 'I could have asked him in for a cuppa, but he wouldn't have been interested.'

'You never ask me in for a cuppa!'

'Do you want to come in for a cuppa?'

He grins. 'Nah. Better get on.'

He waves a pair of electric shears that he's been holding. He's wearing his steel caps for some serious gardening.

'I can come and do yours when I've finished with mine,' he says.

'Thanks Brian, but Harry likes to do it.'

'Doesn't look like it.' It's become a running joke in the neighbourhood – a sure sign that they've settled in.

'Think of it this way, Brian,' she says. 'It makes your place look even better.'

'True,' he says, and brandishes his shears again. 'Any time but.'

Louisa waves him off, and heads back inside to see how Harry's going with the dhal.

CHAPTER THIRTY-SEVEN

Out of a clear blue sky a tiny meteor seems to have fallen to earth. Just before the point of disintegration it hits Buddha, shattering him.

Louisa is standing at the kitchen bench before a small stack of dishes, staring through the window as the sink slowly fills with hot water. Buddha flies to pieces before her eyes. At that point, Louisa, and everything around her, is frozen in time. The sky remains still, clear and empty. The water from the sink overflows and Louisa comes to, turning off the tap in a little panic. She calls out to Harry, causing Buster to send up a shrill bark.

'Harry! Come here.'

'What is it?' He appears from the bedroom half dressed.

'It's Buddha.'

He pulls on his dressing-gown against the cool morning and they venture outside to get a closer look. Buddha lies broken amidst the clover. They search around the pieces, but can find no likely culprit: no small piece of metallic rock; no nearby honky nut from the gum tree. Nothing jettisoned from a passing aircraft joy-riding out of Jandakot airport. There has been no light aircraft for over half an hour.

'What happened?' he asks. 'Did you see anything?'

Louisa tells what she saw and what she believes. There will be a rational explanation. They just haven't found it yet. She feels sad as she looks at the shattered pieces of Buddha.

'It's a shame,' says Harry, 'but they have them down near the markets, so we can easily get another one.'

Louisa leans her head on Harry's chest. 'I miss Tom,' she says.

'I know you do.'

'I feel like if I stop thinking about him, or if I stop suffering over him, it will be as if he never existed. What if I let him go and he disappears?'

'He won't.'

'What if I forget him?'

'You won't.'

'You think so?'

Harry nods.

'I've spent so much time thinking about him that I don't know what would happen to me if I stopped. What if there was nothing left? What if that's all I am, Harry?'

'It's not.'

'Yes, I guess.'

'You won't forget him.'

'I know.'

'I'll be here,' Harry tells her. 'I'm here.'

'I don't even know what I want. I don't know if anyone does. Do you?'

'When?'

'Generally.'

'No. Yes. Just to be happy and to get by.'

Louisa grins. 'That sounds achievable,' she says. 'To survive.'

'Not just that. Together.' Harry gives her a squeeze. 'Anyway, we ought to aim higher than survival, Lou.'

He points to the rounded edge of a tennis ball lodged in the rosebush. 'Look at that.' He extracts it. 'Here's the culprit.'

'I still think it was a meteorite,' she says.

He throws the ball across the road, and returns to the house to finish dressing.

She stands for some time staring down at the green and white ceramic pieces scattered amongst the winter grass.

'Poor old Buddha,' she says. 'Shouldn't have got attached. That'll teach me.'

She decides that she won't replace the statue. In the Himalayas Buddhists put up prayer flags and every time the wind blows, their prayers are taken up. Sometimes they might be heard and answered. Maybe she could do that – write a prayer on a rectangle of silk and place it there for the breeze to catch.

Standing in the sunlight Louisa is startled by the fluttering of wings and a small rush of wind by her face. A common grey dove flies in, landing on the birdbath, and a second later its mate lands beside it. One stands guard while the other bathes.

ACKNOWLEDGEMENTS

I am grateful to all those who helped me to bring this, my first novel, to its realisation: my partner Andrew for his unwavering enthusiasm throughout the process of the book's inception and realisation, and to Hamish for his inspirational antics. I am grateful to all of my family for their interest and support, to Norm and Beryl for the use of their home-as-writing-retreat, my daughter's friend Linda who showed me that it is possible to stop talking about it and just do it, to all of my friends, especially Jill, David and Denise, and to Dr Helena Grehan, Natalie Kon-yu and Lucas North for their reading, and their thoughtful and encouraging responses to the early manuscript. I am particularly indebted to Dr Chris McLeod, who mentored me with such generosity, and without whose insight, expertise and encouragement, I don't think I would have felt sufficiently confident to complete this novel; and to Sylvia McLeod for her support. Thanks also to Tom Flood for the later manuscript appraisals and a fresh viewpoint, which was so helpful in further progressing the work; and to Chris and Tom for their wonderful letters of support. Finally I want to express my heartfelt appreciation to Georgia Richter and Kate O'Donnell who guided me with patience, skill and sensitivity through the editing process. Thank you, Georgia, for the great compliment of paying such close attention to this novel in its final incarnation.

First published 2013 by
FREMANTLE PRESS
Fremantle Press Inc. trading as Fremantle Press
PO Box 158, North Fremantle, Western Australia, 6159
fremantlepress.com.au

Cover design Ally Crimp
Cover image Michael Cogliantry, 'Dog in lying in grass sleeping'

 A catalogue record for this
book is available from the
National Library of Australia

ISBN 9781921888540 (paperback)
ISBN 9781921888557 (ebook)

Fremantle Press is supported by the Western Australian State Government
through the Department of Cultural Industries, Tourism and Sport.

Fremantle Press respectfully acknowledges the Whadjuk people of the
Noongar nation as the Traditional Owners and Custodians of the land
where we work in Walyalup.

www.ingramcontent.com/pod-product-compliance
Lightning Source LLC
Chambersburg PA
CBHW020557030726
47497CB00007B/1972